JULIA JUSTISS

The Untamed Heiress
"Justiss rivals Georgette Heyer in the beloved *The Grand Sophy* by creating a riveting young woman of character and good humour... The horrific nature of Helena's childhood adds complexity and depth to this historical romance and unexpected plot twists and layers also increase the reader's enjoyment."
—*Booklist*

My Lady's Honour
"Julia Justiss has a knack for conveying emotional intensity and longing."
—*All About Romance*

ANNIE BURROWS

"Annie Burrows is an exceptional writer of historical romance who sprinkles her stories with unforgettable characters, terrific period detail and wicked repartee."
—*Cataromance*

TERRI BRISBIN

Surrender To the Highlander
"...rich in historical detail, laced with the perfect amount of passion, Ms Brisbin continually delivers highly satisfying romances. Don't miss it."
—*Romance Reviews Today*

The Duchess's Next Husband
"Brisbin offers a novel of manners with high sexual tension and just the right Regency flavour."
—*Romantic Times BOOKreviews*

Julia Justiss wrote her first plot ideas for a Nancy Drew novel in the back of her primary school notebook and has been writing ever since. After such journalistic adventures as publishing poetry, composing the wording on the envelope enclosing the death benefit cheque for an insurance company and editing an American embassy newsletter, she returned to her first love, writing fiction. Her Regency historical novels have been winners or finalists in the Romance Writers of America's Golden Heart™, *Romantic Times* magazine's Best Historical Fiction, Golden Quill, National Readers' Choice and Daphne du Maurier contests. She lives with her husband, three children and two dogs in rural east Texas, where she also teaches high school French. For current news and contests, please visit her website www.juliajustiss.com

Annie Burrows has been making up stories for her own amusement since she first went to school. As soon as she got the hang of using a pencil she began to write them down. Her love of books meant she had to do a degree in English literature. And her love of writing meant she could never take on a job where she didn't have time to jot down notes when inspiration for a new plot struck her. She still wants the heroines of her stories to wear beautiful floaty dresses and triumph over all that life can throw at them. But when she got married she discovered that finding a hero is an essential ingredient to arriving at "happy ever after". Please visit her website at www.annie-burrows.co.uk

Terri Brisbin is wife to one, mother of three and dental hygienist to hundreds when not living the life of a glamorous romance author. She was born, raised and is still living in the southern New Jersey suburbs. Terri's love of history led her to write time-travel romances and Historicals set in Scotland and England. Readers are invited to visit her website for more information at www.terribrisbin.com, or contact her at PO Box 41, Berlin, NJ 08009-0041, USA.

Regency

CANDLELIT
CHRISTMAS

JULIA JUSTISS
ANNIE BURROWS
TERRI BRISBIN

M&B™ and M&B™ with the Rose Device
are trademarks of the publisher.
Harlequin Mills & Boon Limited, Eton House,
18-24 Paradise Road, Richmond, Surrey TW9 1SR

A REGENCY CANDLELIT CHRISTMAS
© Harlequin Books S.A. 2009

*The publisher acknowledges the copyright holders of the individual
works as follows:*

Christmas Wedding Wish © Janet Justiss 2008
The Rake's Secret Son © Annie Burrows 2008
Blame It On the Mistletoe © Theresa S. Brisbin 2008

ISBN: 978 0 263 87711 3

26-1009

Harlequin Mills & Boon policy is to use papers that are
natural, renewable and recyclable products and made from
wood grown in sustainable forests. The logging and
manufacturing processes conform to the legal environmental
regulations of the country of origin.

Printed and bound in Spain
by Litografia Rosés S.A., Barcelona

CONTENTS

Dear Reader,

Christmas is by far my favourite holiday and, for me, the heart of it is family. Especially now, as my children have grown and gone off to college and jobs, having everyone home together to share meals and fun and laughter is the highlight of the season. So when I began to craft a Christmas story, my thoughts immediately returned to the Wellingfords, the family about whom I have written off and on since my very first book, *The Wedding Gamble*.

After her older sister Sarah's marriage, second-eldest sister Meredyth took over Sarah's role as chatelaine and protector of the Wellingford estate and family. When her beloved fiancé was killed in India, she resigned herself to spending the rest of her life as competent manager, devoted sister and doting aunt.

As the story opens, while joyously welcoming her sisters and their children to a Christmas celebration at Wellingford, she cannot suppress a secret, bitter envy that they have husbands to love and children of their own. Then her brother Colton returns from Oxford with his best friend Thomas – accompanied by Thomas's elder brother Allen. Though two years younger than she, the mesmerising Allen Mansfell begins to make Meredyth doubt whether her heart and her senses have been entombed forever. But could this fascinating younger man truly be interested in her?

I hope you will enjoy watching Meredyth's awakening to all the possibilities of love and joy inherent in the Christmas season.

Julia

CHRISTMAS WEDDING WISH

JULIA JUSTISS

To my family, Ronnie, Mark, Catherine and Matt,
who bring me joy at Christmas and always

Chapter One

‘**M**erry! Merry, they're here! Come quickly!'

From the dining room, where she was supervising the footmen placing another leaf in the long table, Meredyth Wellingford heard her younger sister's urgent voice summoning her to the entrance hall. ‘Coming, Faith!' she called.

A lilt in her step, Meredyth smiled as she walked to the front hall. How she loved the Christmas holidays! The scent of greenery adorning stairs and mantels mingling with the spicy tang of simmering wassail and the mouthwatering smell of roasting meat; mistletoe kissing balls and sharp-edged holly; carols sung around the hearth before the blazing Yule log. But especially she loved having her family at home— the siblings gathered once again under the Wellingford roof, as they had been for all their years growing up.

The first to arrive should be her younger brother Colton, returning from Oxford with his best friend Thomas Mansfell. Since Wellingford was on the way from university to his friend's home farther north, Thomas was a frequent visitor, normally spending a few days with them each time the boys made their way to and from college.

Just as Meredyth met her sister in the entrance hall they heard boots tramping up the front steps, followed by a sharp rap at the wide front door that Twilling, their old butler, hastened to throw open.

'Faith! Merry!' Colton cried, sweeping them into a hug as they ran to greet him. 'How good it is to be home!'

'How good it is to have you,' Merry replied, an ache in her heart as she stepped back to inspect the youngest member of the Wellingford clan. With their mother having never really recovered after his birth, Meredyth and her older sister Sarah had tutored and cared for Colton all his life before he left for school. In place of the smiling, eager boy she'd sent away to Eton now stood a young man taller than she was, his burnished brown locks highlighted with gold, his blue eyes glowing. Her little brother was becoming a handsome young man, Meredyth realised with a shock.

'The hall certainly looks festive,' another masculine voice said, pulling her from her contemplation of Colton.

'Thank you, Thomas, and welcome,' she said, turning her attention to her brother's friend. 'You are planning to stay for a few days before journeying home, I hope? I've had your usual room prepared.'

'Oh, yes—do say you'll be staying!' Faith interposed. 'It is so agreeable to see you again.'

'Good to see you too, brat,' Thomas replied, giving one of Faith's gold curls a careless tug before turning back to Meredyth. 'I should love to rest here for a few days before returning to the rigours of Christmas at the Grange. And I hope you don't mind, but I took the liberty of telling my brother Allen that he could stay here as well. He arrived from London to join us on the trip north just as Colton and I were leaving Oxford.'

'Of course he's welcome,' Merydth replied. 'You've spoken of him so often, although we've never met, that I feel I know him already.' Indeed, over the years Thomas had frequently recounted the exploits of the older brother he admired—his prowess at riding and fencing, his service as a dashing young subaltern carrying messages for Wellington during the Waterloo campaign, the expertise with which he'd taken over the management of the family estates.

Thomas grinned. 'I'm glad! It would have been most embarrassing to have to send him on his way alone! He stopped to see about the horses—but here he is now.' He gestured to the tall, dark-haired gentleman, whom Twilling was just admitting into the hallway.

'Ladies, may I present my brother Allen? Allen, here are Merry and Faith Wellingford—two of Colton's sisters.'

'Miss Faith, Miss Wellingford—a pleasure!' the newcomer said, bowing over their hands in turn. Addressing Meredyth, he added, 'I've heard so much about Wellingford from Thomas. I'm delighted to visit at last—if you are certain, as he insisted, that having an extra guest foisted upon you without notice won't be an inconvenience.'

As the gentleman straightened, Meredyth barely suppressed a gasp. Unlike her fledgling brother, Allen Mansfell was a man already fully mature—and a strikingly handsome one. Though Meredyth was tall for a lady, the visitor towered over her. Sable brown locks brushed the forehead of his square-jawed, slightly smiling face, while eyes of an arresting green captured her gaze, making her feel for an instant as if the two of them were the only occupants of the hall.

A little disconcerted, she dropped her eyes, letting her appreciative gaze travel from his broad shoulders down a trim torso to muscled thighs, well displayed by his chamois riding breeches. When, cheeks pinkening, she forced her eyes back up to his, a tingle of attraction sizzled through her, stronger than anything she'd felt since the death of her fiancé James, a heartbreak ago.

Shaking her head, she tried to regather her wits. 'If

you've listened to what Thomas says about me, I'm surprised you dared venture to the house.'

He laughed, that disturbing, shiver-inducing stare still fixed on her. 'I assure you, everything he recounted was most complimentary.'

'I hope you left us some decorating to do,' Colton said, glancing around the garland-hung hall. 'After being cooped up with musty old books for a term, Thomas and I are keen to ride about the countryside.'

'Faith and I began with the hall, but we haven't progressed much further. We shall have need of you gentlemen to fetch more pine, holly and mistletoe. I thought we'd leave some of the gathering until Sarah, Elizabeth and Clare arrive with their clans. Riding out with you should amuse the children.'

Colton grinned at her. 'That's Merry—already managing everyone and half the group aren't even here yet.'

'She is an excellent manager,' Thomas pointed out. 'Viewing Wellingford now, Allen, you cannot imagine what it looked like when I first visited here! The manor in disrepair, cottages falling into ruin, fields lying fallow. Merry's done a wonderful job of refurbishing the house and farms and seeing the land brought back under cultivation.'

Were Thomas not almost as close to her as a sibling, Meredyth might have been embarrassed by his bald description of the sorry condition of Wellingford at the time of their father's death. As it was, knowing that via Thomas his brother Allen would be fully aware of how badly their gamester father had neglected Colton's inheritance, she felt no need to explain or apologise. 'Time, a competent estate agent and an influx of funds can accomplish a great deal,' she replied.

'Having wrestled with the upkeep of my own papa's properties, Miss Wellingford, I am well aware that it takes much more than those to keep a property in good heart,' Allan said. 'The land and farms we rode through looked exemplary, and this house is lovely. Your hard work is quite evident.'

'Oh, indeed!' Colton interposed. 'Merry is so excellent a manager I believe I shall keep her on when I marry and return to Wellingford for good.'

'I doubt your bride would care for such an arrangement,' Meredyth replied tartly, feeling her face heat. She knew that Colton, with the blunt insensitivity of a young man didn't realise he'd just branded her as his spinster sister, well and truly on the shelf. Which, of course, she was—but it was not a fact she appreciated his pointing out in front of the very attractive Mr Mansfell.

Though some eight years senior to the seventeen-year-old Thomas, Allen Mansfell was still two years younger than she. Her discomfort intensified by that lowering thought, Meredyth told herself sternly that she must get over the unseemly sensual response he'd sparked in her.

Noting from her expression that her sister was piqued at being left out of the conversation—and conscious of a sudden need to escape Allen Mansfell's too-compelling presence—Meredyth said, 'Faith, why don't you take our guests into the front parlour? I'll have Twilling bring in some spiced wine while I see about preparing a room.'

Turning to Mr Mansfell, she added, 'I'll have your chamber ready shortly. If there is anything I can do to make your stay at Wellingford more comfortable, please don't hesitate to ask.'

To her surprise, Allen took her hand and bowed over it. 'I'm sure you will make me comfortable indeed,' he murmured, the warmth of his voice and the heat of his gloved hand sending another little shock through her.

Hastily withdrawing her tingling fingers, Meredyth curtseyed and turned away, acutely conscious of his gaze upon her back as she ascended the stairs.

Escaping from his view down the hall, Meredyth proceeded to the guest wing to inspect the room she meant to assign Allen, wishing to determine if anything more than fresh linens would be needed. As her gaze lingered on the large high bed, she recalled Mr Mansfell's velvet-voiced remark about how comfortable she would make him. A surprisingly intense flush of heat suffused her body.

She was being ridiculous, attributing to his idle remark an innuendo a gentleman would never direct towards a gently born spinster. It was bad enough that she'd blushed like a schoolgirl under his gaze. She'd best get hold of herself around him before she did something that alerted him to the effect he had upon her. The thought of him realising it and reacting with distaste—or, even worse, pity—was too humiliating to contemplate.

Fortunately he would only be at Wellingford for a few days. With the rest of the family arriving at any time now, she'd be too busy overseeing meals, lodgings and entertainment for her sisters, their spouses and their children to reflect on the mesmerising effect of a pair of vivid green eyes, or the quivering in her belly produced by a handsome face and a virile physique.

It wasn't as if she'd encountered no attractive men in the years since her engagement had ended. What was it about Allen Mansfell that sparked her body to a sensual awareness she'd thought submerged for good after James's death?

The dull ache that had replaced the first searing pain of losing her fiancé throbbed in her chest. Swallowing hard, she drifted to the window, staring sightlessly down at the winter garden as the memories overtook her.

How in love they'd been! How vividly she recalled

the excitement of kissing him—the way she'd felt as if she were melting from the inside out when his tongue caressed hers and his strong hands fondled her breasts. Not for the first time she regretted the sense of honour and responsibility that had made them curtail those thrilling explorations short of complete fulfilment.

They'd have all the time in the world to enjoy each other when he returned from his posting in India, James had promised as he gently pushed her away. Drawing a finger over her kiss-swollen lips, he'd pledged to pleasure every inch of her once she was his bride, when they need no longer fear that their joining might create a child.

That last night before he'd left she'd been tempted—oh, so tempted—to draw him back into her embrace, to rub her breasts against his chest, fit her body around the hardness in his breeches and coax his lips open, touching and teasing until his control broke and he took her then and there down the path to ecstasy. Only the knowledge that conceiving his child would mean disaster had stopped her.

Faced now with the probability that she'd never bear a child of her own, she wasn't so sure she'd made the right choice.

It wasn't that she'd set her face against marriage. Of course for the first year or so after losing James she'd not thought it possible she would ever wish to wed anyone else, but time had worn away that certainty as it had muted her grief. In the intervening years the necessity of remaining at Wellingford to tend her dying mother, followed by a succession of other needs and duties, had kept her here, far from the ballrooms of London where she might have found another love.

Not that it was completely impossible that she might yet marry. She'd go to London with Faith in the spring, accompany her little sister to all the events of the Marriage Mart. But by then she'd be more than ten years older than her sister and the other girls making their bows, she would likely be consigned to wearing caps and sitting with the dowagers.

Besides, unlike many of the maidens soon to join Faith in the drawing rooms of society, Meredyth cherished no dreams of wedding for wealth or title. She'd already sidestepped the rich neighbour who'd come wooing, wishing to join her dowry lands with his. And gently rebuffed an old family friend—a widowed viscount looking for a new mama for his clan. Possessed of a valued place among her family, a budding brood of nieces and nephews to spoil, land and a dower house in which to live once Colton brought home a bride to be the new mistress of Wellingford, she would not give her heart, her worldly possessions and her future to a husband in exchange for anything less than a love as powerful as that she'd felt for James.

Turning to give the bed one last lingering glance, Meredyth sighed and walked out. Despite Allen Mansfell's ability to make her senses zing, demonstrating that passion burned within her still, for a lady as long in the tooth as Meredyth Wellingford, finding true love again would take a miracle.

Savouring a glass of spiced wine in the parlour below, Allen Mansfell propped an elbow against the mantel and looked on indulgently as Miss Faith Wellingford tried—with no success—to flirt with his brother Thomas, who alternately teased and ignored her while discussing with Colton a proposed hunting expedition for the morrow.

A pretty enough child, Miss Faith resembled her older sister Elizabeth, said to be the beauty of family, who'd recently married his friend Hal Waterman. With her lovely face and artless charm, Miss Faith would probably have little problem finding a suitable husband next spring when, as she had earnestly informed him, she'd be making her debut.

At the thought, Allen suppressed a quiver of distaste. Next spring would probably find him back in London as well. Though after Susanna's faithlessness part of him recoiled at the thought of ever offering his hand and name to another lady. Once his initial hurt and fury had abated, he had recognised that the reason he'd first sought her out—a desire to marry, settle down on his estate and delight his mama by providing her with grandchildren—would propel him back to Marriage Mart again. Not that he had any intention this time of risking his heart.

Unfortunately the London Season provided the most convenient and comprehensive gathering of maidens of suitable breeding and lineage from which a gentleman might find a wife. Though it was ludicrous to think of choosing an infant like Faith.

It had been Susanna's confident self-assurance that had first caught his interest last spring. Unlike most of the other maidens, she had been able to converse intelligently—and flirt alluringly—instead of falling into giggles or blushing at every word he uttered. To say nothing of the blatant promise of her lush body…

Angrily he thrust away the memories. He'd raged and mourned long enough. He would not allow her perfidy to cast a damper over his spirits any longer.

If he were compelled to wade into the waters of the Marriage Mart once again, he thought, Miss Faith's sister Meredyth would be much more to his taste. Tall, slender, her hair a paler blonde that the gold of her little sister's, her eyes grey-blue rather than cerulean, she carried herself with a graceful elegance. And then there'd been that surprising spark of awareness, accompanied by a jolt of warmth that had fairly burned through his gloves when he'd foolishly uttered that naughty remark about how comfortable she could make him. Elegance and—unlike Susanna—integrity in one subtly sensuous body made for quite an arresting combination.

Nor had he been mouthing empty phrases when he'd complimented her on the management of Wellingford. He'd been genuinely impressed by the well-tended fields, fences and cottages past which they'd ridden, their excellent condition all the more impressive considering in what a shambles the entire estate had been just a few years ago.

Randolph Wellingford's profligate habits, addiction to gaming and shocking neglect of his estate had been quite the *on-dit* when Allen had first left Oxford for London. Indeed, many at his club had murmured it was a blessing for the family when the man met an early death, riding out half-foxed one cold winter morning in an attempt to win some ridiculous wager. Meredyth Wellingford must be intelligent, diligent and a thrifty manager to have accomplished so much at Wellingford.

A thought struck him then, as appealing as it was sudden. If he must marry—and marry he must—why not choose a more mature lady? One he knew by reputation to possess a sterling character and by personal observation to have the skills necessary to be mistress of a large estate? An older lady who might be as amenable as he to a marriage based on similar tastes and mutual respect? A lady whose subtle attractiveness promised satisfaction of his appetites without the torment of lust and jealousy Susanna had roused in him?

A lady who just happened to be planning to accompany her little sister to London for the upcoming Season...

Allen swallowed the last of his wine and set down his glass, smiling. He'd use this few days' sojourn at Wellingford to become better acquainted with his charming hostess. And if he continued to be as impressed—and titillated—by Meredyth Wellingford as he'd been upon their first meeting, he might just have found the answer to his marriage dilemma.

Chapter Two

At midmorning the next day, Meredyth left the housekeeper and proceeded to the drawing room. Noting with approval that the extra side-tables she'd requested to accommodate serving refreshments for a houseful of guests were already in place, she walked to the window. Stealing a moment's respite from the array of chores still before her, she gazed over the front lawn towards the forest.

Colton had announced at breakfast his intention to hunt later in the Home Wood, boasting that he'd bring back some pheasant to grace their Christmas table. Having not seen their other guests yet this morning, she didn't know if Thomas and Allen Mansfell had accompanied him or not.

Excited as she was by the imminent arrival of the rest of her family, Meredyth still felt on edge. Despite the severe lecture she'd given herself before going down to dinner last night, upon encountering Allen Mansfell she'd experienced the same pull of attraction and quiver of response he'd surprised from her at their first meeting.

If anything, she recalled with a little frown, her reaction had been more intense. Attractive as Mr Mansfell was in casual riding clothes, in formal black dinner dress, his arresting green eyes mirroring the glow of the Christmas candles Faith had added to the table in honour of the season, he'd been handsome enough to steal her breath. Even after her pulse had steadied she'd had to remind herself to stop staring and turn her attention to her other guests, so automatically had her gaze seemed to drift back to him.

And when he had looked at *her*... Though her dinner gown had boasted only a modest *décolletage*, it had seemed she could almost feel his gaze burn the bare skin of her chest and shoulders.

Which was, of course, ridiculous. With only two ladies present at dinner, one of them many years his junior and trying to catch the eye of his younger brother, naturally Mr Mansfell had often looked her way during the meal. She should hope her conversation was more sophisticated and interesting than that of a chit just emerging from the schoolroom.

Though she couldn't now recall what they had discussed.

'Miss Wellingford, will you be riding out later?'

The sudden appearance behind her of the very gentleman about whom she'd been thinking made her jump. As she turned to face him, a guilty flush heating her cheeks, the sweep of his gaze across her completely clothed neck and shoulders elicited a quiver deep in her belly, while the deep velvet timbre of his voice made her think of murmured confidences in the bedchamber.

Heavens, what was it about him that produced such an effect in her? Feeling herself flush hotter, she cursed her fair skin as she tried to wrestle her unruly senses under control. 'Colton and Thomas mean to hunt this afternoon,' she replied. 'If you wish to join them, I'm sure our head groom can find you a suitable mount.'

With a wry grimace, he shook his head. 'Thank you, but I'll leave the pheasants to them. Unless Thomas's marksmanship has improved dramatically since the last time we went out, the birds are safe enough. After my stint in the army, I've lost my taste for unnecessary hunting.'

Merry nodded her head in quick sympathy. 'You were at Waterloo, Thomas informed us. Though it must have been dreadful, he told us you provided gallant service, galloping from unit to unit carrying Wellington's messages, despite the hail of rifle balls and cannon shot.'

Mansfell's mouth turned grim. 'Don't be thinking me a hero. 'Twas blind luck only that I survived the battle unscathed. Nor was there anything heroic about carrying orders that sent scores of men to their deaths.'

'And prevented the collapse of the Allied lines,' she inserted swiftly, castigating herself for having brought up the subject. Even deep in the country as Wellingford was, she was acquainted with three families whose sons or brothers had not returned from the battle, and the soldiers she knew who had survived seldom talked of it.

Before she could apologise, Mansfell gave her a smile. 'Forgive me for snapping at you. 'Tis Christmas—no time for such dismal reflections! One thing about surviving a catastrophe is that it makes you all the more eager to savour every delight of the present. In that regard, if you are riding out this afternoon, I should very much like to accompany you. I'm eager to see more of Wellingford.'

Such a simple request, but Merry found herself unable to return a quick answer. Allen Mansfell seemed to possess some…force—an aura that surrounded him and drew her to him, stirred her senses, made her intensely aware of him all the time she was in his presence. Attracted as she was—and she *was* so attracted—she was not at all sure she wished to invite his company. Particularly if the two of them would be riding alone.

Still, being on horseback would require her to maintain her distance—perhaps far enough away from him to extinguish the idiotic desire that kept creeping over her to brush the hair back from his brow or rest her hand on his arm. Besides, an excellent natural rider, she knew she showed to advantage on horseback.

She might be a spinster past her last prayers, but she still couldn't help wanting such an attractive man to see her at her best.

While she hesitated, he said, 'Excuse me! I didn't wish to impose. I know you must have many duties.'

It was tempting to agree—except he'd found her dawdling in front of the window, obviously not in a tearing rush to finish some urgent task. He was also a guest whom it was her duty to entertain, and there were few enough amusements to be had in winter, far from the inducements of London. And she had intended to ride out…

'I do need to inspect the Yule log and check the progress to the repairs at the Dower House. You are welcome to join me—if you're certain you wouldn't find tagging along on such trivial errands a dead bore?'

'Time spent in your company could never be boring,' Mansfell replied, and that velvet edge was in his voice again, while the leisurely glance he trailed up and down her body made little shivers stir once again in her belly. 'Repairs to the Dower House, you said?' he continued.

'Repairs and renovations, yes,' she replied, trying to stifle her distressing, seemingly instinctive reaction to his voice. 'As Colton said, some day soon he shall bring home a bride and I shall need another place to live.'

There—she'd just warned him again that she was on the shelf. That should put an end to his gallantry, if such it was.

Mansfell merely nodded. 'I would be most interested to see them. I've just assembled a list of all the dwellings on Papa's properties in need of repair or refurbishment. You have done such an excellent job here at Wellingford that I should very much like to see how you are conducting your repairs to the Dower House.'

So much for gallantry—on his part, anyway. Obviously she was reading far too much into his voice and gaze. He merely admired her abilities as chatelaine of Wellingford and was interested to see a fuller demonstration of them.

Thank heavens she had not tried to flirt with him! They could be friends, as she and Thomas were friends, sharing an interest in estate management, house repair and other such prosaic things. Even with a man as handsome and dynamic as Allen Mansfell, she could handle being friends.

'I'll have Twilling let you know when I'm ready to

ride out,' she said, curtseying as she turned to go. Once again conscious of his gaze resting on her back, she walked to the stairs, ignoring the little voice in her ear whispering that while desire for him simmered in her belly, their becoming 'friends' was as dangerous as it was unlikely.

A short time later Twilling found her, to announce that Sarah and her family had arrived. Delight filling her at the prospect of seeing again the older sister who'd been her lifelong mentor, confidante and friend, Meredyth hurried to the parlour.

'Nicky—Sarah!' she cried, halting on the threshold. After receiving her brother-in-law Lord Englemere's kiss on her cheek, she tossed herself onto the sofa and enveloped her sister in a fierce hug. 'Welcome home!'

'It's wonderful to be back,' Sarah said, returning her hug just as fiercely. 'And how wonderful Wellingford looks! The new marble floor and the hall's plasterwork are beautiful!'

'The workmen finished them just in time for Christmas,' Meredyth said. 'I must thank you, Nicky, for obtaining such a good price for the harvest that we were able to hire the craftsmen. I must admit, decked out in holly and pine, it reminds me of happy Christmases past.'

'Wellingford never looked this well in Christmases

past,' Sarah said bluntly. 'Our being together was the best part of Christmas then. It's your dedicated work that has made the house lovely again.'

'And Nicky's money,' Meredyth reminded her.

'Never could I have made a better investment,' Nicolas replied. 'You've transformed a failing estate into a thriving one in far less time than I'd imagined possible.'

Warmed by her brother-in-law's praise, Meredyth inclined her head towards her sister. 'I had the very best of teachers. But where is my brilliant nephew? So fascinated by his Uncle Hal's engineering projects that he has run straight off to inspect the new water pump in the kitchen?'

Nicholas shook his head ruefully. 'Our son is mesmerised by all things mechanical. I'm afraid he may use this visit as an opportunity to beg Hal to take him along to see his canal project.'

'Aubrey went up to the schoolroom,' Sarah replied. 'As the eldest of the cousins, he said he needed to make sure all was in readiness for the other children. Though I suspect he hoped to find some of Cook's teacakes awaiting him there as well.'

'Dear Aubrey—as serious and responsible as his papa,' Meredyth said, giving her brother-in-law a fond look. 'You certainly married a kind and generous man, dear sister.'

'Didn't I?' Sarah agreed, giving her husband a

smile so warmly intimate Meredyth felt a pang of loss—and envy.

Trying to smother it, she said quickly, 'You must be chilled. Some spiced wine to warm you after the journey?'

To her surprise, Sarah paled and put a hand to her stomach. 'Not for me. Tea and some dry biscuits would settle better, I think.'

At Meredyth's widened eyes, Nicholas grinned. 'I'll wait until the others arrive for the wine.' Striding across the room, he bent to place a kiss on his wife's forehead. 'Is there anything I can do to make you more comfortable, sweet Sarah?'

'You could go and make sure Aubrey hasn't got into mischief.'

'Tell him his Aunt Merry is eager to see him,' Meredyth added. 'He can sample Cook's teacakes just as well in the parlour, you know.'

Nicholas nodded. 'I'll have Twilling send in tea, and leave you two to chat. Let me know if you need anything, sweeting,' he said, squeezing his wife's fingers before walking from the room.

Meredyth waited until he had exited. 'You're increasing again?'

Sarah nodded. 'Nicky is delighted—but concerned.'

As well he might be, Meredyth thought, already worried herself. Sarah had miscarried a seven-month

babe last winter. It had been mostly to console his wife
for the devastating loss and to help her recover her
health and spirits that he'd squired the whole Wellingford clan on a Grand Tour of Italy and Greece last
spring and summer.

'How are you feeling?' she asked anxiously.

'Wonderful,' Sarah replied. At Meredyth's pointed
look, she said, 'Well, mostly. You know I'd suffer
anything to give Nicky another healthy child. But
between feeling sickly and Nicky trying to wrap me
in cotton wool, I'm afraid I won't be much help to
you. I'm sorry to be so useless when the gathering will
be even larger this year with Sinjin, Clare and Bella
staying too. You're sure it won't be too much? Sinjin
and Clare could probably stay with his mother at San-
diford Court and ride over.'

Meredyth damped down a pang of dismay
deepened by what she feared was a tad of resentment.
She had been looking forward to sharing the myriad
preparations required to conduct such a large Christmas house party with her competent, resourceful
sister—especially since she was still catching up on
the many duties neglected during her summer-long
absence abroad with the family.

But how could she resent Sarah? The family
wouldn't be here at Wellingford for Christmas if Sarah
hadn't given up her childhood love Sinjin, then a
soldier on the Peninsular with Wellington's army, to

go to London and find a wealthy husband to rescue the estate from foreclosure. Only the intervention of a kind Providence had spurred Nicholas, the former fiancé of Sarah's friend Clare, into proposing what had been at first a marriage of convenience.

'If Sinjin and Nicholas can co-exist amicably under the same roof, I imagine I can make sure everyone is adequately fed and housed.'

Sarah laughed. 'Don't be silly. You know they made amends long ago. As Clare and I knew from the start, they both realised that Nicholas was better for me and Clare was better for Sinjin.'

Spurred by a sudden, unexpected ache of longing, Meredyth found herself blurting, 'Did you never repine over losing your first love?'

Sarah turned to study her, her look so insightful that Meredyth felt compelled to turn away.

'It was dreadful at first, of course. So compelling and unprecedented a feeling is burned into the soul. But, driven by necessity to make a match before the mortgage came due on Wellingford, everything happened so quickly. I hadn't much time to repine. Certainly not long years, as you have had.' Reaching over, she squeezed Meredyth's hand. 'Both Nicholas and I found that second love can be an even better love. You could too, sweet sister, if you'd only open your heart and mind to the prospect.'

Meredyth blinked back the sudden burn of tears.

'I doubt it would be that easy. I'm seven and twenty now! What passably attractive and eligible man would seriously consider a spinster like me?'

Looking her up and down critically, Sarah said, 'I see an accomplished lady with an elegant figure, lovely golden hair, striking silver eyes—and nary a wrinkle,' she added with a grin. 'True, you are not a chit making her first bow, but I think you would be surprised to discover how many attractive, eligible men would seriously consider you.'

Unbidden, the image of Allen Mansfell's handsome face invaded Meredyth's mind. Before she could thrust it away, Twilling entered with the tea tray.

After he had served them, Sarah sat cautiously sipping tea while Meredyth nibbled a sweet biscuit. 'You are going to accompany Faith to Town next spring, aren't you?' Sarah asked.

'Of course. Faith has talked of nothing since we got home last summer—and is already practising her wiles on Thomas Mansfell, as yet to no visible effect! I've not set my face against matrimony, so I suppose since I shall be in London anyway that I may look about.'

'Good,' Sarah said. 'I do hope you will try to find a suitable gentleman. I hate to think of you denied all the joys of matrimony and motherhood.'

As she reached for another biscuit, Sarah's face

suddenly took on a greenish cast. Putting the hand over her stomach instead, she took a quick sip of tea.

Pointing at her nauseated sister, Meredyth grinned. 'Indeed, I'd hate to miss *that*.'

Sarah made a face at her. 'The instant you hold your first babe in your arms you'll realise it was worth all the times you felt sickly or peevish or huge as a cow. It's worth everything.'

At that moment Twilling appeared at the door. 'Miss Clare and Miss Elizabeth are here,' he announced.

'No, keep your seat,' Meredyth urged Sarah, and she went to the door to greet the newcomers, accepting a kiss from her sister's best friend Clare, a hug from her husband and their neighbour, Sarah's first love Sinjin, then a fond embrace from her younger sister Elizabeth. With only a bit of hesitation she exchanged a handshake with Elizabeth's beaming husband, Hal Waterman—Nicky's best friend and Uncle Hal to all their offspring.

'We sent the children up to the nursery with their maids,' Clare announced. 'After being cooped up for hours in a lurching carriage with a chattering child, we ladies need calm. Ah, I see there is tea. Bless you, Merry!'

'Would you prefer spiced wine?' Meredyth asked.

Elizabeth and Claire winced, Claire putting a hand to her mouth.

Her eyes widening, Sarah said, 'You are *both*…?'

'Increasing? I am,' Clare said, and looked over at Elizabeth, who nodded.

'And you too, Sarah?' Clare asked, turning her keen gaze to her friend. When Sarah nodded too, Clare laughed. 'I would say something about the effects of Italian air, but the malady seems to have afflicted Elizabeth as well, and she never left England.'

Meredyth's beautiful younger sister was gazing at her husband Hal. The rapturous joy of being newlyweds shone in their eyes. 'Cupid is not bound by geography,' Elizabeth said.

While the husbands offered each other hearty congratulations, Meredyth looked away and sipped her tea. How fortunate the happy news had captured everyone's attention, making it unlikely anyone would sense the discomfort she felt, meeting Hal Waterman again for the first time since his marriage to her sister.

Meredyth had known and admired the tall, quietly-spoken Hal since Sarah's marriage to his best friend. She'd even, after the rawness of her grief at losing James had eased, once thought she might try to fix his interest.

Thank heavens she'd never put a word in Nicky's ear about it! she thought, her face burning anew.

Observing the hungry gaze the couple shared, Meredyth could understand why Society's disapproval had not been sufficient to dissuade Elizabeth,

whose elderly first husband had died last summer
while they were all abroad, from wedding before the
end of her year's mourning. A bolt of envy and
longing shot through her.

'Best sit,' Hal was telling Elizabeth. 'Not feeling
too well,' he explained to the group.

'Have you tried ginger tea?' Sarah asked.

'Are you always ill in the morning?' Clare interposed.

Meredyth looked up to see Sinjin winking at Hal.
'Megrims and vapours! We'd better go and find Nicky.
Being only recently wed, you're new to this, Hal, but
trust me—the conversation is about to disintegrate
into woman talk.'

Clare sniffed. 'Since you men are the cause of our
megrims and vapours, perhaps you should take your-
selves off.'

'Virago,' Sinjin said fondly. 'Her temper's been
uneven ever since she realised she was with child—and
now that long carriage ride… Ladies, we'll rejoin you
after you've refreshed yourself with tea and sage
advice.'

Clare stared after her departing husband. 'My
temper *has* been unsteady. I never suffered a day with
Bella, but this child has sickened me from the first.'
She sighed and patted her stomach. 'It must be a boy.
Only a man could cause this much trouble!'

While Elizabeth, already fond mother to a son, exclaimed in protest, Sarah said, 'Have you tried dry soda crackers and weak tea before rising in the morning?'

'A peppermint leaf tisane may help,' Elizabeth added.

'I'll just go check on the children,' Meredyth murmured, and walked out, leaving the other ladies to exchange recipes and advice.

Thrilled as she was to have all of them at Wellingford, and as genuinely as she rejoiced at the news of babes to come, the twist of bitter sadness squeezing her chest compelled her to distance herself. She loved them all dearly...but she could not quell a deep, searing sense of envy.

Envy for the children they'd already borne and these new babes, for the obvious love expressed by their husbands in teasing words and fond glances.

Had she been wrong to turn aside the proposal of their neighbour and deflect the suit of the family friend?

It was too late to regret decisions already long since made. Besides, sickening with the child of a man she didn't love would be no bargain, for a good part of those ladies' joy was in the adoring circle of a family they'd created.

No, she'd made the right choice, the necessary choice, and if she were to live through it all over again would choose no differently. Except, perhaps, being too prudent to lie with James.

But if she had found joy in his arms and conceived she would never have been able to keep the child of their love. Worse than the appalling shame and scandal, she would have had to give up the babe.

Which brought her back full circle. She would expire of longing and envy before she let her family suspect how deeply their joy wounded her. She'd have to fix her mind and heart more firmly on being the valued sister, the loving aunt.

With a house to refurbish to her taste, property of her own and an independent income, she was far more fortunate than most spinster ladies, who were often shuttled from household to household as family needs dictated—unpaid and dependent servants, who became, once age diminished their usefulness, a burden.

No, she would visit her siblings, love their children, and assist them as necessary. But as an independent lady of means she would return to her own home when she chose and travel if she wished. And if a small voice murmured that such an existence sounded sterile and empty, she suppressed it as firmly as she had the whispered warning against befriending Allen Mansfell.

Chapter Three

As Meredyth crossed the hall on her way up to the schoolroom, a scamper of feet on the landing alerted her to the presence of children an instant before she saw them, skipping down the stairs. Led, as they usually were, by Sarah and Nicky's son Aubrey, oldest of the cousins, as soon as they spied her they accelerated their pace, tumbling over one another in their haste.

'Aunt Merry! Aunt Merry! We're so glad to be here!' they cried as they reached her. Aubrey and David halted to make her a bow, while little Bella hugged her skirts. Meredyth drew them all close, savouring the warmth and scent and wonder of them.

'Papa, Uncle Hal and Uncle Sinjin have gone off to hunt with Uncle Colton and Mr Thomas, but I told Papa I would stay here and help you,' Aubrey said.

'We can help too, Aunt Merry,' Elizabeth's son David said.

'Me too,' Clare's daughter Bella inserted. 'Mama says I'm a "strong-willed termagant", which Papa says means I know how to do lots of things. I am going to be a beauty, you know.' Turning to Aubrey, she added, 'Then I shall marry you and be a countess too.'

'You know I'm not going to marry,' Aubrey said firmly. 'I shall devote my life to science.'

Bella narrowed her eyes, her smile fading. 'I can marry you if I want to,' she replied.

Noting the worried crease in David's brow at this exchange, Aubrey said to him, 'Bella means no harm. She's just a bit…difficult sometimes.'

Bella put her hands on her hips. 'Am *not*!'

'Indeed you are,' Aubrey replied, turning back to her.

'I. Am. Not!' Bella cried, stamping her foot.

'Children, there's some lemonade and ginger cookies for you in the kitchen,' Meredyth inserted hastily. 'Your favourites, Bella.' With a sudden flash of inspiration, she added, 'After that, you can all come with me in the gig to inspect the Yule log.'

Her aggrieved expression replaced by a blazing smile, Bella said, 'Can I ride my pony?'

'It will be better if we all go in the trap. Then you can help John, the groom, gather holly and mistletoe for the swags and kissing balls,' Merry said. And I will have a collection of attention-demanding escorts during my ride with Allen Mansfell, she added silently to herself.

'I love ginger cookies,' Bella pronounced. 'And I *will* marry Aubrey if I want to—you'll see. Race you to the kitchen!' In a froth of white petticoats, she suddenly dashed towards the service stairs, the two boys pelting after her.

Pleased with herself for averting a squabble—and for having cleverly acquired an audience that would make flirtation difficult, should Allen Mansfell have that in mind—Meredyth headed back to resume her work with the housekeeper.

Frowning at the unwanted tingle of anticipation it produced, she sent Twilling to inform her guest that they would ride out in an hour.

A half-smile on his face, Allen Mansfell stood beside his horse next to the pony trap, watching Meredyth Wellingford field questions, offer opinions and compliment the diligence of her young relations as they ran about the woodland clearing, dragging the pine and holly John the groom had cut for them back to the carriage.

The smile deepened as he acknowledged the success of Miss Wellingford's ploy. When she'd greeted him at the stables two hours ago, he'd hardly needed the fetching blush that had coloured her cheeks while she explained to him the unexpected appearance of a gig full of children to realise she'd decided to provide herself with a group of chaperons.

The fact that she'd chosen to enlist the children only confirmed what he'd suspected: she was as conscious as he of the sensual attraction that simmered between them. However, rather than using her knowledge of his vulnerability towards her to tease, tantalise and entice him, she'd chosen to retreat from it, like the modest, virtuous maiden she was.

After Susanna, he found her reticence both quaint and vastly appealing. Her maintaining a proper distance now only whetted his appetite and made him keener to court her.

Cheerfully allowing her the victory this time, he'd refrained from any attempt at gallantry during the ride—so far. But he wasn't about to let a gaggle of infants discourage him—not when everything he saw and sensed about her continued to reinforce how attractive he found her and what an excellent wife she would make.

As her swift countermove in recruiting the children had increased his estimation of her cleverness, so their dawdling ride across Wellingford land had reinforced the high opinion he'd already formed of her excellent management abilities. And though she'd obviously brought along the children to keep him at a distance, she hadn't neglected him.

Rather, in between conversing with the youngsters she had provided him an ongoing commentary about the planting plans for the fields they'd passed, the building materials being used to refurbish the cottages, the winter repair of tools and harness, and other such topics which she hoped, she said, might be of interest to a man with his responsibilities.

As the ride had continued, he'd also been able to observe her affection for and skilful handling of her young charges. She'd kept even the restless Bella entertained, pointing out horses in one field, puppies trotting along the fence line in another, even squirrels frolicking in the trees overhead, all while patiently answering the children's many questions and defusing potential squabbles. She would be as excellent a mother to some lucky gentleman's children as she would an exemplary helpmate in tending his estate.

Add that beguiling hint of passion just waiting to be kindled to her other abilities, and Miss Meredyth Wellingford possessed every quality he could wish for. His last-minute decision to accompany Thomas on their journey home was looking more and more fortuitous, Allen concluded, an expansive feeling of well-being settling over him as he walked over to help the groom stack the pile of fir boughs and holly branches into the gig.

While the two men worked, the children made their

final inspection of the Yule log—a huge oak that had been felled at the end of summer to allow it to dry properly and burn well on Christmas Day. While the boys clambered up to sit on it, little Bella remained on the ground, stamping her foot in frustration that her long skirts hampered her from following them.

'Don't fret, Bella,' Miss Wellingford consoled her. 'It's time to return to the house anyway. Once the log is limbed and ready to bring back you shall ride upon it too. Your mama and papa and all your aunts and uncles will come with us. We'll have drinks and teacakes and sing carols, and at all the farms we pass, the tenants will come out to wish us good luck and sing a carol or two. When we finally place the log on the hearth you may help light the fire with a taper from the remains of last year's tree.'

The little girl's eyes widened. 'I can start the fire? You promise?'

'I promise. So back in the gig with all of you, and home we go. I imagine by now Cook will have baked some fresh ginger biscuits for you.'

As she settled the children back into the carriage, Colton and Thomas rode into the clearing. 'Excellent work, troops,' Colton pronounced upon viewing the overflowing greenery. 'I think you've gathered enough for two houses.'

'Was the hunting good?' Aubrey asked them.

Thomas shrugged, but Colton proudly held up a

haversack. 'Bagged two pheasants for Christmas dinner—just as I promised, Merry.'

While the children clamoured to see his prizes, Miss Wellingford said, 'If you're planning to take the birds straight back to Cook, can I ask you to escort the children home? I need to stop at the Dower House.'

'Of course,' Colton replied.

'Thank you! Children, you can inspect Colton's birds when you get back,' Miss Wellingford told them. 'I'll see you at the house later.'

'What do you say, infants? Shall we see if this old pony can gallop?' Colton asked.

The boys clapped their assent while Bella shrieked, 'Yes, yes—let's gallop!'

Miss Wellingford watched them leave, concern on her face as Colton told the driver to 'spring it!' Her teeth clamped down on her lip, as if she had to restrain herself from warning Colton not to be too reckless.

'Mind if I continue to ride with you?' Allen asked her.

She started, as if surprised to find him still beside her. Turning to him with a hesitant smile, she said, 'You're not yet bored to flinders? Between the children's antics and me prosing on about farming, I thought you'd be anxious to return to the Hall and a warm glass of wine.'

'Not at all! I enjoyed the children—and your commentary. Besides, I could never be bored in your company.'

She raised an eyebrow. 'Gallantry indeed, sir.'

'Merest truth,' he assured her, turning upon her the full force of his admiring gaze.

Her silver eyes rose to his face and their gazes locked. Once again he felt that powerful zing of connection. As if scorched, she looked quickly away.

'You can ride along if you wish,' she allowed, her cheeks going rosy.

Hardly a heartfelt invitation, but he intended to avail himself of it anyway. In her cautious voice and wary stance he read clearly her hesitance to be alone with him.

He would never force his company on a truly unwilling maid. But in this instance all his instincts told him Meredyth Wellingford's reluctance stemmed not from fear or distaste for his company, but rather from its opposite…an attraction she felt as strongly as he did, but for some reason was trying to repress.

He'd have to proceed carefully. While he wished to leave her in no doubt about how appealing her found her—he doubted he could conceal that fact in any event—he must also keep his conversation free of any innuendo that might make Miss Wellingford uncomfortable. There would be no deep kisses and fondling on balconies for her. No taking liberties with her person until she was well and truly wed. He respected, even admired that. After all, he'd not want a wife who gave a come-hither smile to every passing rogue each time his back was turned.

A wife like Susanna who, with heavy-lidded eyes and an unspoken invitation on her pouting lips, had imbued her every utterance with sensual overtones, driving him mad with lust and jealousy.

'Thank you,' he replied. 'Shall we go, then?'

Giving him a nod, she signalled her mount to a trot, taking care to maintain some distance between the horses. With his body already urging him closer, faster, he found her caution frustrating, intriguing— and very enticing.

Like a beautiful, high-strung, unbroken filly, Meredyth Wellingford would have to be soothed and gentled if he wanted her to come to him. Allen found it unexpectedly appealing that to woo *this* lady he would likely have to win her mind and heart before he could beguile her senses. And the better acquainted with her he became, the longer he spent in her company, the more fervently he desired her to do just that.

'Thomas told us you took over the daily management of your father's estates after your return from the army,' she was saying. 'You seem to relish the responsibility?'

'I do,' he affirmed. 'I enjoy watching the fields go from damp earth after spring ploughing to fragile shoots to vigorous stalks and to the gold of harvest. I like consulting with the tenants on ways to increase yields, improve the land and keep the property in good repair.' He chuckled. 'I like beauty, order—and the smell of whitewash and paint.'

'Then you shall definitely enjoy stopping at the Dower House,' she replied with a grin.

At that moment a quail burst from the woods. Miss Wellingford's mare reared up, neighing and fighting the bit. Before Allen could signal his mount to assist her, she had soothed the animal and settled her back to trot.

'Well done!' Allen said. 'For an instant I feared your horse might bolt, but you controlled her beautifully. What an exemplary horsewoman you are!'

Miss Wellingford shrugged off his compliment. 'Growing up in the country as I did, I expect 'twas inevitable.'

'Not at all. My sisters both ride, but neither can match you. You move as one with the horse. It's a pleasure to watch.'

Though he truly had not intended to imbue the remark with any innuendo, her eyes widened as she lifted her wary gaze to his. Once again he felt almost compelled to draw near her. His fingers itched to brush the golden tendrils from her brow, to trace along the fine leather of her gloves to the soft bare skin of her wrists.

Her silver eyes turned smoky, almost as if she could

read his thoughts. When she sighed and ran the tip of her pink tongue over her lips, leaving them moist and glistening, his pulse jumped. His heart hammered in his chest and he felt such a surge of desire he nearly lost his seat.

Shaken, exulting, he struggled to get himself back under control. Ah, yes, passion ran deep in Miss Wellingford. He ached to explore it. *Now*.

Maybe he wouldn't wait until the beginning of the Season to begin openly courting her…

Chapter Four

While he reached that pleasant conclusion, Miss Wellingford's mount had trotted on ahead. 'Are your father's holdings far-flung?' she asked as she turned back.

She'd increased the distance between them again. But not for long, he vowed. 'The Grange is his principal estate, but several other sizeable properties have come into the family through marriage and purchase,' he replied, urging his mount nearer. 'I visit them every several months.'

'You get to travel, then? Does that suit you?'

'I enjoy it. Papa does not—all the jolting about on horseback tires his bones, he says. Besides, since my sister married the owner of a neighbouring estate Papa prefers to remain at home and enjoy his grandchildren.'

'Your family is expecting some from you soon?' she asked, carefully avoiding his eyes.

Was that a glimmer of interest? He certainly hoped so. Encouraged, he replied, 'They are not pressing me to marry, but I'm sure they would welcome it. Nor am I averse to the idea, if the time—and the lady—are right.'

Once again a slight blush tinged her cheeks. 'As an exemplary young man of good family and excellent prospects, I'm sure you'll have your pick of the Marriage Mart. The Dower House is just down this lane.'

He turned his horse to follow, admiring the bounce of her trim posterior on the sidesaddle. If he could assume her remark was sincere rather than idle flattery—and nothing he'd yet seen of her led him to expect she would indulge in that—it appeared she found his character as appealing as he found hers. A most gratifying prospect. Mutual admiration might easily lead to the friendship and tender regard he now believed created the best foundation for a happy union.

She pulled up at the Dower House, a compact but spacious half-timbered building that appeared to date back to Elizabethan times, and waited for him to assist her. He did so with pleasure, savouring the feel of her trim waist under his fingers as he helped her from the saddle.

Before he could make any more of that momentary closeness, an older man, having apparently heard their approach, trotted out the front door. 'Good day, Miss Wellingford—sir,' he said, bowing. 'We've just finished the front parlour. Would you like to inspect it?'

'Very much,' she replied. Nodding at Allen to follow, she set off after the foreman. Not sure what he would have done had they not been interrupted, but sorry he'd not had the opportunity to find out, he trailed after them.

They crossed the entrance hall, its wooden floor sanded and its walls bright with fresh paint, and entered a side room, also freshly painted and boasting a handsome coffered ceiling.

'The heater be fully installed now,' the foreman said. 'You sure it warms better than the old fireplace, miss? It's not so big.'

'True, Baxter, but the smaller size draws less cold air from the room and allows less heated air to escape up the chimney, while the shallow sides and angled back reflect more of the fire's heat into the room,' she explained.

The workman still looked dubious. 'If you say so, miss. Now that we know how to do it, refitting the other rooms will go more quickly. I'll be getting back to it.'

'Thank you, Baxter.'

'You're having Rumford fireplaces installed in all the rooms?' Allen asked.

'You're familiar with the design?' she asked, sounding surprised.

'Yes. After reading the Count's treatises on heating devices, I sought out some examples. I've also seen the double boiler he developed, and a model of his stove.'

Her eyes brightened with enthusiasm. 'I viewed his stove in London too. I'd like to install one here, but his design is too large for the kitchen.'

'You sound quite knowledgeable,' Allen said, surprised in turn—and impressed. 'Have you read Rumford's treatise?'

'No, but Hal—Mr Waterman—told me about them. So many new devices are being developed! Preferring this house to the Hall—and such a drafty, crumbling wreck it was then one could scarce blame her!—my mama moved here after my father's death, living here until her own demise. Nothing about the house has been altered since before my grandfather's day. Since it required renovation anyway, I decided to incorporate into its refurbishment as many of the new designs as I could.'

'So Hal has interested you in his technologies too? His zeal is contagious. He's been a good friend since Oxford, and the breadth of his knowledge still amazes me.'

'Quite true,' she agreed. 'I've known him for years—since my sister Sarah married Lord Englemere.'

A brief blush came and went in her cheeks, making Allen wonder if she'd ever had a *tendre* for Hal. A surprisingly intense satisfaction filled him that his friend was now safely wed to the lovely Elizabeth.

'Have you invested in any of his ventures?' she asked.

'Alas, working the land does not allow one to quickly accumulate the extra coin necessary for investing. I do hope to give him some blunt towards a proposed scheme for rail transport, but in the main I've focused on domestic improvements. As you seem to have.'

'Let me show you what else I've had installed, then,' she said.

To his surprise and delight she took his arm. Enjoying the little sizzle of contact, he let her lead him out of the parlour.

'How I wish I might have interior gas lighting as well, such as I have seen at several houses in London!' she told him as they walked down to the kitchen. 'But I expect it will be years before we have a gas works near enough. Still, along with the Rumford fireplaces we shall have a saltpeter vat for chilling, and a Sidgier washing machine in the laundry. Are you familiar with that?'

'No. Do tell me how it works.'

For another half an hour, her gestures animated, her manner friendlier than it had been at any time previously, Meredyth Wellingford took Allen through the house. She showed him the double-caged rotary washing machine, the improved gas lamps Hal had brought her back from Scotland, and described how the workmen were altering all the fireplaces to accommodate the shallower, narrower Rumsford stoves.

Allen followed her about, charmed, delighted and impressed that Miss Wellingford not only shared his interest in household improvements but demonstrated a thorough knowledge of how the new devices functioned. Enjoying the discovery that she possessed so unusual and unexpected an understanding assuaged somewhat his body's disappointment that her tour did not include the bedchambers.

It required but little imagination for him to envisage himself slowly disrobing her before a glowing Rumsford hearth, combing those golden tresses through his fingers as he pulled her head close and took her lips…

His chest and his loins tightened at the thought. Dispelling the image with reluctance, he told himself that for the moment he would have to be content with fanning the small flame of friendship their shared interests had created in Miss Wellingford. More carnal pleasures would have to wait for later...but not too much later, he promised himself.

They ended their explorations where they had begun, in the front hall. 'Shall we return to Wellingford Hall now?' she asked. 'You must be famished!'

'A glass of ale does sound appealing,' he admitted. 'But I've enjoyed this afternoon tremendously. Thank you so much for the tour.'

'You're very welcome.'

She looked up at him, smiling faintly. A warmth seemed to envelop them, binding them closer, making him fiercely glad he was standing with her, inhaling her sweet rose scent, savouring the feel of her hand on his arm. Just one small movement and he could lean down and kiss her...

His head had angled downwards before he halted abruptly, his brain warning his eager body that it was too soon. Loath to rush into something that would frighten her off, or spoil the camaraderie they'd just enjoyed, he stepped back.

Ignoring the clamouring of his disappointed body, instead of claiming the kiss he craved Allen offered her his arm and walked her down the front steps to the waiting horses. Allowing his hands to linger at her waist just a moment longer than necessity dictated, he assisted her into the saddle.

'It's a handsome property,' he said after he'd re-mounted his own horse, determinedly pulling his thoughts from admiring the luscious curve of her hips. 'I can understand why you are lavishing such attention on it.'

She shrugged. 'It will be my home some day, when Colton brings home his bride.'

'Are you so sure? I'm already surprised the gentlemen have left so lovely a lady unclaimed,' he said, glad for this opening to question a fact he found increasingly puzzling.

To his surprise, a sadness settled over her face. 'There was one gentleman. Like you, my fiancé was a soldier. He died in India several years ago.'

Saddened for her—but relieved to know she was not irrevocably set against marriage—he said, 'I'm sorry. It was not just in Waterloo and on the Peninsula that we lost good men. Did you…abandon society after his loss?'

Keeping her horse beside his this time as they rode, she said, 'Not exactly. I went to London when my other sisters Emma and Cecily were presented, while James and I were still engaged. Just after he died Mama's health declined, and she could no longer leave Wellingford. I stayed with her until her death. Since then there has been one thing or another—repairs to the Hall, overseeing the manager in bringing the farms and fields back into order, attending my sisters at their lying-ins, and most recently the trip abroad. But I plan to accompany Faith to London for the Season next spring.'

'I've heard a great deal of what Miss Meredyth Wellingford has done for her family,' Allen said as they started down the gravel drive to Wellingford Hall. 'But what does Miss Wellingford want for herself?'

She looked down at her hands on the reins. 'A place to belong,' she said, so softly he had to strain to hear her. 'Where I am loved and valued. Not a burden.'

'Here among your family I can see you already have that.' Reaching the front entrance, he jumped down from his horse, handing the reins to a waiting groom, who led away their mounts away while he helped her to alight. 'Do you not long for…more?'

This time he could not resist the temptation to leave his hands on her waist well past the time necessary for her to steady her balance. Loath to remove them, he stared down at her, forgetting his question, oblivious to any answer she might have given him, lost in silver eyes that widened, then darkened, in lips that parted in seeming invitation. His breath drying in his throat, once again Allen fought against the urgent need to kiss her.

Abruptly she stepped back, breaking the spell. 'Th-thank you for your escort, Mr Mansfell,' she said, her voice breathless to his ears—or maybe it was the sudden thunder of his heartbeat that made her sound faint. 'I shall see you at dinner, I'm sure.' After giving him a quick curtsey, she hurried up the steps.

Watching her walk away with a lithe grace, while

he stood silent, waiting for his pulse to steady, Allen found himself smiling. Though his desire for her was even sharper after the interlude they'd just shared, somehow, with a sense of euphoria and calm expectation filling him, he felt less impatient.

He meant to wed Meredyth Wellingford, he realised, the decision resonating with a satisfying feel of rightness. He'd seen enough of women to know what he wanted and didn't want in a wife. Indeed, he wondered suddenly, was it truly necessary to wait until next spring's Season to go down on his knee before her?

Having known each other by reputation for years, they had no need of a long courtship in which to discover each other's character. His time thus far at Wellingford had demonstrated that they shared even more interests than he'd suspected. Better still, since the moment they'd met he'd known there lay between them a deep vein of sensual attraction just waiting to be mined—one he was more than eager to explore.

Tasting her loveliness was a pleasure worth waiting for—an eventual delight anticipation would make even sweeter. He'd earn that moment by building on the rapport this afternoon had created, coaxing her along the path from admiration to affection down which he felt himself already tumbling, until her resistance to the pull between them vanished and she willingly gave him her hand.

Without being too conceited, he felt he could offer her as much as she offered him. Lovely as she was, Meredyth Wellingford *was* a bit old for the Marriage Mart. In their bedazzlement with the fresh young beauties making their first bows, less thoughtful men might overlook her. She deserved a man who truly appreciated her charm, her unique talents…and her passion.

If he could induce her to reciprocate his regard as she already reciprocated his desire, and to look as favourably as he did on the idea of marriage, perhaps they could reach an understanding even before he and Thomas left Wellingford for the Grange.

An understanding, he thought, his enthusiasm for the idea building, that might allow them to announce their engagement at once, sparing him having to waste the crucial start of another agricultural season trapped in London trolling the Marriage Mart.

A spring in his step, Allen mounted the stairs to Wellingford Hall. He could think of no more delightful a Christmas gift than having Meredyth Wellingford agree to become his bride.

Chapter Five

Dismissing her maid after dressing for dinner, Meredyth lingered in her chamber, hoping a moment of reflection might settle her nerves.

Settle them she must. Otherwise, perceptive as Sarah was, Meredyth couldn't be certain her sister's current condition would distract her from noticing the agitation still afflicting Meredyth after her ride with Allen Mansfell. The chaotic mix of confusion, yearning, anxiety, and raw desire churning within her was so distressing and embarrassing she didn't feel she could bear discussing it—not even with the sister to whom she'd disclosed every other secret of her life.

Just how had Allen Mansfell invaded her placid, well-ordered existence, and within the space of two short days shattered all her hard-won calm and contentment? Making her burn with desires she'd thought permanently extinguished and yearn for an intimacy she'd long felt impossible to ever recapture.

Even with the children accompanying them she'd been unable to harden herself to his charm. With a good-humoured amusement that made him all the more appealing he'd displayed neither surprise nor annoyance at this addition to what was to have been their private ride. Instead, with the twinkle in his eye telling her he'd recognised her ploy, he'd joined in her efforts to entertain her young charges and helped them cut and load their greenery.

While she had deliberately limited her conversation to a prosaic discussion of agricultural life—hardly the stuff of which flirtation was made—he had responded with such intelligence and genuine interest that, forgetting she meant to resist him, she'd been drawn to him anew.

And once the distraction of the children's presence had been removed...oh, how much stronger the urge to draw near him had become!

By then the force pulling her towards him had become more than just the ever-present temptation of his very attractive person. And, astounded and thrilled at the Dower House to discover he possessed an interest in innovations as lively as her own, she'd allowed him to lure her into prattling away...and ended up enjoying his company far more than was good for her.

His company and the closeness of his far-too-attractive body.

Her recollection of what it felt like to anticipate a kiss might be several years out of date, but some memories—the most vivid, searing memories—never faded. She was certain he'd almost kissed her twice. First outside the Dower House and then beside her own front door.

That such a handsome, vital young man desired her sent a purely feminine thrill through her. And, oh, how she'd longed to lean up and taste his lips!

Hers burned anew at the thought.

The fact that he had made her yearn for him so desperately when they stood not ten feet from Wellingford's front windows, where one of her guests or servants might have seen them should they have embraced, had sent her scurrying into the house in a near-panic.

How was she to deal with Allen Mansfell?

Too restless to remain seated, she jumped up and began to pace.

For a virile man like Mr Mansfell, immured in the country as he had been lately, it was probably natural to flirt with whatever feminine company was available. As the only unmarried female of appropriate age, that had to be her.

His flirtation was most likely only casual—wasn't it?

Except…the marked attention he was paying her was beginning to attract notice. Even the not normally discerning Colton had sent her a questioning look when Mr Mansfell had remained in her company instead of riding back with the rest of the party.

He was a gentleman of impeccable reputation; she was a lady of quality and his hostess. To tempt her into dalliance would be unthinkable.

Could he be serious?

Mayhap he *was* interested in her. She was only two years his elder. Younger men sometimes did marry older ladies.

Usually rich ones, though. Thanks to Nicky's generosity she'd not enter marriage a pauper, but neither was she by any means an heiress. Except for the neighbour who'd courted her because the lands she'd inherited marched with his, she'd always assumed any man who pursued her would do so mainly for her charms alone.

Which brought her right back to the same question. Would a handsome man with excellent prospects who, as she'd so baldly told him, might have the pick of the ladies in the Marriage Mart truly favour a maiden years his elder? Or was he just trying to pass the time with an agreeable flirtation?

She didn't know him well enough to judge. But, alas, she wanted to know him better. Already she liked him far more than was prudent. And unfortunately, her desire to respond to his sensual appeal, to reach up and pull his mouth down to claim a kiss should he ever offer one again, was great and growing, whether he was earnest in his regard for her or not.

She sighed, thinking how marvellous it would be to have a companion who shared her enthusiasm for country life, for building, cultivating, preserving and enhancing the rich heritage entrusted to her. Someone of intelligence with whom to confer and question and debate and entertain.

A man of powerful physical attraction to excite her appetites and slowly, thrillingly, satisfy them…

Warmth swept over her as she pictured the vivid green of his eyes, the little dimples in his cheeks she longed to trace with her finger when he smiled, the thick dark hair curling over his brow through which she imagined running her fingers, and more…

Closing her eyes, she envisaged those broad shoulders and strong arms bared to embrace her, the muscled thighs that controlled his mount so easily gripped about her as he drove her deep into the warmth of a feather mattress—

Goodness! She halted her by the window with a gasp, fanning herself. This was awful! Never before had she indulged in such lewd, wicked fantasies.

What was she to do? Abandon resistance and let herself follow her emotions and senses wherever they might lead? Respond in a way that would betray her interest and risk embarrassing herself by discovering that he was only trifling with her?

She simply didn't know.

How could she recapture any sense of calm when all her instincts warned that Allen Mansfell posed a more serious danger than any other man she'd encountered in all the years since losing James? A man who might lead her to jeopardise her self-respect, her independence and her health in the pursuit of pleasure…who could tempt her to abandon caution and risk not just her body but her heart.

She'd just begun another agitated turn about the room when her chamber door swung open and Bella waltzed in. 'Aunt Merry! Isn't my new dress beautiful? Mama had it made specially for Christmas.'

Gladly Meredyth put aside her agitation to focus on the child. 'It is lovely,' she told the little girl pirouetting before her. 'I'm surprised, though, that your mama is letting you wear it before Christmas Day.'

'Oh, she wanted me to wait. But I asked and asked. The last time I asked she was lying down with a cloth on her head, and she told me to wear it and go to the devil.'

While Meredyth choked back a laugh, Bella continued, 'Your dress is pretty too, Aunt Merry. But gentlemen will like it better like this.' Reaching up, the child tugged the neckline lower, until it revealed the rounded tops of Meredyth's breasts.

Appalled, Meredyth stared at the little girl. 'Heavens, Bella, who told you that?'

'Nobody,' the little girl said. 'When we were in Italy last summer, I watched the gentlemen who met Mama. If her gown showed some of her bosoms, they stared at her all night.'

Merciful heavens—the child was barely six years old! Meredyth thought, aghast. She was wondering whether she ought to warn Clare when Bella added, 'Mr Mansfell will watch you too. You like him, don't you?'

Meredyth was about to reply that she liked all her guests, but then her mind caught on the image of Allen Mansfell, looking down her bodice, his eyes lingering on her breasts. At the idea, her nipples swelled and burned, while a slow melting started lower, in her core.

She didn't realise she'd gone silent until Bella, with a little clap of glee, said 'You *do* like him!'

'Of course I like him, Bella,' Meredyth replied, belatedly attempting a recovery. 'His brother Thomas has been Colton's best friend for years.

'He's almost as handsome as my papa,' Bella allowed. 'He likes you too. During the ride today he watched you all the time.'

Had he been staring at her during their drive? Half-pleased, half-alarmed, Meredyth felt a blush warming her cheeks even as she protested, 'I'm just the sister of his brother's friend.'

'He *does* like you,' the child insisted. 'Mr Mansfell likes Aunt Merry!' she sang, dancing around the room. 'Aunt Merry likes Mr Mansfell!'

Now, that was just what she needed—the mischievous Bella drawing attention to her conduct towards Allen Mansfell while she was still at sixes and sevens trying to decide how to act around him. Searching for a way to silence the child, she said, 'A lady never announces her interest in a gentleman—'tis terribly vulgar and your papa would be most disappointed in you. You must promise me you won't say anything.' While Bella stared at her, considering, she added a little desperately, 'I'll make sure Cook bakes ginger biscuits every day.'

Bella nodded seriously. 'I promise, Aunt Merry.' Her solemn expression giving way to an impish grin, she cried, 'Ginger biscuits every day! You like Mr Mansfell very much!' Giggling, she skipped out through the door.

Meredyth wiped a handkerchief over her flushed brow. She could only hope Bella didn't take it into her unpredictable head to do say or do something awful.

Given that appalling observation about lowered bodices, she wouldn't put anything past the child. Whether she'd persuaded Bella to silence or not, though, she didn't dare mention the matter further. No matter how aghast she was at having to rely, in such a delicate matter, on the dubious discretion of a precocious six-year-old.

Now, however, she must descend to the parlour lest she be late for dinner. More jittery than ever, Meredyth pulled on her gloves and walked out.

Several hours later, Meredyth sat before the mirror at her dressing table, brushing out her hair for bed. The events of the evening replaying in her head heightened her agitation and indecision, and she knew it would be hours before she could capture sleep.

In honour of the family's first night together they'd dined early, so as to include the children. Entertaining the youngsters while she conferred with Twilling to keep the dinner service running smoothly had helped to occupy Meredyth—and dilute the unsettling effect of having Allen Mansfell in the same room. Though she admitted, with a reminiscent shiver, she'd still *sensed* his presence, even when her eyes and attention were directed elsewhere.

She'd had a respite when the ladies withdrew, leaving the gentlemen to their brandy and cigars while the feminine contingent escorted the children up to bed. But from the moment the men had rejoined them in the parlour Allen Mansfell had singled her out to receive his particular attentions, joining her at the tea tray, remaining by her side as she poured, chatting with the company while he assisted her in distributing cups.

By the time he'd solicited her to be his partner at

whist more members of the company than just Colton had been casting speculative glances at them. She had tried to avoid looking at him and focus on the game, but even that innocuous entertainment had seemed to underline the intellectual connection they'd made at the Dower House. Somehow they'd seemed to antici- pate each other's hands, nearly always choosing the correct cards to play, as if they had been partners for years.

After they'd carried the rubber, Mr Mansfell had leaned over to murmur, 'I love the way you follow my lead.'

'I follow when it pleases me,' she'd responded, feeling her cheeks heat.

'Then I shall strive always to please you,' he had replied, his eyes gleaming with approval and the promise of something more.

He meant to pursue her. There was no other way to interpret the remark, was there?

As the evening had continued, it had seemed his gaze was always on her. Seeking to escape his scrutiny even as she'd enjoyed the heady thrill of knowing she was the object of his attention, she had gone to the pi- anoforte, meaning to quell her agitation in music.

Once again he had followed, standing so close as he turned the pages that she'd made a number of blunders in performing pieces she'd long since mastered. Rattled, she'd switched to playing a simple folk tune, but when she had begun to sing he had surprised her by joining in, his deep bass a pleasing counterpoint to her soprano.

While the company had clapped their enthusiastic approval of the duet, he'd bent to murmur in her ear. 'See how beautifully we blend together?'

With his lips lingering just above her ear, his virile body a mere touch away, her mind had skipped immediately to other things they might blend. She'd had to beat her senses back from a heated contemplation of bared bodies and tangled limbs.

And though she ought to resent his ability to so easily fluster her, paradoxically she also found it immensely appealing that he understood and appreciated the same things she did—from farming to thatching cottage roofs to the concept of the washing machine. She liked it that he could anticipate which card she would play, that he enjoyed making music with her. It had seemed so natural to have him at her side, watching her, smiling that intimate smile, engaging her in animated discourse…making her burn with a longing that demanded satisfaction.

Yes, she concluded with a sigh, she could all too easily envisage blending Allen Mansfell into her life—and her bed.

His final comment of the evening had been the most disturbing—and thrilling—of all.

While discussing Faith's upcoming presentation,

Clare had expressed the hope that Faith might make a match quickly, sparing the family the necessity of remaining in town for the entire Season.

'Faith should take all the time she needs to make her choice—or not make one,' Meredyth had protested. 'Several Seasons, if necessary.' With a fond glance at her younger sister, she'd added, 'She mustn't settle for any man but the one who can make her happiest.'

'A girl in her first Season should be allowed to revel in the admiration of her suitors,' Mr Mansfell had commented unexpectedly. 'Though an older, more experienced lady might well be able to come to a decision more quickly. Do you not agree, Miss Wellingford?'

He had fixed intense green eyes on her, making her stomach flutter and her breath grow short. 'Y-yes,' she'd allowed, 'I expect a more mature lady would know her mind quickly.'

Sarah had shot her a glance, her eyebrows raised. Meredyth looked away, but had seen the same inquisitive expression on the faces of Nicky, Clare and Sinjin. Only Hal and Elizabeth, gazing at each other raptly, had seemed oblivious to the undertones.

The party had broken up soon afterwards, allowing her to escape to her room before Sarah or Clare could corner her and ask the nature of her relationship with Mr Mansfell. How could she answer them when she didn't know herself?

Nothing formal had been stated. Yet the innuendo of his speech combined with the marked attention he'd paid her under the full gaze of her family must mean Mr Mansfell harboured serious intentions towards her...mustn't it?

And, should he actually have such intentions, how should she respond to them?

Hardly daring even now to contemplate so flattering a possibility, she allowed herself to consider the answer.

There was heat aplenty between them. Of that she had no doubt. She liked him immensely. He amused her. She felt herself increasingly drawn to him. Yet she still had no desire to bestow her hand on a man whom she did not truly love, who did not vouchsafe a similar passion for her in return.

Was there, could there be more, if she abandoned caution and let her emotions run free? If he convinced her he had in fact fallen in love with her?

Exuberant, heedless, full of the optimism of youth, she and James had tumbled into love without consideration or reflection. Wiser now, with her emotions tightly leashed, she knew the growth of her affection for the man she was striving to resist was so different a process from her first foray into love that her previous experience was no help to her at all.

Throwing herself fearlessly open again to the possibility of love...leaving herself vulnerable to the kind

of heartbreak which had once nearly destroyed her…
Did she dare attempt it?

A sudden rap at the door made her start. Hoping
that her caller wasn't Sarah, come to demand what
was transpiring between her and Allen Mansfell,
Meredyth bade the visitor enter.

Chapter Six

To her relief, it was Faith rather than her perceptive
older sister who walked in. Automatically Meredyth
shifted her attention from her own worries to whatever
concern had brought her little sister calling.

'Too excited about London to sleep?'

'Yes, that too,' Faith said. 'Although if I do no
better at attracting other gentlemen than I have with
Thomas Mansfell I shall vastly disappoint all of you.'

'Nonsense,' Meredyth said roundly, giving her
sister a hug. 'With your grace and sweetness of character, the London beaux will fall at your feet. And
don't despair of Thomas either. He may not realise
how grown-up and lovely you've become until he sees
your beauty reflected in the admiring eyes of other
men.'

'Perhaps,' Faith said. 'I do so like him. But then, as

you said—and I do thank you for it, sister—I hope to enjoy the attentions of a number of suitors before I choose one to wed. But that's not what I wanted to talk about.'

Feeling a niggle of unease, Meredyth said, 'Then what did you want to discuss, my dear?'

Faith grinned at her. 'I may pine for a Mansfell admirer, but you, big sister, already have one—and how very particular he is!'

When Meredyth tried to demur, Faith shook a finger at her. 'Even Sarah, ill as she's feeling, noticed how marked his attentions are. Then Colton told us Mr Mansfell rode with you to inspect the Dower House, subjecting his elegant apparel to the hazards of paint and plaster. Now if that doesn't show the seriousness of his intentions, I shall eat my lace fichu!'

'He's interested in renovation,' Meredyth protested. 'He's soon to commence similar work at the Grange.'

'Perhaps,' Faith allowed. 'But he's also *very* interested in you! Which only shows how clever he is, for he could never find a more excellent a lady than my darling Merry! Only promise you will not wed before the end of the Season, for I've quite counted on having your support.'

'Of course I shall stay to support you!' Meredyth replied, trying to decide how little she could get away with revealing to her sister. 'I'll admit Allen Mansfell has paid me some attention—but only, I expect, to pass the time. You make far too much of it.'

Faith shook her head. 'Not at all! Do you not know what happened last Season?'

Another pang of foreboding resonating within her, Meredyth said, 'Perhaps you'd better enlighten me?'

'Colton says Thomas told him his brother went to London last spring to look for a suitable wife. Clare and Sinjin were in town then, and Clare says soon after Mr Mansfell arrived he fell headlong in love with Miss Susanna Davies—a great beauty who had many suitors vying for her favour. Though she showed a great partiality for Mr Mansfell, she never entirely discouraged her other admirers, driving poor Mr Mansfell quite distracted with jealousy! Just after she finally accepted his proposal Lord Wildemere came to town, and was immediately smitten with Miss Davies. Wildemere, you may recall, is connected to the Howards, and a number of the old families of rank and position. With her father's and His Lordship's persuasion, Miss Davies was induced to break her engagement to Mr Mansfell and accept Lord Wildemere instead.'

Though she'd listened to this narrative already knowing in her bones what must have happened, Meredyth still felt touched by the cruelty of Allen Mansfell's disappointment. 'How awful for him,' she murmured.

'Indeed,' Faith continued. 'Clare says all of Society felt quite badly that such a fine young man had been so callously jilted.'

'And because he began last year to look about for a wife, you think he must be set upon completing the matter this spring?' Meredyth asked.

'Quite the opposite!' Faith replied. 'Apparently his mother asked him just such a question. He told her quite sharply he was not yet interested in continuing the search. Nor did he plan ever again to pay particular attention to a lady unless she possessed not just breeding, accomplishments and manners, but a beauty of character to rival that of her countenance. A description which could have been written expressly to describe *you*, dear sister. The consideration he is showing you must mean he has reached the same conclusion!'

'Perhaps. But more likely, as he recovers from his disappointment, he simply wishes to pass the time by engaging in a bit of light-hearted gallantry, sure that within the confines of a family party no one will take his attentions seriously,' Meredyth contended, as much to herself as her sister.

Faith shook her head. 'Thomas told us his brother does not normally flirt—that in fact he'd never danced attendance on any lady until he began courting Miss Davies. I'm so glad, after how shabbily she treated him, that he's found you. For though he is rather old, he's quite handsome and dashing, and I think he deserves to be happy, don't you? Which he will be, if he manages to secure your affection.'

'Though I allow Thomas must know his brother better than we do,' Meredyth replied, feeling both thrilled and cornered by Faith's revelation, 'I am still not convinced he is trying to fix his interest with me.'

'Oh, he is,' Faith replied confidently. 'Colton and Sarah and Clare all think so. They wonder only whether he has engaged your affections in return. Are you in love with him?'

Was she? Could she be? Unwilling to confess how distraught the query made her, she exclaimed, 'Please, Faith, no more questions! If you wish to attract Thomas or any gentleman you must appear at your best, not bleary-eyed and yawning. To bed with you.'

'Very well. I won't tease you any more. But I do think it would be splendid if you fell in love and married him…after I find my own special gentleman, of course. Then we can all be as happy as Sarah and Elizabeth and Clare!'

Giving her sister another hug, Meredyth walked her to the door. 'You deserve to be so happy, dearest. And never fear—I mean to enjoy every moment of watching you become the Belle of London.'

'Promise me you will be happy too,' Faith said as she opened the door.

'I shall certainly try,' Meredyth said with a smile.

A smile that faded as soon as the door had closed behind her sister. So Allen Mansfell had been passionately in love and bitterly disappointed? How devastating the loss of one's love could be! she thought, feeling for him a reminiscent pang.

Apparently her entire family now believed Mr Mansfell had turned his attentions towards her. But, unlike her romantic younger sister, Meredyth couldn't convince herself he had truly fallen in love with her.

For one thing, their personal acquaintance was far too short. And the sad tale of his deception and betrayal at the hands of an acclaimed young beauty just reinforced her original doubts about the nature of his attentions to her.

The idea that she had bewitched Allen Mansfell had seemed too good to be true, even for the few moments she'd entertained it. After what her sister had confided it seemed far more likely to Meredyth that, having arrived at that time of life when he'd decided to marry, and having been frustrated in his first attempt, Mr Mansfell was simply looking for a more suitable replacement.

And what more ideal lady than she? Well-bred, skilful at managing an estate, possessing an easy manner with children, reasonably amenable and attractive—but not so dazzling as to attract a great deal of attention from other men—she possessed all the nominal virtues she supposed a gentleman *would* seek in a wife. In addition, at her advanced age she might be expected to snap up so advantageous an offer, coming as it did from a handsome, well-born gentlemen of excellent character.

So why did she feel so disappointed?

Many, indeed most women of her class, would be honoured to entertain a match based on friendship and mutual esteem in order to gain a handsome husband, a home of her own and the opportunity for children. Moreover, there existed between she and Allen Mansfell a sensual fire that promised she would experience all the delights of the bedchamber she had denied herself with James.

Delights for which she yearned with an intensity she'd not previously imagined. Acknowledging that desire, how should she reply if he did make her an offer?

Even suspecting what she did, she was tempted to accept him. But if Allen Mansfell proposed to her out of admiration and a polite esteem, he offered nothing—save for passion—she did not already or almost possess. The Dower House probably wasn't as grand as the manor adorning the Grange, but it belonged to her. She hadn't given birth to them or suckled them, but with Clare's children and her sisters' offspring she had children to dote on and spoil and love.

Besides that, she would be marrying a very attractive

man in a marriage of convenience that only *seemed* to be advantageous to both parties. She'd watched that scenario play out to a bitter conclusion with her own mother.

Not to put too fine a point on it, despite a genuine affection for his wife, her father had been a flagrant philanderer. It had been his rampant womanizing, Meredyth was convinced, far more than his irresponsible gaming that had led to his wife's decline. Remaining at Wellingford bearing babe after babe, her mother had watched her husband jaunt off to London, Newcastle, Oxford—or wherever the gaming was deep and the women beguiling and easy of virtue. Worn down by childbearing and grief, by the time of Colton's birth her mother's health and self-esteem had been ruined.

Of course Allen Mansfell was a man of a much superior character to her late, unlamented father. If Mr Mansfell pledged her his troth she knew he would intend to honour his vow. But the world was full of unattached women who, looking for security, advancement or simply adventure, would be attracted to a handsome man of means.

Such a gentleman, confident of the affection and loyalty of his wife, and tied to her only by the claims of duty and mild affection, would be vulnerable to any enticing widow looking for brief affair, or any beguiling doxy trolling for a new protector. Indeed, the mores of their society, in which marital fidelity was considered quaint and conquest a matter of masculine pride, would positively encourage such affairs—particularly if the gentleman took care to protect his wife from outward knowledge of his little peccadilloes.

No less for her than for her mother would such a relationship lead to heartache, anger, and a bitterness that would destroy the affection upon which the union had initially been based.

Tempted by passion or not, having known what it was to truly to love and be loved, she could not settle for anything less.

In fact, the longer she considered the matter, the angrier she grew that Allen Mansfell should think her so meek, mild and biddable that she would accept a tepid marriage of convenience—as if she were a poor spinster, desperate for a man to give her his name and protection. As if she *didn't* possess the spirit, fire or brilliance of soul to inspire a man to lose his heart to her.

She might be on the shelf, past her last prayers and an ape-leader—and all the other cleverly derogatory terms by which her society disparaged women who had reached a certain age still unwed. But, praise heaven, she was neither meek, biddable, nor in need of a husband's protection.

Better to be aunt and spinster than suffer as her mother had suffered. So, she vowed, she would turn aside any man's attentions unless or until she was convinced he sought her not for her sterling character but because he loved her as totally and passionately as she loved him.

Chapter Seven

Two days later, Allen Mansfell sat at the table at the conclusion of their informal nuncheon, watching Meredyth Wellingford chat with her sisters. Since their ride together on his first afternoon at Wellingford, observing its mistress had become quite an absorbing pastime for him.

He'd listened to the delightful sound of her laughter as she played hide-and-seek with the children. Observed the sparkle in her eye and her cry of triumph when she bested her brother-in-law Nicky at chess. Watched her rapt concentration and the grace of her movements as she played the pianoforte in the evenings. Noted the tenderness on her face as she assisted her ailing sisters or carried one of their sleeping offspring up to bed.

He'd observed all this because—though she still

appeared to admire his character, enjoy his wit and share his interests—the object of his attentions had determinedly deflected any attempt at gallantry and sidestepped every opportunity to be alone with him.

By now, with a disappointment sharper than he cared to contemplate, he should have given up his efforts, concluding that his initial impression that she favoured him had been in error. Except that despite her elusiveness she continued to give him signs that their attraction was not, after all, one sided.

Like the afternoon after their ride when, having gone in search of her, he'd come upon her playing at jackstraws with the children. He'd read surprise and approval in her eyes when he had plopped down on the carpet and joined the game, which had continued until just the two of them remained.

Intent on her play, she'd lost her wariness, applauding his dexterity as enthusiastically as Aubrey and Bella, crowing with delight when she outmatched him. She'd looked so winsome, sitting there in a crumple of skirts, placing her straws with analytical precision, then looking up to beam at him, her smile both shy and challenging, that his chest had tightened. He'd wanted to scoop her up and carry her off on the spot.

Or last night, after he'd joined her again at the pianoforte to sing duets. He'd asked her to play several of his favourite folk tunes, content for that moment simply to enjoy the sound of her voice mingling with his.

As during the game of jackstraws, after a time she had relaxed, her fingers caressing the keys, head tilted and eyes closed as she gave her heart to the music. While the company had applauded afterwards, she had gazed up at him, her eyes aglow with approval and affection as she squeezed his hand, setting his pulses racing. Until, apparently realising what she was doing, she had blushed and snatched her hand back.

Then there had been this morning, when he'd ridden out with her again. After several hours of in-specting fields and barns and cottages, talking with farmers while he asked questions and solicited her opinions, her reserve had melted away. By the time they had returned she'd been interrogating him about the practices he used at the Grange, and listening attentively to his answers.

When he'd lifted her from the saddle at the end of the ride, once again compelled to let his fingers linger against the tantalising warmth of her waist, desire had smouldered in her eyes. For a moment she'd grasped his shoulders and lifted her face towards the kiss he'd ached to give her. Until at the last moment, with a little gasp, she'd hastily pushed him away and hurried into the house.

He felt sure she wasn't simply trying to entice and frustrate him—though frustrated he was! He'd learned enough of coquettery at Susanna's talented hands to recognise that Meredyth Wellingford's encouragement was unconsciously given, her retreat instinctive rather than calculated.

She seemed to be trying so hard to keep him at a distance that only in moments when shared interests or amusements distracted her did her innate desire and affection break through. That she felt a strong partiality for him, he was sure. Then why was she so hesitant to show it?

Surely she couldn't think he was only trifling with her? His attentions had been too marked and too public for her to believe that.

He was only a man—a simple being who, once he'd determined what he wanted, went straight for it, entirely lacking the subtlety of which ladies seemed capable. His affection and desire for Meredyth Wellingford only increased as he spent time with her, making him surer than ever that she was the woman he must wed.

But his visit to Wellingford was fast approaching its end. And as he'd become convinced he wanted Miss Wellingford for his wife, so had his intention solidified not to wait until the Season in London to ask for her hand.

He must act this afternoon, he'd decided. Whatever he must do to contrive it, he would get her alone, make his declaration, and ensure once and for all that

Meredyth Wellingford would, if not accept him outright, at least agree to consider him as a potential husband.

Satisfying as that decision was, as he rose to follow the company out of the room, his stomach began churning and he felt the chill of perspiration on his brow. He'd thought that nothing could approach the agony of the jealousy and uncertainty Susanna had made him suffer. But he was discovering that being unsure of his fate at the hands of a virtuous maiden could inspire a torment no less painfully sharp.

'Miss Wellingford?' he called as she walked out on Sarah's arm. 'Can I persuade you to show me the rose garden? I wish to design something similar at the Grange, and would like to observe how yours is planted.'

She looked back at him, the flare of interest in her eyes almost immediately overshadowed by wariness. 'I've promised Sarah to help her sort silks for a baby blanket.'

'We can do that later,' Lady Englemere interposed. ''Tis a lovely afternoon for a walk, Merry.'

To Allen's delight, behind her sister's back, Lady Englemere gave him a smile and a wink. He returned the smile, heartened to know that at least her family understood and approved his intentions.

'Yes, Merry—do go for a stroll,' Lord Englemere said. 'While Colton and Thomas have the children occupied, I thought to steal a little time alone with my wife.' As he spoke, he walked over, slipped his wife's hand out of Meredyth's and clasped it in his own.

With a sigh of mingled exasperation and amusement, Miss Wellingford said, 'Since everyone is so determined, I suppose walk I must. Give me a moment to fetch my bonnet and pelisse, Mr Mansfell, and I'll join you on the terrace.'

So, ten minutes later, wrapped in his greatcoat and stamping his feet against the cold, Allen waited outside for Miss Wellingford, feeling far more nervous than he'd anticipated.

A moment later she appeared, her blonde curls and grey eyes set off fetchingly by a deep rose pelisse and bonnet. As he looked at her, her eyes modestly downcast, her long golden lashes casting half-moon shadows on her soft cheeks, a giddy sense of awe swelled in his chest at the idea that very soon this lovely and accomplished lady might be his wife, to love and cherish for the rest of his days.

He clasped her mittened hand, feeling the heat of it penetrate through his gloves and settle in his loins. Ah, yes—the 'loving' part couldn't begin soon enough!

But first he had to successfully negotiate a proposal. Resolved to clear difficult ground as quickly as possible, as soon as they had entered the privacy of the walled rose garden Allen walked her to a bench.

'You wished to discuss the design of the roses?' she asked as he motioned her to a seat.

'Among other things.' Trying to ignore the rapid tattoo of his heartbeat, Allen began. 'Miss Wellingford, I know our personal acquaintance is rather short. However, I soon discovered that Thomas, who has long sung your praises, exaggerated neither the excellence of your character nor your many admirable qualities. My initial admiration has grown enormously as I've come to know you better and discovered how many interests we share. In addition, I feel between us a strong and compelling attraction that I believe over time would deepen into a tender regard that can ensure us a long and happy life together.

'So, Miss Wellingford…' He paused, dropping to one knee. 'Would you make me the happiest of men and do me the honour of becoming my wife?'

Though she left her hand in his grip, for a long moment she said nothing, her grey eyes intently examining his face. While she hesitated, his heart slammed in his chest and panic curled through him.

Had his proposal been too abrupt, too precipitate? Might she refuse him? A howl of protest, shockingly more intense and vehement than anything he'd expected, rose up in him. He must say something more—tease her out of uttering a refusal. But the breath seemed to have dried in his throat.

While he fumbled for speech, she said, 'I too

admire the excellence of *your* character and accomplishments, and am honoured and flattered by your proposal. But why do you want *me* for your wife?'

Confused, he blinked at her. 'Why? I thought I'd just told you. I admire and respect you. We have many common interests. You make me laugh. I enjoy your company. And I hope I am not arrogant in believing we share the sort of attraction that leads to a strong and permanent affection.'

'Affection?' She shook her head. 'I'm sorry, Mr Mansfell, I find "affection" a rather fragile basis upon which to entrust my future. I once experienced a much more consuming emotion, as I believe you did too. Do you not think you would at some later time feel cheated if you were to settle now for a union based on mere affection?'

So she'd heard about his engagement to Susanna. He wasn't surprised; Thomas might have mentioned it. Was she piqued that he'd not vouchsafed a violent passion?

'I did experience a previous attachment,' he admitted. 'Indeed, it is precisely because of that... unhappy affair that I've come to believe a marriage between like-minded partners, based on mutual esteem and a genuine, deepening affection, is more likely to lead to a happy union than extreme emotion, which can as easily cause acute misery as intense delight. You too have lost someone very dear to you. Do you not think it possible I might be correct?'

She nodded. 'It is possible. But what if you're wrong? What if affection does not grow and deepen? What if, instead, it were to fade...perhaps in the face of some new, much stronger passion? Is that not equally likely?'

Did she question his commitment to the bargain he was asking her to make? 'Not if both partners pledge their lives and honour to each other. I know you are drawn to me. That you like me at least a little. Do you deny that?'

She smiled slightly. 'No. I like you a great deal.'

'Then why have you tried so hard to resist the attraction between us—a connection I'm sure you felt, as I did, from the moment we met? Do you think that because I offer my affections to you so soon after severing a prior attachment that I will prove inconstant? Though I crave your consent now, I'm perfectly willing to prove my steadfastness. Only allow me to show you—over the course of the Season if I must—how devoted I can be.'

Anxiety and a driving need to win her overwhelmed his caution. Raising her hand, he turned it over to nuzzle the soft skin where wrist and glove met, filling his nostrils with her sweet rose scent. 'Won't you give me that right?' he whispered, kissing the skin he'd caressed.

As if burned, she jerked her hand away. 'I…I don't question your honour or your constancy. I am sorry to…disappoint you, but I must refuse your offer. I want a husband who proposes to me out of passion and ardour, not mere esteem. Fortunately your attachment to me has been of short duration. I hope you will recover from it as quickly, and offer my most sincere wishes for your eventual happiness.'

Though he had known she might possibly refuse him, still he found himself shocked. 'That…that is all? Can I not hope to persuade you otherwise when we meet again in London?'

Pressing her lips together, she looked away. 'I think it would be best if you did not. And as I shall not refer to this…matter again, we may go on as we have been for the rest of your visit here. I expect I shall see you at dinner.'

Still not believing she would turn him down so completely, Allen continued to kneel, frozen in stupified silence as she rose, dipped him a quick curtsey and headed off down the pathway. Belatedly standing up, he watched until seconds later she exited the rose garden and disappeared from sight.

As, in just a few days, she intended him to disappear from her life. Shoving his hands in his pockets, Allen set off at a furious pace on a circuit around the garden.

How could he have miscalculated so badly? He'd

been so sure that, even if she felt his offer precipitate, she would agree to his continuing to court her during the Season. He had never allowed himself even to contemplate her rejecting him completely.

A wholly unexpected sense of desolation rose in him. They'd seemed to complement each other's interests and strengths so completely…how could she just walk away? Dismiss him as if he'd been nothing more to her than an amusing and casual acquaintance?

Anger followed on the heels of desolation. Dammit, she *did* feel more for him than she was willing to admit—he was certain of it! But for some unfathomable reason she wasn't prepared to risk the small possibility that their union might be unhappy against the much greater probability that it could be joyous and fulfilling. Uttering another oath, he kicked at a stone cherub in the dormant rosebed that had the misfortune to be within reach.

Miss Wellingford's refusal had been even less gracious than Susanna's. She at least had been apologetic when she had admitted to him that her parents were forcing her to break her engagement to him and marry the Earl.

Not that she'd looked coerced, he recalled, his lip curling in distaste. And she'd certainly thoroughly enjoyed the savage, angry goodbye kiss she'd invited him to give her. Indeed, rubbing her lush body against him, she'd whispered that she couldn't bear to give him up completely, that she was sure she could find some way to be together with him after her marriage. That then, when conception was no longer a risk, she could give him all he desired.

The memory of it still curdled in his gut every time he thought about it. As if he'd profane his honour by willingly committing adultery…or allowing a child of his get to be claimed by another man.

The mode of their parting had, however, helped temper his anguish by giving him a first hint of her true character—one that had led eventually to a distaste that finally allowed him break the hold she'd established over his mind and senses. In time he'd come to believe a kind Providence had intervened to prevent his marrying a girl who could hold her wedding vows so lightly.

This time he'd been attracted to a woman of un-questioned honour and integrity—a woman he was convinced was as attracted to him as he was to her on both a physical and intellectual level—only to be once again deceived. A shaft of hurt and disappointment lanced though him, making the future that just half an hour previously had seemed so ripe with promise look bleak and empty. Turning away from Meredyth Well-ingford was going to be a great deal harder than for-getting the duplicitous Susanna Davies.

The very idea brought an instinctive swell of protest. Damnation, he thought, setting his jaw, he would *not* just walk away. If Miss Wellingford meant to discourage him, she would have to bring forth more convincing reasons than she'd thus far offered.

For the remainder of his visit he would accept her invitation to go on just as they had. A roguish smile creased his lips as the hazy outlines of a plan began to solidify. *Exactly* as they had.

She wanted 'passion and ardour', did she? he thought, with a new sense of purpose energising him. A gentleman ought never to disappoint a lady. He would avail himself of every opportunity to pique her intellect, beguile her with his charm…and tempt her with the desire that simmered ever hotter between them.

Until Meredyth Wellingford's own innate honesty forced her to acknowledge that refusing him had been a mistake…and realised she had no choice but to give her heart and her hand to Allen Mansfell…

Chapter Eight

After escaping the walled garden, Merry set off towards the stables at a near-run. Her rendezvous with Mr Mansfell was so widely known that it would be nearly impossible to return to the house without encountering someone who would quiz her on it. Scraped raw by conflicting emotions after refusing him, she simply couldn't dissemble, nor did she feel she could bear to tell the truth. Especially since her entire family seemed to have conspired in encouraging Mr Mansfell's pursuit of her.

These last two days, every time she'd walked into a room, whoever was sitting next to him had risen to insist she take that seat. Her sisters had deserted her at the tea table, ceding their place to Mr Mansfell. She had only to begin a game of cards or chess and her opponent would invite him to join them. And the company positively clamoured for the two of them to perform at the piano every evening.

Breathless, she ducked inside the stables, to her relief finding them empty of human inhabitants. From the box stall opposite, her mare, Frolic, nickered at her.

Gratefully inhaling the comforting, familiar odours of hay, harness and horseflesh, Meredyth walked over and stroked the horse's neck.

She shouldn't condemn her family when she was equally at fault. She simply hadn't been able to resist the temptation of Allen Mansfell's company. The unhappy fact was that she enjoyed chatting with him at breakfast, discussing politics in the parlour, matching wits with him at chess and matching voices in song. She'd broadcast her plan to ride this morning, virtually inviting him to join her and secretly delighted that he had. She was energised by his company, his wit, his intelligent and penetrating observations.

She'd found herself shamelessly seizing every opportunity to enjoy his touch, from allowing him to take her arm into dinner, to grasping her fingers to assist her from a chair, to lifting her down from her horse…where his hands burned into her sides and his lips, so tantalisingly close above her, made her body clamour to rise up and claim the kiss he seemed quite ready to offer.

Oh, how she wanted that kiss…and more!

Which made the proposal she had been trying to forestall doubly tortuous. First because—as she'd suspected—he could not offer her the love she craved. Second, and worse, because she had been so tempted to accept his offer even without it.

Her family would be as unlikely as Allen Mansfell to understand her reluctance to wed him. Sarah herself had made a marriage of convenience to a friend—based initially on nothing warmer than mutual esteem—which had ended up becoming spectacularly happy.

But Sarah had been lucky; such unions did not always prosper. Nor had her sister spent long years with their mother as that lady had slowly slipped towards death, listening to the tales of bitterness and regret that were all that remained of her own marriage of convenience to the handsome man she'd once adored.

Was Meredyth being foolish in categorically refusing Allen Mansfell's offer?

Uttering an angry oath that startled her horse, Meredyth paced away from the stall. She wouldn't do this. No more agonising. Allen Mansfell was everything that was gentlemanly, intelligent and witty; he made her burn with desire but he did not love her, and that was an end to it.

Tempted as she was to try and recapture the rapture she'd experienced with her James, she would not invite disappointment and heartache by settling for less. She wouldn't allow Allen Mansfell to insult her by offering less, bartering for her acceptance as if she were simply a suitable brood mare on the block.

Of course, unable to fathom how a proposal most women of their society would consider flattering could conceivably be thought an insult, at this moment Allen Mansfell was probably as angry and frustrated as she was. But by the time she met him in the spring he would likely be well over her, already courting some more rational and amenable female.

Which was a very good thing, she concluded. Even if, as she exited the stables to return to the house, she couldn't quite make herself believe it.

Through that evening and into the next day, Meredyth was reminded of the adage that it was wise not to yearn too fiercely for something lest it be granted. After having assured Mr Mansfell they could go on for the rest of his visit as they had been, she had discovered that it was apparently much easier for him than it was for her.

Indeed, she was beginning to suspect darkly that, as if to punish her for the sensual delights she'd spurned, he was being even more devilishly attentive than before. For instead of keeping his distance, as she'd supposed he would, he lingered closer than ever.

In the parlour before dinner he stood behind her,

one leg bent so it touched the back of her thigh, the point of contact sparking and burning so that she could barely converse coherently. He leaned down when he replied to her, his breath teasing her ear as he murmured his remarks. He clasped her arm tightly as he escorted her to table, caressing her fingers before releasing them.

Several times while seated his knee 'accidentally' bumped hers, then rubbed over her leg before moving away. When, after several such instances, she gave him a pointed look, he merely raised his eyebrows and smiled benignly at her.

At the tea tray after dinner he managed to tangle his arm in hers while supposedly reaching for a teacup, sliding his fingers along the inside of her wrist and causing a bolt of sensation so intense she almost poured hot tea all over his sleeve. When they sang those now obligatory blasted duets later, he propped a hand on the pianoforte and leaned so far forward that his torso nearly touched her back. She misplayed more notes than she had in her first piano recital at the tender age of six.

Throughout this display her family looked on, smiling indulgently at what they doubtless believed was a courtship in progress.

She supposed she ought to be grateful—for had Mr Mansfell suddenly grown cold and distant one or another of her sisters would surely have cornered her privately to ask what had transpired between them. But, with her senses in a continual uproar that kept her nerves on edge and made her brain go stupid, she sometimes felt like slapping him.

He was at it again now, this morning, all obliging smiles as he somehow managed to bump into her, nudge her or touch her as they gathered food from the sideboard and sat at table.

She'd just about decided she would drag him somewhere private and demand he cease tormenting her when, as they walked out the breakfast room door, they were halted by a beaming Bella. Giggling with delight, she pointed to Aubrey, who stood on a hall table beside the door—holding a mistletoe kissing ball above them.

'Kiss her! Kiss her! Now you must kiss her!' Bella cried.

'Yes, you must,' Aubrey exclaimed. ''Tis tradition.'

Allen Mansfell, devil that he was, merely nodded and said, 'One must always respect tradition.' And before Meredyth could think to protest, he yanked her into his arms and kissed her.

This was no light peck on the cheek, but a brazen, tongue-in-mouth, ferocious all-out assault that she felt down to her toes. After a rigid instant of surprise, Meredyth felt herself leaning into him, her senses exulting as she kissed him back just as fiercely.

Light, voices, the children's laughter—all faded as

they stood there, tasting each other with the frantic urgency of lovers long parted. When he finally broke the kiss, with her pulse hammering and her knees gone limp, Meredyth might have fallen had Mr Mansfell not grabbed her shoulders and held her upright.

'Never again tell me I lack ardour or passion,' he said in a fierce undertone, before pushing her roughly away and striding off without a backward glance. Leaving her standing scarlet-cheeked while Thomas and Colton hallooed, the children clapped, two maids gaped, and Clare and Sarah stared with bemusement.

How dared he make spectacle of her like that and then just walk away?

Too furious to worry about what she would tell everyone later, she turned on her heel and ran after him.

Catching up to him in the downstairs hall, she grabbed his elbow and all but dragged him into the parlour, slamming the door after them before turning to face him.

'Whatever possessed you to kiss me like that?' she demanded.

'I've wanted to kiss you like that since the moment you welcomed me to Wellingford,' he retorted hotly. 'Lately I've wanted much more—but, excuse me, you've already rejected that. I'm sorry that honesty, honour, loyalty and affection aren't enough. That you found an offer based only on those insulting.'

'Of course I'm not insulted by honesty, honour or loyalty,' she replied, equally incensed. 'But since you seem to find my refusal inexplicable, you force me to put it more bluntly. I know you were recently disappointed in your pursuit of a wife. Perhaps you thought that at my advanced age I would be eager to accept the offer of any respectable gentleman. But I'll have you know I have no wish to be an interchangeable cog inserted into your matrimonial plans—a suitably skilled, suitably qualified replacement for the part you discovered would not fit.'

'Is that what you think I'm trying to do?'

'I think it's quite possible,' she retorted, glad finally to have baldly stated what she most feared.

'You truly think I would choose so casually the woman with whom I will spend the rest of my life? I may not be able to profess a grand passion, but a marriage of like-minded partners is hardly unusual. In your own sister's case it has resulted in the happiest of matches! Given the interests and the attraction we share, I think it very likely we could build the same kind of relationship. Yet you spurn me for honestly admitting my feelings, for wanting to establish a home with an amenable wife and family...even for controlling my desire and treating you with respect!' He shook his head angrily. 'I don't know what women want!'

''Tis not so complicated,' she responded. 'I seek to

be loved for myself alone. Not because I possess the correct virtues—like a…a horse of pleasing paces who will pull a carriage well! I have known what it is to be loved and I do not wish to settle for less. I have property of my own, a valued place among my family, nieces and nephews to cherish. Is it so unreasonable that I refuse to give up my comfortable life unless I know my *love*, not just my talents, is craved by the man who seeks my hand? A man who entreats me to accept him because he vows his happiness will be forever blighted if I do not?'

'One who can avow a mindless, intemperate passion, then?' He shook his head impatiently. 'We are not likely to agree on the desirability of that, and nor do I believe that sort of love exists much past one's hot-tempered youth. Or is all this talk of grand passion only an excuse? Is it that you *prefer* to stay here, content to experience life second-hand as Colton's housekeeper, the children's aunt? Immersing yourself in memories of a lost love that over the years you've polished into such perfection no mortal man could ever match it rather than accepting the risk of pursuing a new and real relationship? If that's so, I am sorry you are too much a coward to seek the love you say you want.'

'*I'm* a coward?' she gasped, incensed. 'Content to settle for a safe and easy life? Is that not just what you are doing? After having lost your heart's desire, you now seek to make a safe, practical bargain based on mutual interest and esteem, selecting a woman who may not inspire you with grand passion but who will never cause you doubt or concern? You claim I should throw my heart away, but what of yours?'

'Yes, we've both been heart-wounded,' he acknowledged. 'But while I'm ready to risk seeking happiness, you are not. It makes me angry to see you waste such potential for intimacy. But I shall say no more.' He made her an exaggerated bow. 'I apologise for making you the object of speculation by behaving in a less than gentlemanly manner. I shall not so trouble you again.' He raised her hand as if to salute—and then, his eyes smouldering, unexpectedly pulled her back into his arms.

At first he bound her against his body, assaulting her with his lips. But even as she stiffened in resistance his touch gentled and his mouth turned coaxing. Every sense responded while a little voice in her brain whispered that here she belonged, in his arms, exulting in his hardness and strength. With a sigh, she relaxed against him and opened her lips, inviting his tongue.

He took full advantage, exploring the soft depths of her mouth, nipping, stroking and teasing her tongue while his arms wrapped around her and his hands caressed her back. She raised her hands in turn to clutch him, her nails biting into his shoulders, desire turning her molten and aching, sparking a response in every nerve.

She might have gone on kissing him for ever, but some mindless time later he turned his head away, cradling her on his chest where his heartbeat thundered in her ear. Then, setting her away from him, he said harshly, 'Don't ever try to deny what we might share.'

He pivoted and walked out, leaving her gazing after him, her heart still racing. In a fog, she stumbled to the sofa and sat down heavily.

Once again he'd kissed her nearly senseless and then left her. More than that, before distracting her with those mind-numbing kisses, he had called her what—a coward?

Shaken and trembling, Meredyth felt her anger revive. How dared Allen Mansfell judge her life and brand her a coward for not embracing the challenge he offered? What could he, a mere man, know about the risks a woman took by granting her hand in marriage?

He did not lose ownership of all his worldly goods. *He* did not give all power over his body to someone who could beat or even kill him without risk of prosecution. *He* did not suffer the danger of childbirth, or chance being left alone to care for his offspring while a spouse idled elsewhere—or risk having them taken away if their father chose to do so.

But as her initial indignation faded she found herself troubled. *Could* there be some truth in his accusations? *Was* she a coward, holding on to a past she'd burnished to unrealistic perfection in order to avoid risking her heart and her happiness again?

What if she abandoned caution and poured all her hope and passion into making a life with him? Liking him, desiring him as she did, she suspected she might easily fall in love; indeed, she was more than half in love with him already.

But there was no guarantee he would become similarly enraptured with her. Perhaps the pain of losing the lady he'd adored was still too raw for him to admit the possibility of finding such rapture again. But what if she accepted him and he did later meet such a lady? Would he not soon resent the wife he had so precipitately wed?

She knew she was not capable of turning a blind eye to her husband's indiscretions. If Allen Mansfell did not come to love her too much to be tempted by another lady, with her mama's unhappy example to caution her the chance that a union begun so hopefully could sour into anger, hurt and bitterness was still high—unacceptably high.

If that made her a coward, so be it.

At least he'd agreed to cease his unsettling attentions. Angry as he'd been, she didn't think he'd change his mind about renewing them in the two days remaining before he left. When, praise heaven, she could find peace again.

Of course during the upcoming Season they would inevitably meet again. She could only hope that before that happened he would have begun courting another suitable matrimonial candidate, ensuring that the strong connection still sizzling between them did not prompt him to renew his attentions.

Because if he should…the mere thought of kissing him again made her dizzy with want and need. After the little interlude they'd just shared she could no longer pretend to be indifferent. He'd seen how easy it would be to disarm her with talk of friendship and then use his physical appeal to lure her near, and so befuddle her mind that should he propose again she might well accept him, whether he'd come to love her or not.

If he should entice her with passion again, how would she find the strength to resist him?

An idea flashed into her brain, so outrageous and impossible she tried to immediately reject it. But sneaky, insidious, it refused to be banished.

There *was* a way she could satisfy her desires and savour all the delights she now regretted she'd refrained from experiencing with James. Afterwards, Allen Mansfell would never again be able to call her a coward, unwilling to seize what she wanted, or think of her as a genteel, biddable spinster willing to settle for mild affection and bland mutual respect.

No, if she travelled this path she would so shock and disconcert Allen Mansfell that he would strike her name permanently from his list of proper matrimonial prospects.

And never tempt her again.

Not that this scandalous plan wasn't risky, but she was no longer a penniless young girl. Mistress of her own household, answering to no one, she possessed the means and resources to discreetly cope with any eventuality.

She would do it, she decided. Tomorrow, before he left Wellingford, she would seduce Allen Mansfell.

Chapter Nine

After the scene over the kissing ball, her sisters were too discreet to press her for more than the carefully rehearsed explanation she offered upon her return. Also, to her relief, Allen Mansfell took himself off to hunt with Thomas and Colton, not returning until dinner, during which he maintained a scrupulous politeness before excusing himself immediately after. The rest of the company also retired early, allowing Meredyth to seek the solitude of her own chamber.

Though she determinedly closed her eyes, vivid imagination kept her senses simmering. Torn between a reckless eagerness to proceed and the more prudent hope that Allen Mansfell would rebuff her, Meredyth ended up hardly sleeping the night before her disturbing guest's last full day at Wellingford.

She rose early and breakfasted before the rest of the

family. Fortunately, with the arrival of her sisters Cecily and Emma due the day the Mansfell brothers departed, she had a long list of preparations to distract her and make the hours pass more quickly.

Those duties also kept her away from company until she joined everyone for nuncheon. The air sizzled with tension the moment she walked in, conversation faltering as everyone looked from her to Allen Mansfell. That gentleman sent her a glance that scorched her eyelashes before turning back to resume his chat with Lord Englemere.

During the meal that followed, her stomach churning at the prospect of what was to come, Meredyth did little more than push food around her plate. Afterwards, as the others walked out, she fixed a smile on her lips and intercepted Allen Mansfell.

Motioning him to follow, she walked to the windows overlooking the garden, away from the other guests.

'Mr Mansfell, I should not wish us to part on bitter terms. Will you allow me to apologise? I should be very pleased to have you accompany me to the Dower House this afternoon. The renovations are nearly complete, and I believe you would find it interesting to inspect them.'

For a long moment while she held her breath he studied her in silence. Despite her nervousness, just being the subject of that intense green-eyed stare sent a flame of desire sparking through her.

Finally he nodded. 'Yes, I should like to see your vision one last time.'

Had he imbued that phrase with more than casual meaning? she wondered. If her plan succeeded, he was going to see a great deal more of her…enough to satisfy him and then drive him away for ever.

Setting a time to meet, already light-headed with both dread and anticipation, she went up to her chamber to prepare herself for what might well be the most momentous afternoon of her life.

Conversation was limited on their ride to the Dower House—she too tied up with nerves to be able to manage any, he apparently lost in thought. But when he helped down from the saddle, and she leaned forward to brush her torso against his chest, the sudden clenching of his fingers on her waist told her that despite the disagreement between them he was still as affected by her nearness as she was by his, giving her some reassurance that he might not humiliatingly refuse her.

As they entered the deserted dwelling her heart commenced thrumming in her chest and her stomach turned even queasier, but she steeled herself keep to her plan: trailing her finger down his sleeve after he released her arm. Halting close beside him as she showed him the converted fireplaces, almost but not quite touching him. Pausing before she spoke to draw the tip of her tongue out to moisten her lips.

She felt a surge of excitement and satisfaction as she saw his gaze riveted on her mouth.

By the time they'd finished touring the downstairs rooms she wasn't sure how he felt, but she was on fire with eagerness to kiss him. 'If you'll follow me upstairs, I'll show you the new gas lamps.'

Upstairs—where the bedchambers were situated. Though he raised an eyebrow, he nodded assent and took her arm. Heart pounding in earnest now, she led him into one, its renovations complete though its furnishing were still cloaked under Holland covers. After pointing out the gas lamp, her fingers trembling with impatience and dread, she pushed her cloak back over her shoulders and turned to face him, feeling her breasts swell in the low-cut gown she'd chosen.

As Bella had predicted—blast the little flirt—his gaze dropped immediately to her bodice.

His smouldering green eyes rose to meet hers. 'Just what do you think you are doing?'

She took a deep breath, making her bosom strain against the confining cloth. 'What do you think I'm doing?'

His gaze returning to her breasts, he drew in a sharp breath before replying, 'Since you think I've insulted you already, I hardly dare say it.'

'And if I *were* doing what you hardly dare say?'

'As a gentleman, I ought to escort you back to the Hall before something…improper happens.'

'Do the proper thing? The safe thing?' she taunted. 'And you called *me* a coward.' She stepped closer and angled her face up, brazenly offering him her lips.

For a moment he hesitated, the heat in his eyes like to scald her face. 'I'm a gentleman, not an idiot,' he muttered and seized her, his fingers biting into the soft skin of her shoulders as he pulled her into his arms.

He kissed her with hungry fury, just as he had outside the dining room. She kissed him back as fiercely, revelling in the feel of his tongue invading her mouth, pursuing it with her own.

He groaned, his kiss becoming more voracious still. His hands rose to the exposed tops of her breasts, stroking over them and cupping them. His thumbs sought her stiffened nipples, circled and flicked them, each caress sending a sharp current of need blazing to her centre. Moaning, she pressed herself against the hardness in his breeches.

He broke the kiss and looked down at her, his eyes wild and unfocused. 'This is madness,' he gasped. 'We must stop now, while I still can.'

She put her hands over his and pressed his thumbs back against her nipples. 'Don't stop,' she whispered, and drew his head back down, invading his mouth and suckling his tongue.

After several marvellous moments he broke the kiss again, his breathing shallow and rapid. 'You're sure?'

Daringly she moved a hand down to caress the tented front of his breeches. 'I'm sure,' she breathed.

He gave her a wolfish grin. 'As my lady wishes.'

He tilted her head and kissed her again—deep, then shallow, then deeply again, before he moved his mouth to nip and suck her lips. He bound her against him, dizzy and faint with pleasure, his mouth nuzzling her eyelids, her chin, drawing in the shell of her ear and nibbling delicately. While his lips worked wonders he insinuated his fingertips under the material of her light stays until they found her nipples.

She gasped and shuddered, almost fainting at the intensity of the sensation. Excitement pulsed in her chest as he wound the sensual tension tighter and tighter, rubbing and caressing her. She gasped again when he suddenly replaced his fingers with his tongue, creating a pattern of heat and ice as he licked her, the moist warmth of his tongue followed by the chill of air passing over the wetted skin.

Her legs buckled, and she would have fallen if he'd not caught her. Laughing softly, he supported her across the room, tossed his cloak atop hers before guiding her down on the bed.

Leaning back against the headboard, he pulled her onto his lap, kissing her while his fingers swiftly unloosed her bodice and stays, then pushed the material down until her breasts were fully bared to him, nipples tight and puckered.

'Lovely,' he murmured, and bent to suckle her.

She cried out then, hands fisting in his hair as she held his head there, pleasuring first one breast and then the other. While he suckled her he worked one hand under her skirts, caressing her leg from ankle to knee to the smooth curve of her inner thigh.

Pillowing her head on the soft material of their cloaks, he lowered her onto the bed and bent over her, parting her thighs as he suckled harder. His fingers caressed between her legs, seeking out the nub that throbbed with each nip and pull of his mouth on her breast.

She cried out as he reached that small, exquisitely sensitive scrap of flesh, her legs tensing around his hand. His finger played in the silky wetness, stroking her there and delving lower, inside her throbbing passage.

Just when she felt she must come apart from the intensity of it, he withdrew his hand. Shushing her cry of protest, he bent and replaced his fingertips with the hot velvet brush of his tongue. Beyond thought or sense, she wrapped her legs around his back, holding him against her until, in a wash of heat and an explosion of light, she shattered like a kaleidoscope into a thousand shards of pleasure.

When she came back to herself, she lay loosely wrapped in his arms. While she felt deliciously satisfied, she knew from his panting breaths that he had not yet reached a similar state. Languidly she reached over to pop open a button on his trouser flap. Excitement pulsed in her anew when she clasped his length and felt him jump in her hand.

Wonderful as the first had been, she wanted more. She wanted everything. Though what came next went beyond all previous experience, into territory from which there was no return, she meant to seize her chance to feel this exciting, vital part of him sheathed within her, to sense it as he found his satisfaction, his lips at her breast as he drove deep within her.

'I'm afraid you are behind me, sir,' she murmured, stroking a finger over the satiny tip.

He gasped before his breathy laugh rumbled in her ear. 'Not yet, but I'd like to be,' he murmured.

'Then we must see if this new mode of heating is as satisfactory as the last,' she replied, unfastening the other button to let the trouser flap fall and expose him completely to her avid gaze.

'Lovely,' she murmured, and bent to taste him.

Thick and rigid, and yet so smooth, she marvelled, exulting in the groans and gasps she drew from him as she explored his length. Suddenly he rolled her sideways, letting her continue to feast on him while he pushed apart her thighs and tasted her again.

His urgent tongue soon brought her to the pinnacle of release. Wanting this time, though, to experience the full measure of delight, she pulled away and settled herself above, straddling him.

Suddenly uncertain how to proceed, she hesitated. With a tender smile he reached up to brush a finger across her lips, then gently grasped her hips to fit her over his sleek length. Murmuring her name, he guided himself in.

Her passage burned as it stretched to accommodate his fullness, and for a moment she almost regretted her rashness. But then, balancing her weight, he slid back and struggled to a sitting position, cupping her *derrière* in one hand and with the other pulling her torso close enough for him to trap one nipple between his lips.

As he rolled the tip between his teeth, nipping and sucking, the tightness within her eased. A new tension began building as she slid him deeper, her body instinctively finding that most ancient and basic of rhythms. Soon she was hovering again on the precipice, until he slipped a finger between them, rubbing her nub from above while his length caressed her within, and the tension dissolved in a burst of sensation.

Amid the waves of pleasure she felt him stiffen and cry out as his own release took him. Then she collapsed on his chest and lay there, exultant, satiated, complete.

Oh, indeed, in this too they were well matched, she

thought, relishing in the feel of him buried within her. While she lay against him he drew her crushed skirts back down over her legs and slid a hand beneath them again, to caress her naked bottom.

Murmuring with appreciation, she wriggled against him...and felt his softening length jerk within her, setting off an answering jolt of pleasure in her. She began to rock gently in time to the ministration of his hands, while his shaft swelled and hardened again.

They took pleasure slowly this time, with Allen rolling her over and propping himself above her, where he could alternately taste her lips and her breasts while gradually increasing the rhythm and depth of his thrusts. Until she was panting with urgency, wrapping her legs around him and begging him to thrust harder, deeper, until they both found ecstasy again.

They must have dozed, for when consciousness returned Meredyth found herself lying in his arms, her head pillowed on his shoulder, while outside the chamber windows the afternoon sun was fading.

She looked up to find him watching her, a tender smile on his face.

Her heart squeezed in her chest, and she knew in that moment she was lost.

'Delightful as our present position is, I suppose we'd better return before they send out a search,' he said.

'I suppose we must,' she replied reluctantly.

'Before we go, I expect I'd better—'

She put up a hand to stop his lips. 'Don't say anything.'

'Am I not allowed to say you were wonderful?'

She smiled. 'Yes, I suppose you can say that.'

'Am I not allowed to acknowledge you totally flummoxed me? I admit, I've always seen you as the most proper of maidens. How delightful to discover you are so much more! I expect, however, that upon our return we'd best announce our engagement at once. We can have the banns called—'

Once again she stopped his lips. 'There's no need to turn this…agreeable interlude into more than it was. I took precautions, I assure you, to ensure there would be no…repercussions. We're safe on my land, far from town and the gossips. There is absolutely no need to make me a "gentlemanly" offer.'

His smile faded. 'Are you telling me…you let me make love to you, but you'll not accept my hand?'

Something cracked and splintered inside her as she made herself laugh. 'Goodness, you can't try to tell me you propose to every woman you bed?'

Sitting up abruptly, he shifted away from her. 'No, but it is the first time I've bedded an unmarried lady. Or at least I thought she was a lady.'

That shot went home, but she let it go. She had to get him out of here, before all resolve crumbled like a child's sandcastle after a wave and she begged him to stay, accepted his hand, catapulted herself into the terror of a future she could not control.

'Life is full of surprises, isn't it? I expect we should get back. You must pack, and I have the preparations for Emma and Cecily's arrival to finish. I shall need your kind assistance, however.' Turning her back, she indicated the loosened laces of her stays.

Silently he began doing them up, while she waited, her heart already bleeding at the cold anger radiating from him. When he'd finished, she moved to slide off the bed.

He caught her shoulder. 'You can't pretend to be so…indifferent. I know you're not!'

Her eyes stung with tears she wouldn't let him see, and it took all the effort she could summon to keep her voice even. 'Indeed, I'm hardly indifferent! Have I not just given a convincing demonstration of how attractive I find you?'

'Attractive. And that is all?'

'Did you not find it enough? *I* thought our interlude vastly satisfying. In any event, I trust I may rely on your discretion?'

'My discretion!' he repeated, his tone bitter. 'I suppose I can promise you that.'

Her heart seemed to be splintering in as many pieces as pleasure had shattered her body. Frantically she resisted the imperative to apologise, throw herself back into his arms and assure him she wasn't the doxy she was trying to appear.

It had seemed so easy when she'd planned it: savour his touch, and touch him in return with a shocking intimacy that would distance him for ever and never tempt her again.

She'd not foreseen it would rip her heart from her body to deceive him and walk away, knowing he would never again approach her with more than chill civility.

Only the thought of Mama, dying neglected and heartbroken in this very house, lent her the courage to continue. Casting about for some remark that would prick him deeply enough to make him depart at once, she said, 'I do thank you, of course. 'Twas a very agreeable entertainment.'

The green eyes studying her turned glacial. After swiftly refastening his trousers, he made her a bow. 'So glad I performed to your expectations, madam. Having *entertained* you, I shall take my leave.'

She managed to keep a smile on her lips as he stalked past her and out through the door. Stumbling to the window, she peeped through the frame and watched him exit the house, mount his horse and ride off.

Wrapping both arms around herself, she returned to sit at the edge of the bed, staring into the rapidly gathering gloom. In mockery of all her clever stratagems, she was very much afraid that Allen Mansfell had carried away with him not just her innocence, but also her heart.

Chapter Ten

Back home at the Grange, Allen had passed the most joyless Christmas he could remember—all because of the perfidious Meredyth Wellingford. He'd thought himself so clever, teasing and inflaming her into finally acting upon the passion between them! So confident their unexpected interlude would lead to an immediate engagement. Fool that he was, she'd gulled him even more completely than Susanna Davies.

By the time he'd reached home, his initial fury over this fact had disintegrated into a black depression no amount of dispassionate reasoning had lightened.

None of the traditional family celebrations he normally savoured had appeased him. His mother's welcoming wassail had lacked the piquant touch of lemon and spice in Miss Wellingford's brew. The blaze of Christmas candles had carried the image of her face reflected in their glow. The children's excitement when they'd brought home the Yule log had made him recall the greens-gathering expedition at Wellingford, while the jackstraws Thomas had given his nieces sparked poignant reflections of the game he'd played with Meredyth on the schoolroom floor, back when he'd still believed he would make her his bride.

And he absolutely couldn't look at a kissing ball.

As unsuccessful as he was at avoiding thoughts of her by day, at night it was worse. Too many times he awoke bathed in sweat, hard and aching, his mind aflame with the image of her astride him.

In vain he argued with himself as he lay there, unable to recapture sleep, trying to dismiss from his mind and senses a wanton who had been as ready to ride him as she'd been to casually send him away afterwards.

He actually welcomed the end of the Christmas holiday, that he might resume the time-consuming, energy-draining tasks of supervising the estate, certain that the work would dim this agony as it had helped him survive Susanna's betrayal.

Except so far the charm wasn't working. Indeed, his work on the estate had, if anything, deepened his unhappiness and kept his anger, disappointment, puzzlement and frustration over Meredyth Wellingford's behaviour at a constant simmer.

He couldn't ride the fields and consult with the tenants without recalling his time at Wellingford, with an intelligent, knowledgeable Meredyth cantering by his side. Nearly every task he undertook—ordering seed, preparing thatch, mending tools—recalled a discussion, an observation, a similar activity he'd shared with Meredyth.

It was more than past time to get on with his life, he told himself as, short-tempered from lack of sleep and frustration, he stamped into breakfast a month after Kings' Day, giving a curt nod to Thomas, who was already at table.

The two brothers ate in silence until, as he rose to leave, Thomas jumped up to follow him. 'Allen—wait! Can I have a word with you?'

'If you want me to increase your allowance,' he said over his shoulder to his brother, 'the answer is no. What with putting more acres under cultivation—'

'It's got nothing to do with my allowance,' Thomas interrupted. 'Just like you to start growling before I even tell you what I want! You've been like a bear with a sore paw since we left Wellingford. After your withering reply reduced poor Mama to tears when she asked you what was wrong last night, she has begged me to speak with you.'

Before Allen could tell him to go to the devil, Thomas held up a hand. 'I don't know what happened at Wellingford—nor do I want to. Though I must say

I always thought you possessed such address I'm amazed you somehow made such mice-feet of courting Merry.'

'Thank you for refraining from comment,' Allen said acidly.

'Dammit, I can at least express my disappointment!' Thomas replied with exasperation. 'I can't think of another lady I'd be prouder to call sister. That bitch Susanna Davies must still be clouding your mind. I had hoped you were over her by now.'

'You should be more charitable, Thomas. Besides, all women are wanton at heart. 'Tis just a matter of degree—'

Allen had scarcely uttered the last word when Thomas shocked him with a right uppercut to the jaw. Propelled backwards, he barely managed to keep from knocking over a dining chair as he righted himself.

'Don't you *dare* compare Merry to that…that witch!' Thomas declared angrily. 'Not all women are like Miss Davies—though I'm glad she revealed her true character before you succeeded in marrying her. She tried to seduce *me*, you know.'

Engaged in rubbing his sore jaw, Allen froze. 'Tried to seduce you?'

'When I called to congratulate her on your engagement, she invited me to walk through the shrubbery. There she rubbed herself against me, offering me her lips, murmuring how glad she was that we would be *close.* I never told you—blind with adoration as you were, I doubt you'd have believed me. Not content with bewitching you, Susanna Davies wanted every man she met to be wild with desire for her.'

A woman who bewitched a man with desire? Allen thought, pressing his lips together against the temptation to tell Thomas a thing or two about his revered St Meredyth. But though Meredyth Wellingford might not be the lady everyone believed her, he was a gentleman—and he had promised her his 'discretion'. A surge of outrage over her ill-treatment of him rose again to choke him.

'I do apologise for my maladroitness,' he said, when he could speak.

'It's your foul temper that's plaguing everyone now,' Thomas retorted. 'Why don't you either get over it or go beg her pardon and start again?'

'Ah, the astute advice of a experienced gentleman of ten and seven summers,' he shot back.

'I may not be old and experienced,' Thomas replied, 'but I'm not such a selfish oaf as to inflict my black-tempered moods on the whole family.'

That well-aimed barb hit home with the sting of truth. 'Pray convey my apologies to Mama and Papa,' Allen replied, remorse emerging through the weight of misery that lay like a soggy blanket over his soul. 'Let me hasten to remove my objectionable presence from the house.'

While Thomas sighed, and denounced him without heat as a blockhead, Allen bowed and strode from the room.

The chill, grey morning fog had disintegrated into a steady rain driven by bitter wind. Impelled by raging anger and unhappiness, Allen set off on a tour around the Grange, forcing his shivering mount past field after field deserted by farm workers intelligent enough to have left work to a more auspicious day.

Finally, exhausted, soaked and chilled to the marrow, Allen rode home. In the bleakness that succeeded his burst of activity, as he paced back to the house, he asked himself why he was having such difficulty ridding his mind and senses of Meredyth Wellingford. Even in the depths of his anguish over Susanna he hadn't been so out of sorts and snappish with his family.

Get over it, Thomas had advised…or start over again. A pang of longing rose in him. Oh, that he might turn back the clock to the moment just after their lovemaking at the Dower House, when he'd thought himself the luckiest man in the world! Exulting at his good fortune in winning for his wife a woman who combined all the virtues of a lady with the sensuality of a siren. A lady who would surprise him, delight him, and captivate him for a lifetime.

Until she'd uttered those blighting words about their 'amusing interlude'. Acid drenched his stomach anew that she had casually dismissed the event that had so shaken his world as an afternoon's frolic.

Meredyth Wellingford was a wanton, despite what Thomas believed. Whatever her other qualities, he'd as soon saddle himself with the misery of a loose-moralled wife as he would mortgage his birthright.

But then another of Thomas's remarks rang in his head, stopping him in his tracks.

The fact that Susanna had made advances to Thomas, then a stripling of sixteen, no longer shocked him. As Thomas had alleged, a wanton's behaviour would find her out sooner or later. But in all his dealings with Meredyth before the afternoon at the Dower House no one he'd observed with her— workmen, foreman, tenants, neighbours—had betrayed the slightest hint they suspected Meredyth Wellingford to be a lightskirt.

Absent that episode at the Dower House, he would not have believed it himself.

The whole conundrum of her behaviour crystallised around that one point. If she wasn't a wanton, why had she deliberately set out to make him believe she was?

Why she would seduce him if such were not her normal practice was a mystery too devious for his simple male mind to sort out. However, it should be rather easier to discover her true character. If Meredyth were lacking in morals, having lived nearly all her life at Wellingford, someone in the country thereabouts would surely know it.

Perhaps confirming that fact would set him at ease and allow him to begin forgetting her.

And if he could not confirm it… He was not the sort of man to seduce—or allow himself to be seduced by, he amended—a lady and walk away for no more reason than she had given him at the Dower House. He would have to confront Miss Wellingford face to face one more time and demand that she explain herself.

The thought filling him with more energy and enthusiasm than he'd felt since riding with her to the Dower House that fated afternoon, he strode into the house. He wasn't sure how, but one way or another he meant to discover the truth about Meredyth Wellingford.

The opportunity to investigate occurred sooner than he could have hoped, at dinner that night, when his father mentioned the possibility of acquiring a property in the country adjacent to Wellingford. Immediately Allen volunteered to inspect it. Though he wasn't yet sure exactly what he meant to do, Waring Manor was located only a day's ride from Wellingford. Once he had completed the business for his father, he could stay overnight at the inn at Swansden, the small village closest to the Wellingford demesne.

* * *

A week later, his tour of the prospective new property complete, Allen strode into the Swansden Arms. The innkeeper in the deserted taproom hurried over to assist him. After he had requested overnight accommodations and given his name, the man asked if he were related to the Mr Thomas Mansfell who frequently visited the young master at Wellingford.

Pleased to discover, as he'd hoped, that the proprietor of the only inn for twenty miles around was familiar with the owners of the local estate, Allen confirmed that he was. If Meredyth Wellingford had lovers, they must have either met her here or travelled through here. Accepting a pint of the landlord's homebrew, he settled beside the bar to discover what he could.

The next half-hour's conversation was wonderfully illuminating. Mr Sweeney, the innkeep, had nothing but praise for Meredyth Wellingford, whose care and diligence had brought the property neglected by her sire back into a productivity that benefited the entire countryside.

'Aye, what a good mistress she is! Took my Betsy into service at the Hall, she did, and knows as much as the parson about any in the county who be ailing or in need. Though I'm surprised you mean to stay here, being acquainted with the family. We've not housed visitors to the Hall since repairs to the house been finished, five or so years ago. Though she been good to bring us custom, often sending her guests here for a homebrew after a day's hunting.'

'Her suitors didn't stay here?' he pressed.

The innkeeper chuckled. 'Being a neighbour, Lord A paid his calls from home, and that other gent, though he stayed up at the Hall, didn't last long. Folks hereabouts think Miss Wellingford never got over losing the young soldier she was promised to. A pity, for she'd make some gent a fine wife!'

At that moment another party entered, and the garrulous innkeeper excused himself to go tend them.

Allen sipped his ale, considering what he'd just learned. It seemed the local innkeeper had as high an opinion of Meredyth Wellingford's character as Thomas did.

Of course she might have conducted her affairs in some deserted outbuilding on the Wellingford grounds. But with whom? He couldn't see her dallying with her elderly steward. No, there had been no cavalcade of suitors, nor were there any other estates in the area to host the calibre of gentleman which was the only creditable type for a tryst with a lady of the manor.

Which meant…despite her insinuation to the contrary…that perhaps she hadn't trysted. The evidence he'd just gathered and every maligned instinct he possessed told him that Meredyth Wellingford was no wanton.

For what incomprehensible reason could she have

deliberately tried to deceive him? He had no idea. But he intended to ask her first thing tomorrow.

A rising excitement intermingled with joy bubbled up at the prospect of seeing her again, watching the expressions play across her mobile face as he matched wits with her. Anticipation sizzled in his blood at the thought of inhaling her rose scent, touching the softness of her hand, her lips.

Whatever her game, Meredyth Wellingford was going to find him much more difficult to fob off than she had at the Dower House.

It was then, smiling at the image of her, that the truth dawned on him, so clear and simple he wondered why it had taken him so long to see it. The reason he'd been so distraught at her deception, so angry at the thought of her with another man. The reason he'd been in such a black despair since he'd left Wellingford, forced to abandon the idea of making her his wife.

He was in love with Meredyth Wellingford. He threw back his head and laughed at the giddy delight of it, attracting a curious look from the newcomers across the taproom.

Tomorrow he would demonstrate to her just how much passion, persuasion and persistence he was prepared to exert in order to win her love in return.

After breakfast the next morning, Meredyth wandered through the rose garden, warmed by the

morning sun within its sheltering walls. It had been a
month since the last of her Christmas guests had left—
Sarah bearing Faith off to help plan her Season,
Colton going to visit a friend in the next county. And
almost two months since she'd last seen Allen
Mansfell. Yet she found him still constantly invading
her thoughts.

She went over to sit upon the bench where he'd
proposed. In the long days and even longer nights
since he'd departed she'd been unable to shake the
suspicion that in refusing him she might have made a
dreadful mistake.

She was sure, however, that she'd not erred in suc-
cumbing to her desire for him. If, as seemed quite
probable, she would never again experience the heights
of bliss to which he had raised her that fateful afternoon, she would always have the memory of it to
cherish.

A memory, since her courses had arrived on
schedule, that would remain untarnished by shame or
scandal.

However, rather than that fulfilment satisfying her
hunger and setting her at peace, it seemed the long-
slumbering appetite Allen Mansfell had awakened in
her was not to be quenched by a single splendid afternoon. Knowing what it was to pleasure and be plea-
sured by him, she still burned for his touch.

Nor did she know how to prevent herself from

reliving the moments they'd spent together, recalling the sound of his voice, the timbre of his laughter, the change in hue as his green eyes turned smoky with passion. How to stop savouring the memory of his touch every time she closed her eyes to sleep, or aching with loss every morning she awoke, alone and bereft.

Had she given her assent to the engagement he'd proposed at the Dower House, would her loving him have been enough for them to find happiness?

Fool she was, despite all her good intentions, to have fallen in love with him anyway!

Further fuelling her unhappiness was the advice Sarah had given her before leaving Wellingford. 'Though I don't mean to pry,' her sister had assured her, ''tis clear something extraordinary developed between you and Allen Mansfell. What happened to disrupt that I know not, but I urge you not to let it go without seeing him again. Love, I can assure you, does not always run smoothly, but it is precious. And it is always worth fighting for.'

Could she be any more miserable with him than she was now without him? What if she were to take Sarah's advice at the beginning of the Season and seek him out?

If she were the strong, confident woman she'd always believed herself to be she should embrace the risk of confessing her love and discovering if it was possible to end their estrangement. He might, of course, hand her a humiliating rejection. But at least then she'd know there was no hope for the longings she was unable to banish.

The confident, joyful, eager-to-experience-life Meredyth of ten years ago would have accepted the challenge. She'd let more of her spirit drain away than she could bear to admit if she were no longer capable of such courage.

She must go to him.

As she reached that brave but unsettling conclusion, she became aware of approaching footsteps. Blinking into the morning sun, she turned in the direction of the sound.

And then blinked again when her first hazy glimpse told her Allen Mansfell was walking towards her. Though she shook her head in amazement, a second glance confirmed that impossibility.

Excitement, gladness, and a wild, fierce desire to throw herself into his arms coursed through her. She was on her feet before she could check her enthusiasm.

'Mr Mansfell, what a…surprise.' She substituted the word at the last minute for 'delight'. 'Has something happened? Thomas? Colton? All the family are well?' she asked with sudden anxiety.

Then she closed her eyes, swept away by the power of his touch as he took her hand and bowed.

'The family is fine,' he replied, retaining her fingers in a light grip that resonated down every nerve. 'Something did happen, but to me alone, and it has left me so very far from "fine" that despite the anger of our parting I had to see you again.'

Urging her down beside him on the bench, he fixed her with a steady gaze. 'You suffered no...repercussions from the events of that afternoon at the Dower House, I trust?'

'None,' she assured him, feeling herself blush.

Giving her a look whose tenderness sent a shock of surprise and gladness through her, he continued, 'You're not the wanton you tried to appear that day, are you?'

So thankful that he was treating her without anger, despite her inexcusable deception of him, she felt tears prick her eyes. 'No,' she admitted.

He gave a cry of triumph. 'I knew it could not be true! Oh, you convinced me thoroughly enough at first that I rode away in a rage, determined to put you from my mind. But you refused to be banished. Memories of you kept slipping into my consciousness. Your voice. Your smile. The taste of you, and the incredible pleasure you brought me. And while I suffered from recollections I had no wish to recall,' he continued, 'it suddenly occurred to me that the episode at the Dower House was so out of character with everything I knew of you, something just wasn't right. Why then, my wanton, did you try to deceive me?'

'You tempted me too much!' she blurted. 'I feared if you kept after me my partiality for you would eventually lead me to accept your hand, whether you loved me or not. I hoped if I sent you away in disgust you wouldn't trouble me again and I could go on as before.'

'Ah, my "passionless" offer!' he replied with a grimace. 'Along with the other truths bedevilling me, I reluctantly came to acknowledge you were right. I was just as much a coward as I accused you of being, counselling you to open your heart while holding mine close. As if love could be politely restrained, broken to bridle like an untamed colt. Small wonder you despised a proposal offered out of tepid affection, holding yourself worthy of so much more! Had you not sent me away, who knows how much precious time I might have wasted before realising how much I adore you? I came here determined to throw my heart at your feet and beg you to let me try and capture yours. Will you do so?'

By some miracle she had not dared hope for he now loved her. She could follow her heart without reserve or worry of consequence, with the wild abandon and reckless enthusiasm she'd possessed before pain and loss had shackled her joy in life.

'You don't need to convince me,' she said softly,

love for him swelling in her chest. 'The afternoon you left the Dower House, you took my heart with you.'

That avowal won her a dazzling smile as he dropped to one knee. 'Then will you marry me, my darling? Not because I esteem you and all your virtues, but because you are indispensable to my happiness. Can I not persuade you that I am equally indispensable to yours?'

Joy like an effervescent wine bubbled in her veins and she gazed down at him, still on one knee before her, his impassioned gaze locked on her face.

'Just how do you intend to "persuade" me?' she asked, caressing with one finger the hand that clasped hers.

Immediately heat darkened his eyes. 'By every means I possess—soul and body.'

'Ah, that sounds promising. Did I mention that work at the Dower House is now complete, with all the gas lamps and Rumsford stoves in place?'

A devilish smile creased his lips. 'New technologies must be tested, do you not think? Particularly those in the upstairs bedchamber.' In one fluid movement he stood and offered her his arm. 'Will you come with me, my love—now and always?'

'Now and always,' she promised, and lifted her mouth to his kiss.

* * * * *

Dear Reader,

When I was asked if I would like to write a story for this anthology, I decided I wanted to celebrate the very essence of Christmas which, for me, is not about presents and feasting and putting up decorations. It's about a baby, born to a poor family as a symbol of hope for the whole world.

So my story is about forgiveness and second chances and the miraculous transforming power of love.

I hope it touches your heart,

Annie

THE RAKE'S
SECRET SON

ANNIE BURROWS

To all the other Harlequin Historical authors
(proud Hussies) who have welcomed
me into their loop.

Prologue

...Joseph, being a just man, was not willing to make her a public example...

Harry Tillotson barrelled through the church door and up the aisle, wiping his runny nose on the back of his torn jacket sleeve.

It was just two weeks to Christmas, and at Sunday school they had been learning all about the coming of the Christ child. Mary was going to have a baby, but it was not her husband's, Reverend Byatt had said.

Some of the older boys had sniggered, and looked at him, and on the way home they had begun to make nasty remarks about his mother. He had tried to make them stop, but there had been too many of them. All of them thinking they were better than him because they had a proper ma and pa, most of them married in this very church.

Harry glared up at the stained glass window where a glowing Madonna smiled serenely at the baby on her lap. Reverend Byatt had said God sent a baby at Christmas time to show He wanted to forgive sinners.

So why wouldn't anyone forgive his ma for having a baby? For having him? When she was the kindest, and cleverest, and hardest-working of all the mothers in Barstow?

He sniffed, angrily dashing a tear from his mud- and blood-caked face. People in the Bible just weren't like real people at all. Take that Joseph, the carpenter, Mary's husband. He had somehow known he wasn't the baby's real father, but he hadn't gone round telling everyone Mary was wicked, then gone off to war and got killed! No, he had stayed and looked after her.

'Why couldn't Ma have married someone like Joseph?' His words burst from the misery deep inside him, startling him as they rang out through the empty church.

You weren't supposed to talk in church. Only to say your prayers.

He whipped off his cap, clasped it between his hands, and bowed his head in a penitent attitude.

But his voice was still throbbing with resentment as he muttered, 'She should've had a husband who would stick by her no matter what. Then nobody would ever have known she had done anything wrong. And the other boys wouldn't think they have the right to make my life as horrid as they can just because I've never had a proper father! They wouldn't call my ma those names either. I do try to stick up for her, but—' he hiccupped, remembering the crowd who had circled him, taunting and jeering not five minutes earlier '—I'm too small!' Another tear ran hotly down his face to soak into his collar.

'The Reverend said you sent Jesus to get born in a stable, to prove you wanted to reach the poorest and lowliest and forgive their sins. Well,' he complained, '*everyone* looks down on us. So that makes us the lowliest. And Squire Jeffers says my ma's the greatest sinner in these parts. So I should think you'd jolly well want to send us a man like Joseph to make things right for us. And then—' he lifted his face defiantly towards the high altar '—I might believe there's some point in having Christmas!'

A sudden shaft of sunlight pierced the Mary window and lanced down to strike the floor right in front of his scuffed boots.

He flinched, guiltily acknowledging that he shouldn't have shouted at God.

A hell-born brat. That was what Squire Jeffers said he was. Even though Reverend Byatt argued that *nobody* was beyond God's forgiveness.

Harry turned on his heel and pelted back down the

aisle. He wasn't sure which of them had it right about him, but one thing he did know. He had to make it back to the one place he knew he would always be welcome, even though he *was* a bastard.

Chapter One

The sky was leaden, but at least the ground was soft. Nell wrapped a shawl over her head, took a long-handled fork, and made her way down to the vegetable plot. The recent frosts would have sweetened the parsnips nicely.

She had just carefully prised the first root from the end of the row when she heard a footstep behind her. Whirling round, she saw a man in a threadbare coat and scuffed boots had come up the garden path and was standing behind her, looking at her with that intent, hungry look all beggars had.

'I am sorry to have startled you,' he said gently, when she took a hasty step back, raising her fork as though to ward him off. But her heart-rate did not slow down.

An ordinary beggar she could have dealt with. She

might live alone save for her six-year-old son, on the very outskirts of Barstow, but she had learned over the years how to take care of herself. But this was no ordinary beggar.

She shook her head in disbelief, her stomach plummeting to her boots.

They had told her Carleton was dead. Five years ago there had been a letter, saying he had been hanged as a spy in some town in Portugal she had not even *tried* to pronounce.

She had not believed it then. Carleton! Spying! The man she had married had not been capable of engaging in activity that required any degree of cunning. The very moment a thought occurred to him it came exploding out of his mouth.

No, she had never believed he could have been a spy.

But she had believed he was dead.

So this man, standing on her garden path now, could not possibly be him. Even though he looked so very similar. Apart from being older, and thinner, and completely lacking in that arrogance that had oozed from Carleton's every pore.

'I was looking for Mrs Green.' He frowned, as though confused. 'Is this not her house?'

'It used to be—' she began. But that had been many years ago. The place had already stood empty when the man who had become Viscount Lambourne on her husband's death had sent her here.

But before she could explain all that, the man who reminded her so much of her late husband raised a trembling hand to his brow, muttered, 'I think I am about to…' and promptly collapsed.

And while he was toppling sideways into her blackcurrant bush it came to Nell that it had not been just his facial features but the very timbre of his voice that had jerked her so disconcertingly backwards through the years.

Just as the very gracefulness with which he was now passing out struck a resounding chord. Most men would have gone down any old how, probably landing flat on their faces, but not him. Oh, no! Even on the verge of losing consciousness *he* had instinctively managed to preserve his exceptionally good looks by choosing the nearest bush to cushion his fall.

She had to ram her fork into the ground and lean on it as the overwhelming and unpalatable truth sank in.

Carleton was not dead after all.

Somehow, against all the odds, he had survived and returned to…no, she shook her head, squeezing her eyes shut in pain. He had most definitely not returned to her. He said he had come here looking for Mrs Green. He had not expected to see Nell at all. Nor did he even seem to have recognised her. But then, why should he? When their brief, disastrous relationship had always been so one-sided? It had always been her gazing at him, never the other way round. She had been the one peering over the balcony railings to watch him when he had escorted one of her cousins in to dinner. On the rare occasions they had come face to face, during that ill-fated house party her aunt had thrown, he had always looked through her, or down his nose at her, taking her for one of the servants rather than a member of his hostess's family.

Even on the night that had changed the course of their lives so irrevocably he had been oblivious to her presence. She had sat with her knees drawn up to her chin in the window seat, marvelling at how completely sleep had wiped all traces of arrogance from his face. In repose he had looked, she recalled, almost vulnerable.

Just as he did now.

She drew a little closer in spite of herself. The years had inevitably wrought changes on the man who had treated her so cruelly. But though lines had appeared around his eyes, and his cheeks had hollowed out, his long limbs sprawled across the jagged clumps of broken branches with as much elegance as they had draped over her aunt's silken sofa cushions all those years before. And though she would never have believed her extremely fashionable husband would have been seen dead in such a downright shabby coat, there was no longer any doubt in her mind that this was him.

'Oh, Carleton,' Nell moaned, wrapping her arms round her suddenly churning stomach. 'What am I to do with you?'

It was the heavens that answered her. The clouds that had been lowering all day finally began to shed their burden. As the first fine flakes of snow sprinkled Carleton's gaunt cheek Nell knew she had no choice.

He must be desperate to have come here seeking help. He was already weak, probably ill, or he would not have keeled over as he had. She could not leave him lying out here in the cold.

Heaving a sigh, she went into the cottage and fetched a blanket from her bed. She placed it on the ground next to where he lay, and rolled his unconscious body onto it. Then, grasping hold of two corners, she dragged him inch by laborious inch over the uneven pathway.

For all he looked so thin, there was still a lot of substance to Carleton. By the time she got to her back door she was panting from exertion. And she still had to somehow manhandle him up over the stone step to get him indoors. She did not think her method of getting him up the path would work. She might bang his head as she heaved him over the step and knock him out…if such a thing as knocking out a man who was already insensible were possible…

No. She shook her head, her moment of levity swiftly passing. She doubted she could do him any real damage, but she did not want to risk bruising his skull and giving him a headache. She never wanted to face Carleton with a headache ever again.

She hid her face in her hands, recalling the morning after their wedding when, stiff with affront and paper-white from the after-effects of too much brandy, her handsome bridegroom had torn into her, ripping her last flimsy hope to shreds. She had not been able to credit then that lips that looked so beautiful, that kissed to such devastating effect, could form such cutting words.

She had not really known him. She sighed, dropping her hands and looking steadily at him. Not then.

Not until much later.

Pulling a face as she steeled herself to touch him again, Nell squatted down at his head and, hitching up her skirts, spread her legs indecorously on either side of his body.

She blushed. Oh, please let him not wake now! She would shrivel up and die of mortification if he ever knew she had wrapped her legs round his hips and tucked his head against her shoulder like this. But she could think of no other way. By wrapping her arms round his chest and shuffling backwards on her bottom Nell managed to raise his dead weight up over the back step and into the warmth of her kitchen.

She sagged against the leg of her solid table,

waiting for her breath to settle into a normal, steady rhythm again, his head still cradled in her lap.

His hair felt soft and fuzzy under her fingers. It must have been shaved off not so very long ago. He would have hated that, she thought, remembering the carefully arranged, silky dark locks of the handsome young buck he had once been. Of their own volition, it seemed to her, Nell's fingers swept the crown of his head one last time before she eased herself out from under his body. Then she carefully lowered his head to the flagged floor and knelt up beside him.

What should she do next? She had got him out of the snow, but he could not stay here on her kitchen floor for ever. Though the closed stove kept the room warm, she was certain his body heat would only seep away again through the stone flags on which he lay.

If only he would wake up, get up and walk out!

She reached out on a spurt of annoyance to shake his shoulder, then as quickly drew it back, mocking herself. If hauling him along the garden path and up over the back step had not roused him, shaking him was not going to do it.

If she only had some spirits in the house! She could tip some into his mouth, and perhaps that would revive him. Moodily, she began to chew at her already bitten fingernails. There was not even any tea to offer him. She had rather hoped the Vicar might bring her a quarter-pound as a Christmas gift, but by then she was sure Carleton would be long gone.

She had done all she was capable of doing for him. She had brought him in out of the cold, at least— which was more than he would have done for her, were their situations reversed.

On that sobering thought she got to her feet and pushed the back door closed. For several minutes she leaned against it, simply looking at Carleton and chewing her fingernails.

She had been so naïve to have hoped for anything from the handsome devil she had married. With hindsight, she should have known that no true gentleman would pass out drunk on a sofa during the course of a house party whose guests included several young ladies of gentle birth. Nor would a decent man, upon waking, have vented his wrath in such an intemperate fashion upon a girl he had just discovered was not only not a servant, but barely out of the schoolroom to boot.

It was the sound of footsteps pounding up the garden path that eventually jerked her out of her reverie.

Harry came bursting into the kitchen with the desperate air of a criminal seeking sanctuary, and would have tripped over Carleton's body had she not caught fast hold of his arm.

An extra weight descended on Nell's shoulders

with the arrival of her son. Through the dirt that caked his face she could just discern a reddening along one cheekbone that presaged a black eye. The snowflakes peppering his silky black hair announced the fact he had lost his cap somewhere. In short, it was obvious he had been in a fight.

Again.

In spite of all she could do, there was no denying that he was beginning to grow wild. She knew she was too soft with him, but she could never bring herself to beat him—even though Squire Jeffers insisted such strict discipline was the only way to stop him from becoming gallows-bait.

And even though she knew she ought to at least be reprimanding him for coming home in such a disreputable state, she simply did not have the energy right now. Someone would beat a path to her door soon enough, telling her exactly what he had been up to and demanding recompense.

'Cor!' he said now, his guilty expression transforming to one of awe as he wriggled out of her hold, making straight for Carleton's inert body. 'Ain't he big?'

Then, inexplicably, he whirled round to look over his shoulder through their little kitchen window towards the church, the spire of which was just visible over the tops of the yew trees bordering the churchyard.

'Is he just, though?'

'Just?' She frowned. She could not keep up with the strange words he picked up from the village boys. 'I don't know what you mean by that, but he's certainly big.' She ached all over from the effort of getting him indoors. Then she eyed her son's small but sturdy frame. 'Do you think you could help me make him more comfortable?'

''Course, Mama,' he said, puffing out his chest. 'We got to look after him, haven't we?'

'Yes,' she blinked, somewhat taken aback by his enthusiasm. 'Though as a rule one should not really bring beggars into the house. But he fainted in our garden, and I could hardly leave him lying out there in the cold…'

''Course you couldn't,' he beamed. 'Not at Christmas.'

She supposed the Reverend Byatt had been teaching them about charity in his Sunday school. She was a little surprised that the lesson appeared to have made such an impression on Harry, but nonetheless she was pleased.

'Exactly,' she smiled, proud that he was showing, at last, some signs that he was not going to grow up to be as self-centred as his father. 'Between us,' she said with determination, 'I should think we could get him onto the sofa in the parlour. And then I want you to run to Squire Jeffers with a letter about him, so that someone can come and take him away.'

'Take him away?' Harry's face fell.

'Yes,' she said firmly. She could not very well have left him out to die in the cold, but nor did she want him staying one moment longer than he had to. 'This man may look like a beggar, but he comes from a wealthy family. He does not belong here, with the likes of us.'

For a moment it looked as though Harry was going to argue with her. He was doing that more and more lately. Answering her back, asking awkward questions and never being satisfied with her answers. So it was a relief when, albeit with a mulish expression on his face, he obeyed her prompting to take Carleton by the feet and help her manoeuvre his dead weight through the kitchen and into the front parlour, where, with a little ingenuity and a great deal of effort, they managed to get him onto the sofa.

'Run and fetch him a pillow for his head, and another blanket,' she said, with a sinking feeling as she realised she was going to have to dig into her precious reserves of fuel by lighting a fire for him.

While Harry clattered up the stairs to her bedroom, Nell bent to undo the buttons of Carleton's coat, which had rucked up round his neck. As the backs of her fingers brushed his throat she flinched at the searing heat that was pouring off him. His face, which she had avoided looking at since Harry had come home, for fear she would reveal her feelings, was beaded with sweat.

No wonder he had collapsed in her garden. He was running a very high fever.

Forgetting just who and what the man was for a few minutes, she began to strip him of his clothing. Years of experience in nursing her son through his various ailments had taught her that sponging a body did as much good as anything a doctor might suggest, had she ever been able to afford to send for one.

It was not very hard to get him out of his clothes. They slid off him as easily as if they had been made for a very much larger man.

But when she rolled him to one side, to ease off his sweat-stained shirt, she reeled back, gasping. Carleton's back was ridged and furrowed with old scar tissue. It looked as though some considerable time ago he had been flogged!

Her hands shook as she went back to the task of stripping him, her eyes filling with tears. She hated to think of anyone suffering such brutal treatment, but for Carleton it must have been particularly devastating. Not only had he been the only son of extremely indulgent parents, and heir to a venerable title, but he had been blessed with great wealth too. Wherever he went he had expected, and generally received, unqualified admiration.

Thankfully, she had managed to remove his shirt and roll him onto his back before Harry returned with his arms full of bedlinen. She did not feel up to answering a barrage of questions about how a man's back could end up looking like a ploughed field. She felt sick enough just imagining cruel men stripping Carleton, tying him to a whipping post, then beating him until his skin tore to bloodied shreds, without having to talk about it.

'Go to the pump and fetch me some water and a cloth,' she said in a tremulous voice, 'while I pen that note for you to take to the Squire.'

Though disapproving heartily of her, the Squire would make sure a letter got through to Viscount Lambourne, her landlord. Especially if she marked it 'urgent'. For it *was* urgent that someone should come and collect Carleton, give him the care she was so ill-equipped to provide, and restore him to his proper sphere.

Where neither she nor her son belonged.

Chapter Two

Carleton yawned, stretched, and opened his eyes. And wondered why he was looking in a mirror at a reflection of himself at about seven or eight years old.

He squeezed his eyes shut again. The marsh fever must still have him in its grip. Though for once the waking visions that assailed him were of a benign nature. He had even conjured up an angel this time, who had silently ministered to him with soothing hands and compassionate eyes.

Brown eyes, they'd been, set beneath a smooth brow framed by dusky curls.

He sighed. Angels ought to have blue eyes, and hair like flame. So whatever the creature was who had tended to him she was no angel. Even though she had left such a sense of well-being in her wake.

And as for imagining himself a boy again, proudly

examining the black eye he had got fighting with the stable lad… He shook his head impatiently, as though doing so might clear it.

It was because he had dreamed for so long of coming home. And when someone had nursed him so gently it had sent his mind back to a time when he had been safe and life had been full of promise. That must be it. As to where he really was… He gave an involuntary shiver.

'Want another blanket, mister?' the child with his hazel eyes, straight black brows and pugnacious jaw piped up.

Warily he opened his eyes again—to see that the image of himself as a scrubby schoolboy was still hovering over him.

When he came into his right mind this person would probably turn out to be a strapping farm worker, and not a boy of any sort. The last time he had fallen this ill he had mistaken his fellow prisoners for a troupe of demons who had been tormenting him with pitchforks. He had fought their every attempt to care for him, they had later told him, and he'd had to beg their pardon.

He had not fought the angel, though, not once. On the contrary, he remembered being pathetically grateful for her every act of kindness. During one period of relative lucidity he seemed to recall babbling profuse thanks, and being answered by a shake of the head and an expression so sad it had made him feel unaccountably guilty.

'How about a drink, then?' the imp with the black eye persisted.

In English.

A sense of well-being hatched within Carleton's breast and emerged as a fully-fledged smile. He'd made it. He was back in England.

'How about fetching me that angel instead?' he countered. She would bathe his face and body in deliciously cool water. Then, if he could keep his eyes open, she would hold his head against her bosom while she spooned ambrosia into his mouth. He would feel strength returning with each spoonful and lie down at last, knowing he was safe for she was watching over him.

'Mama can't come just now,' the imp replied. 'Viscount Lambourne is with her. On account of you. She says he has come to take you away, but he don't look too pleased. If he don't want you, though, it don't matter. You can stay here with us and be my pa.'

Nothing anyone said when he was in the grip of his fever ever made much sense, so he brushed aside the contradictory elements in what the imp was saying. And as for being this boy's father… He grimaced as the old pain slashed into him with a force that took him by surprise.

Grimly, he pushed himself to a sitting position and

tried to examine his surroundings through the fog that pervaded his mind. All he felt certain of was that his guardian angel was presently busy elsewhere. But when the room stopped spinning he perceived it bore a remarkable resemblance to the best parlour of Mrs Green's cottage. Though he had only ever visited the old lady once, when he'd first come into his title, she had clearly remembered him and given him shelter. A weight seemed to tumble from his shoulders.

It had only been after he had disembarked that it had occurred to him that he had neither the funds nor the strength to make it as far as Lambourne. For a moment or two he had been crestfallen. He'd had no acquaintance in Portsmouth to whom he might apply for help. Nor had his experience thus far encouraged him to expect any practical assistance might be forthcoming from the local authorities.

But he had not survived so much only to lie down and give up on the quayside!

And that was when he had recalled Mrs Green. She had been a great beauty in her youth, and his grandfather's sole mistress throughout the course of his married life. When they had parted company she had told him she had no heart for the bustle of London without him, and asked him to settle her somewhere in the country. The snug little property he'd subsequently bought her lay—providentially—close enough to the bustling harbour to make walking there a feasible option.

Even so, it had been a close-run thing! He swung his legs to the floor and bowed his head over his hands. He had used up the last of his physical reserves before he had even reached the outskirts of Barstow. Will-power alone had kept him putting one foot in front of the other—until that moment when he had lifted the latch of the garden gate and seen the woman digging, and known he could finally let go…

He ran his hand over his face and round the back of his neck. The stubble on his chin felt almost as long as the fuzz that was growing on his scalp. Soft enough to represent a few days' growth. But then he was distracted from his musings on the passage of time by another, increasingly urgent sensation.

'I need,' he said, feeling somewhat discomfited by the discovery, 'to relieve myself.'

The imp, who had been hanging over the arm of the sofa, his keen eyes following Carleton's every move, promptly dived under a nearby table and produced a chamber pot.

'Here you go, sir.'

Carleton regarded the receptacle with distaste. His nostrils were already full of the unmistakable odour of the sickroom.

'Or you could try to get to the midden, if you like. It ain't snowing today.' He sobered, regarding Carleton's frame a little dubiously. 'It is a bit blowy, though.'

Sensing a challenge, Carleton pushed himself to his

feet, and waited to see if his legs would hold him. It would be well worth taking a calculated risk for the pleasure of being able to get outside, and taking care of his personal needs for himself.

'The wind won't blow me over, I shouldn't think, if I could lean on you,' he said. The boy was probably older than he looked, and must in any case be quite strong. For somebody must have carried him in out of the garden, where he had collapsed, and installed him on that sofa. He did not think the angel could have done so alone. And, from his hazy recollection of the time he had so far spent here, this imp was her only attendant.

The imp had in any case decided he was up to the task, for he skipped to Carleton's side with a grin.

Returning that infectious smile, Carleton laid his hand on the lad's shoulder.

'Not that way,' the imp said, when Carleton instinctively made for the passage that led to the back of the house. 'Don't want to go by the kitchen—not with the Viscount in there. Always best to keep out of his way when *he* comes calling, but he's in a meaner mood than ever today.'

'We shall go out through the front door, then, and round the side of the house,' said Carleton, though he was not sure how far he would get before his legs gave out. No matter, he shrugged. He would crawl back if necessary. He wanted to breathe fresh air for at least a minute or two. Real, crisp English winter air, that would scour his mind and his lungs clean.

It was only after he had relieved himself, and done up his breeches, that he realised what had felt so different from the moment he had woken on the sofa this time. He was no longer sweating. Shaking, yes, but he rather thought he could attribute that to his weakened condition now.

Even before this latest bout of fever he had not been in top form. They had urged him to wait longer before attempting the voyage home, but all he'd been able to think of was getting to Lambourne Hall in time for Christmas. Images of roaring fires, soft beds, and sideboards groaning with food had kept him marching doggedly on. All the things he had taken so much for granted during his privileged youth had taken on something of the allure of the Garden of Eden from which he had been so summarily exiled.

He blinked, looking round at the neat but productive garden in which he was standing, then down at the boy. And he frowned.

If his mind was clear, and he was not still in the grip of a fever-induced hallucination, then this was a real boy, not a phantom. He had not known Mrs Green had any children, but if the woman who had been digging up vegetables was her daughter, and this boy her grandson, it would explain why he had thought they looked vaguely familiar.

Well, he could soon find out.

'What is your name, boy?'

'Harry Tillotson, sir,' said the imp, sending him floundering back into the substance of his worst nightmare.

The lad must truly be a demon, to be spouting that name of all names. Dear God, was he still, after all, lying in some filthy hut in France? Would he wake in a few more moments to find that he was still waiting for the British troops to reach his hamlet? Did he have that debilitating voyage to endure all over again?

No, it could not be! This all felt so real!

Besides, if he was only imagining he was back in England, why was he picturing himself here, when it had always been visions of Lambourne Hall that had fuelled his imagination?

Though even this cottage, he reflected, looking back over his shoulder along the neat little flagged path, was a palace compared to what he had become used to. Mrs Green's cottage might be small and out of the way, but it had solid walls and a thick, weatherproof thatch. She even had a patch of land big enough to keep her kitchen well stocked with a variety of produce, and—most importantly—the freedom to come and go as she pleased.

He must not have heard the lad correctly.

'Tillotson?' He bent a stern eye on his diminutive tormentor. 'Are you sure?'

''Course I'm sure,' said the boy scornfully. 'I can even write if for you, if you like. I know all my letters,' he boasted, puffing out his chest, 'and I can reckon up my numbers. Mama says next spring she's going to get the Reverend Byatt to start me on Latin, if she can sell enough eggs, and if she can't she's going to take in laundry.'

Carleton bent down, peering closely at the boy who reminded him so much of himself as a youth, asking, 'How old are you?'

'Seven, come spring. That's why I got to start learning the Latin.'

Seven. He straightened up, swallowing down the bitter taste of bile that rose in his gorge. That was too much of a damned coincidence. There was only one more element necessary to explode this serene vision of England into the hellish reality that being a prisoner of war entailed. And that was to hear him claiming to be Helena's child.

'What is your mother's name?' he grated, bracing himself for the answer.

But in the event the boy just shrugged, and declared, 'Mama.'

He felt ill. Really ill now. 'I need to lie down,' he muttered, groping for the lad's shoulder as the garden dipped and swayed round the edges of his vision.

He had no idea if this was real, or a nightmare, but one thing had just become crystal-clear. There were still obstacles barring his return to his Garden of Eden. And a serpent in residence he would have to tackle once he made it back there!

He laughed mirthlessly to himself. He had focused so completely on getting back to Lambourne Hall that he had pushed aside all thoughts of what had driven him from it in the first place. Or rather who.

Helena, that was who. His bitch of a wife. She would be there right now, with her bastard son, queening it over his servants while he did not even have the means to procure a horse to ride home and confront her. Or, if he did, no strength left to mount it.

He had tottered to within five feet of the kitchen window when the sound of raised voices halted Harry in his tracks. Since Carleton was leaning on him so heavily, he had no choice but to stop too.

'You have no choice, woman!' a male voice thundered. 'Not if you want to keep a roof over your head!'

He felt Harry shudder.

'Viscount Lambourne,' he muttered darkly, as though he were uttering a curse.

'No…' Carleton whispered, swaying on his feet. The man in there could not be Viscount Lambourne. *He* was Viscount Lambourne. At least… He raised a hand to his brow in an attempt to wipe away the confusion. At least that was who he had been when last he was in England.

Staggering up to the kitchen window, he gazed

in—and saw the angel who had nursed him sitting at a plain table with her hands clasped tightly together on its surface. She was gazing imploringly at a man who was striding up and down, the skirts of his coat whirling to dominate the confined space at each turn. His anger was like a tangible force, reaching out to Carleton through the cracks in the windowpanes.

'No—please!' he dimly heard the woman say. 'You could not be so cruel!'

But the man calling himself Viscount Lambourne was so saturated with rage that he was impervious to the appeal in the woman's eyes. He ceased pacing and banged his fist down hard on the table, making her flinch.

Carleton's legs began to shake so much he had to grip the sill for support. How could any man use such threatening behaviour towards such an obviously defenceless woman? And how dared he do so in his name? He must put a stop to this!

He raised his hand to rap on the window, but found his movement curtailed by Harry, who had grabbed the sleeve of his jacket and was hanging on with grim determination.

'Get down here with me,' he whispered. Harry dropped down beneath the lip of the window ledge, the unexpectedness of his action pulling Carleton down beside him. 'Then you can hear it all without them seeing you.'

Two things registered almost at the same time as his legs buckled beneath him.

One was that this young rascal must be in the habit of eavesdropping, and ought to be reprimanded for it. The other was the crushing realisation that he was in no fit state to do anything to help the poor woman who had done so much for him.

'Christmas be damned!' the man in the kitchen was bellowing. 'Do you think it makes any difference to me what season it is?'

Carleton sucked in several deep breaths, whilst grinding his clenched fists into the pebbly soil on which he sat.

The man who was calling himself Viscount Lambourne was an utter disgrace to the name! Threatening to evict a woman and her child, no matter what the season!

Just who *was* he? Carleton thumped his hand hard into the frozen soil yet again, forcing his fogged brain into action.

News must have reached England, he supposed, that he was dead. And the next in line to inherit his title must have stepped into his shoes. That next in line, he recalled, had been his cousin Peregrine.

His heart began to pound.

He could put the whole thing right in a matter of minutes. Peregrine would only need to take one look at him to know exactly who he was. All he had to do was walk into the kitchen, inform his cousin that the report of his death had been made in error, and he could have his old life back. Peregrine was bound to have some form of conveyance nearby. Peregrine would take him home!

But first he would explain how this woman had taken care of him, and whatever she had done that had so enraged Peregrine—perhaps she was behind with her rent?—her generosity in caring for him would surely cancel out any amount of debt…

As he pulled himself to his knees, he bent his ear once more to the conversation taking place indoors.

'All I am asking you to do is make sure Carleton stays dead!'

'But he is *not* dead!' his angel protested.

'He would have been if you'd only had the sense to leave him lying on your path!'

Carleton felt as though he had been turned to stone. Peregrine appeared to be angry with his guardian angel *because* she had helped him.

'Look—' he heard the sound of a chair scraping across the floor '—it is only going to cause everyone a deal of unpleasantness if you persist on taking this line with me. For a start there will have to be a lengthy legal case just to re-instate him. A *costly* legal case. By the time it is over the estate which I have worked so hard to restore will be sadly depleted again. Hardly anything left worth inheriting!'

The woman murmured something so low Carleton could not hear what it was, but it had a stringent effect on Peregrine.

'I know you have no great fondness for me, but surely you cannot hate me as much as I know you must hate your husband? Helena—Helena, for God's sake see sense!'

Helena? Carleton shivered convulsively. Who hated her husband? The woman in there, the woman of whom he had just felt so protective, was Helena? It was fortunate he was already sitting down, or hearing that the woman inside was his wife would have felled him.

'Perhaps I have not been as generous with you in the past as I might have been.' Peregrine's voice took on a wheedling tone. 'Perhaps I could do something for the boy? That is what you really want, is it not? How would it be if I promised that if you take care of this for me, I will always take care of your boy?' He began to sound more sure of himself. 'Provide him with the very best education. Stand sponsor when he decides upon a profession. Think what that would mean for him!'

In a choked voice, the woman he had come to think of as his guardian angel, the woman he now knew was in fact his faithless, grasping wife, said, 'But I am not a murderer!'

'No.' Peregrine's voice turned cold. 'Just a whore.'

Beside him, Carleton felt Harry stiffen.

'If it were not for the fact that I decided to shield you from public censure, you and your bastard son would be on the streets already!' Peregrine was persisting. 'Consider your options, madam, and then tell me it would not be far better if you were to just slip something into his food that would send him into a sleep from which he would never wake up.'

Carleton heard a chair overturn. Then Peregrine said, 'Yes, we can show him more mercy than he showed you, on the day he condemned you to a living hell by repudiating your marriage and your child.'

There was a flurry of pebbles at his side as Harry shot to his feet. He looked down at Carleton with pure loathing.

For a moment, man and boy glared at each other. This was Helena's brat. The child Nicholas Malgrove had sired on her not two months after she had married *him*!

'You're Carleton Tillotson, aren't you?' Harry bit out. 'The Viscount before that one!' His grimy finger stabbed viciously in the direction of the kitchen window. 'You're…you're my…' His face contorted, his cheeks turning red.

But before Carleton had the chance to deny there was any possibility Harry could be his son, the boy had turned and run down the path and out through the back gate as though all the hounds of hell were after him.

Inside, Peregrine was chuckling softly.

'I will return in a few days, when I have obtained some poison. Call it my Christmas present to you, Helena.'

Cold slithered up Carleton's spine from the stony ground on which he sat. He had never felt more alone and afraid in his life. He had made for this cottage, thinking he would find an elderly lady who would be only too glad to help the grandson of the man she had loved so much. Instead he had fallen into the hands of his two worst enemies.

Peregrine, who seemed so determined to hang onto the title he would ruthlessly commission his murder.

And Helena. A woman devious enough to trick a green boy into matrimony so that she could get her sticky paws on his money.

And he was too weak to even attempt to escape them.

Very well. The years had taught him some things. Even when a man had nothing else to rely on, he could still hang onto his pride. Though it took him three attempts, he got to his feet, and with head held high made his way back into the cottage to face the worst they could do to him.

Chapter Three

For several minutes after Viscount Lambourne had left, Nell sat at the table with her head in her hands.

From the moment she'd accepted Carleton was still alive, she'd known he would be trouble.

But she had assumed it would only be her foolish heart at risk. She knew it was stupid to have revelled in the sensation of holding him in her arms. Fanciful of her to think that the way the firelight had played over his torso as she'd sponged his feverish body made him look like some marbled god of ancient legend. For he was no statue, but a leanly muscled man, with the calluses and broken nails that bore witness to a life spent doing hard manual labour. Even more vital than that perfect slender youth, with the carefully manicured, soft white hands, who had once broken her heart. Already it was a constant tussle to remember she was supposed to be nursing an invalid, not indulging in daydreams of what might have been!

And now this!

Who would have guessed Peregrine was so amoral that he would rather have his cousin murdered than relinquish his title?

She would have to warn Carleton as soon as he was well enough… But, no, no…even if she could make him believe Peregrine wanted her to kill him—and she was finding it hard enough to credit herself—there was no telling how long it would be before his fever abated enough for him to attempt to escape on foot. And it would have to be on foot. She had gone through his pockets before laundering his clothes, and he had not a penny on him. And she had never had the money to hire a horse, or any other means of conveyance to spirit him away.

Anyway, even if he did get away safely, where would that leave her? Peregrine would be furious with her for thwarting him. And his wrath would fall on her. And Harry.

Her stomach gave a lurch as she considered what her options seemed to be. Murder her husband or face eviction.

She sat up, and spread her work-roughened hands palm-down on the scrubbed tabletop. Carleton might not be a good man, but for some reason God had spared his life. She had not taken

him in and nursed him just to become his execu-
tioner.

And, speaking of nursing, it was well past the hour
she should have taken her patient some more nourish-
ment. Her face set, she went to the pot she kept simmering on the stove, ladled out a portion of chicken
broth, and marched with it to the front parlour.

She halted on the threshold, the tray almost tipping
out of her hands. For Carleton was awake and in his
right mind.

'Helena,' he bit out, leaning back on the sofa, pale-
faced and bristling with hostility.

She'd been bracing herself for this moment. Even
when in his delirium he had smiled at her, told her she
was an angel, she had warned herself he could only
say such a thing because he had no idea who she was.

How glad she was she had not yielded to the temptation to respond to what had been burning in his eyes
and kissed him that night! Because if she had he
would no doubt be accusing her of taking advantage
of his weakened, confused state.

Mindful of his true station in life, and hers, she
dropped him a curtsey and murmured, 'My lord.'

For all that Peregrine Tillotson held the title,
Carleton was the real Viscount Lambourne.

'I have brought you some more broth,' she said, in-
dicating the tray she held. And then, when he switched
his glare from her to it, went on, 'I know it must be

getting a little boring, but it is all I have to offer you. And so far it has done you nothing but good.'

He took a breath, as though he meant to speak, then appeared to think better of it. He subsided into the cushions and watched while she set out the bowl, spoon and napkin on a low table which she had drawn up to the sofa for his convenience.

When he did not immediately reach for the spoon, Nell asked, 'Do you still require help, my lord? Shall I feed you?'

His face contorted into an expression so fierce she flinched.

'I will eat it myself!' he spat, taking the spoon in a hand that she noted still trembled a little.

He had taken several mouthfuls before it occurred to her that there was no real reason for her to linger. Not now he was beginning to manage for himself. It was blatantly obvious he had no wish to have her hovering over him now he knew who she was. How he must hate the discovery that the woman upon whom he had been forced to rely was none other than the wife he would do anything to be rid of!

She could not bear it. After all this time it should not bother her at all, and yet it still felt like a knife sliding between her ribs when he treated her with such contempt.

But as she began to sidle away he paused, the spoon halfway to his mouth, and said, 'Where are you going?'

She had got as far as the door, and was fumbling for the latch. 'I have chores I should be getting on with. You do not need me here any more. I should—'

'Wait!' he barked at her. 'I have some questions to ask of you.'

She blinked in disbelief.

'Is it not a little late for that?' The time for them to speak had been when they had first married. She had tried to talk to him then, but he had not listened. Instead he had…

'It is never too late. That is one thing I have learned over the past years. Sit,' he commanded her, waving his spoon at the armchair which faced the sofa across the table.

When she had taken the place he had indicated, he said, his eyes narrowing, 'I cannot quite comprehend what you are doing here. Or why you have taken such pains to nurse me. Why you did not simply leave me lying outside on the path, for the cold to finish me off.'

She huffed. 'I would not leave a dog outside in weather like this.'

He took another mouthful of broth, frowning at her. 'You are a puzzle, Helena. The way you have nursed me over these last…' He raised his eyebrows in enquiry.

'Three days,' she explained.

He nodded. 'Yes, that feels about right. But what

does not feel right is the gentle, proficient way you have been caring for me since I fell into your hands. I confess I am surprised to find that the years have changed you so much.'

She lifted her chin. 'I have not changed at all.'

'Come,' he reproved her. 'When you were a girl you thought nothing of compromising me into a marriage I did not want, and when I would not consummate the union you took your revenge by taking a lover and trying to foist your child off as mine.'

'I did none of those things,' she gasped, lurching to her feet.

'Sit down!'

She paused, her fists clenched at her sides. 'You cannot order me about in this house, Carleton. You have no rights over me any more. You cast me aside, left me at the mercy of—'

'And that is what puzzles me the most.' He cut through her tirade. 'Why *are* you living in such poverty?'

He had soon worked out why he had not recognised her on sight. In his mind she had stayed a girl. A girl, moreover, whom he had spent the last few years imagining disporting herself in silks and lace, while he shivered in rags. She had matured, filled out, grown weather-beaten and was dressed like a farmer's wife. And after the initial shock of discovering he had fallen into her hands had worn off, the questions as to how

she had ended up here, in Barstow, had begun to
mount up.

'Why are you not at Lambourne Hall, enjoying
your status as my widow? Or, if you found living in
the countryside too restricting for a woman of your
ambition, why did you not hire a house in London
with the jointure I settled on you? And snare another
rich lover who could pander to your appetites?'

'I have never snared anyone! And as for why I am
living here—in poverty, as you put it—I have never
felt so well off in my life! I answer to no one. I do as
I please. I grow my own food and look after my
child...'

'And what do you tell him about his father?' he
inserted silkily.

Too angry to mind her tongue, Nell blurted out, 'I
tell him the truth, of course. That his father got caught
up in the war and was hanged for spying...'

'You maintain the pretence that he is my child,
then? Is it not rather cruel, even for you, to lie to your
own son?' He was amazed that he managed to keep
his voice level when he felt such blistering anger. If
he'd had the strength he would have been on his feet,
pacing the floor and shaking his fists at her. Instead,
he bit out, 'It is quite impossible that he should be
mine, since you and I have never slept in the same
bed.'

'We did not sleep, no,' she admitted. 'B-but on

our wedding night I came to your room, to try to tell you—'

He shook his head vehemently. 'I woke on the library sofa the morning after our wedding day.'

'You got up straight after,' she said, her face going bright red. 'You looked…appalled at what we had done. You said—' she gulped, looking not at him but at a damp spot on the wall behind where he was sitting '—that you needed another drink. Although you had already had far more than could have been good for you.'

He had been drinking steadily all day, he acknowledged. Not yet twenty, and leg-shackled to a scheming harpy, he had wanted to blot the entire fiasco from his mind.

He had almost succeeded.

But every now and again he had the most disturbing dreams about his bride…

He would dream she came to him with her face alight with love and hope. She was always wearing a lacy white nightgown that left her arms bare, with blue flowers embroidered about the neckline. And when he lowered his head to kiss her it was like sipping at nectar. She always promised him the earth and gave him a taste of heaven.

But at that point the dream always changed. The sweetness of the experience gave way to feelings of being trapped, and tricked, and then he was running—

running away from a piercing light towards a clammy darkness that threatened to swallow him whole. He usually awoke at that point, with a feeling of profound relief at having narrowly escaped a dreadful fate.

The first time he'd had that dream had been on their wedding night. He'd awoken from it horrified that she had featured in a dream of such an explicit nature. And had realised she was far more dangerous to him than he could ever have imagined. If he could have a dream like that about her, when he was so determined to remain aloof... Of course he had been able to recall the very moment his hostility towards her had begun to abate. She had looked so scared of him in church, as she had stammered her vows, that he had experienced a twinge of pity. Not that he hadn't every right to be angry at what she'd done, but he wasn't a brute! He had decided he would have to at least assure her she had nothing to fear from him. All through the wedding breakfast he'd darted covert looks at her as he'd sought for the words to explain himself, and discovered he had, albeit accidentally, married an uncommonly pretty girl.

Was it surprising he had dreamed about what it could have been like? What it should have been like when he married?

His fury redoubled, he had stormed up to her room and reiterated his decision, as much to himself as to her, that just because he had gone through a public ceremony she was not to imagine he would *ever* permit her to share any part of his private life!

And she had stood there in silence, looking at him much as she was looking now.

Just as Harry had looked at him in the garden.

Harry, who had seemed so like his youthful self that when he'd woken that morning it had been like looking in a mirror.

'What were you wearing?' he grated, suddenly feeling horribly sick. He more than anyone should know what tricks the mind was capable of playing on a man. What if those dreams had their basis in some fleeting memory? A memory he had been trying in vain to suppress?

'On our wedding night?' She frowned. 'It was a nightgown I borrowed from Lucinda.'

'Yes, but what did it look like? Tell me some details. See if you can spark any form of memory if you really want to convince me this coupling took place!'

She was shocked to see what looked like agonised self-doubt in his eyes. Her heart picked up speed. Was he at long last offering her a chance to vindicate herself?

'What colour was it?' He slammed his clenched fist into the sofa cushions.

'Wh…white.' She screwed up her face in an effort to recall some specific detail of the night that had brought her so much pain she had done her level best to forget it. For if she could finally convince him he really had made her his wife that night, maybe he would listen to her about all the rest of it too.

An image shot into her mind.

'When I put my arms round your neck the sleeves slid back,' she told him. 'Right up to my shoulders. The gown was too big for me, really. Lucinda was much larger than me.'

Her cousin Lucinda had loved pretty things. She'd had at least three layers of ruffles sewn onto the hems of all her garments. And flowers embroidered onto everything.

'Take this for luck,' she had said, handing over a nightdress so worn from repeated washing it was almost transparent. 'It is old, you are borrowing it, and the flowers on it are blue.' And then, with a snigger that had made it quite impossible for anyone to construe the gesture as springing from a spirit of generosity, 'You are going to need all the luck you can get.'

'It had lots of lace all round the cuffs,' Nell told Carleton. 'And flowers embroidered at the neckline. Forget-me-nots, I think they were supposed to be. Blue, with little yellow centres...'

'Then that boy is mine,' he groaned, lowering his head. 'Mine. The minute I clapped eyes on him I felt...I sensed...'

He ran a shaky hand over his closely cropped hair.

'More than ever now I need to understand why you are not living at Lambourne Hall. That is where my son should be growing up!' He lifted his head to glare at her. 'With servants, and tutors, and decent clothes on his back—not those rags I saw him in today! Why have you hidden him away here, Helena? Is it because he looks like me? Is that it? You are punishing the son for his father's sins?'

'I am doing no such thing…'

'You must have deliberately concealed him from my mother,' he continued, as though she had not spoken. 'She would only have needed to take one look at him to know he was mine. If you really believed I was dead, then Harry should be the new Viscount, and Peregrine should hold the position of trustee. Why did you not insist…'

'Do you really think, after you did such a good job of convincing everyone I was a whore, that your mother would have me or my son anywhere near Lambourne Hall? Or listen to anything I had to say? When you left England I stayed in the hunting box where you left me, shunned by your whole family until Peregrine stepped into your shoes when it seemed you had been executed. He was not content to leave me be. Just one more of your mistakes he had to clean up, he told me when he came to deliver his judgement upon me.' Her mouth twisted into a bitter line. 'Though he did not, as your mother and sister urged him, turn me quite out onto the streets.'

'They would never have done anything so harsh…'

'Of course they would!' she scoffed. 'They said it was all *my* fault you had left the country, apparently. If I had not entrapped you into a miserable marriage, and then played the whore, you would not have felt you could not hold your head up in London society and you would have stayed at home. You would not have died. No punishment was too harsh for the instigator of your downfall, believe me!'

He shook his head, as though he did not want to hear any more.

'Peregrine claimed, however, in that sanctimonious way he has, that he bore me no ill-will personally, and very graciously let me have this cottage, rent free, since Mrs Green had died. He even gives me an allowance!'

'An allowance?' Carleton felt completely baffled. Why did Peregrine say he was making her an allowance when he himself had made perfectly adequate provision for her in the event of his death?

'Oh, yes,' Nell continued. 'Thirty pounds a year is most generous for a woman you would have allowed to starve on the streets!'

'Thirty pounds a year?' He looked appalled. 'I used to pay my valet more than that.'

'Yes, but I suspect you valued *his* services.'

Carleton scarcely reacted to her jibe at the battleground that had been their marriage. It was becoming increasingly obvious to him that Peregrine had somehow managed to swindle Helena out of the money he had willed her. As obvious as it was to anyone with eyes in their head that Harry was his son.

'How dare he condemn my son to this sort of poverty?' he roared.

'*He* did not condemn your son to this,' she flung back at him. 'You did it yourself! You were the one who went round telling everyone he could not possibly be yours!'

'I did no such thing!' he gasped. 'It was bad enough to have to deal with the mockery of the *ton* for getting duped into marrying a schoolgirl. Do you really think I would have gone round telling everyone you had made me a cuckold into the bargain? When I heard you had given birth to a son I left England, for God's sake, rather than have to face the physical proof of what you had done. I did not want to even *think* about your baby!'

'But I always thought you…' She sat down rather heavily. 'You did not brand me a whore, then? You did not declare Harry a bastard and go to the continent as a sign that you had repudiated the marriage?'

'No.'

Nell's face creased in perplexity. 'Well, then, how did that story get about? According to Peregrine, the scandal was all over London. If you did not start up the rumour, then who did?'

Carleton cast his mind back to the evening when Nicholas Malgrove had strolled up to him in White's and said, 'I believe congratulations are in order. I hear your lady wife has been delivered of a strapping baby boy. Your son and heir.'

As the man had raised his glass in an ironical toast Carleton had seen red. He had once caught Nicholas sneaking out of Helena's room. Now it seemed they must still be lovers, since Nicholas had news of the birth before he did.

'You, of all people,' Carleton had drawled, too proud to reveal how humiliated he felt, 'must know that the child cannot possibly be mine.'

Only now did it occur to him how rash it had been to make such a statement while standing within the hearing of any number of other gentlemen. But in any case Malgrove himself would have taken great pleasure in spreading such a juicy titbit of gossip far and wide.

'I confided my supposition to one person only,' he admitted uncomfortably. 'I would never have intentionally dragged my family name through the mud.'

'Your family name? Is that all that concerns you?' Nell seethed. Even if he had not deliberately ruined her reputation and disinherited his own son, the only reason he had not was out of concern for his family's honourable name. Not out of consideration for *her* feelings, or what effect such a statement might have upon *her* future.

'I am very concerned,' he countered, 'by the fact my son has been brought up in far from ideal circumstances. Why, in God's name, did you not make more of an effort to persuade me the child was mine before he was born?'

'And how exactly was I supposed to do that? How could I persuade you of anything when you refused to have anything to do with me? I did not know where you were to tell you when I discovered I was with child. The letters I wrote were returned unopened, and when I tried to get someone to take me to see you I was told they were not allowed to! I was practically imprisoned in that hunting box! So don't you *dare* try to thrust the blame back onto me, or tell me he lacks for anything! Look at how healthy Harry is! He has good food and clean clothing…boots on his feet, unlike some of the village boys. And he can read and write…'

'But can he ride a horse? Does he know how to fish? Shoot a gun? How could you have let him grow up like this?'

'Because you did not want to know. None of your high and mighty family wanted to know. And do you know what?' She leapt to her feet, her eyes flashing defiantly. 'He is better off with me than learning to be cold and proud and cruel, like your horrible relatives. If you had not been such a drunken sot you would have remembered your wedding night. And even if you had not remembered a thing, if you had been a decent man you would have made an attempt to reach some kind of agreement with me about how we should live—instead of just running away and trying to pretend I did not exist!'

'If *you* had not set up a situation where you were so badly compromised I was forced to marry you,' he retorted, 'none of this sorry mess would have happened! Are you surprised I resorted to the bottle to get through that farcical wedding day? I was barely out on the town and knew nothing of the world. I should not have had to even *think* of marriage for years, let alone to a girl from a background like yours. I could have looked as high as I pleased for a bride when I was ready to marry!'

'Then you should have been more careful, should you not, Carleton? Why did you mingle with people like my uncle and aunt if you thought they were so far beneath you? Why did you drink so much you did not know what day it was, never mind where you were or who you were with?'

She slammed the soup bowl onto the tray, whisked it off the table, and marched across the room to the door.

'You are still acting like a spoiled child,' she shot over her shoulder. 'You are trying to blame everyone for the mess you have made not only of your life but of mine and Harry's too, instead of being a man and accepting responsibility for your actions!'

With that, she stormed out of the room, kicking the door shut behind her.

* * *

Dusk was falling before she returned. Carleton had spent the rest of the afternoon before the fire, feeding it from the supply of logs that sat in a basket on the hearth, feeling thoroughly wretched. The room in which he had previously felt so secure now resonated with echoes of their quarrel.

Even the way Helena was banging pots about in the kitchen spoke of shattered vows and bitter regrets.

Once he heard the clatter of boots on the garden path that presaged the homecoming of his son. His heart sped up, and a yearning sensation twisted in his gut. Last time the boy had been in the cottage he had come in here, asked him to stay and be his father.

Now that he knew he really *was* his father, he did not even deign to poke his head round the door to see how he fared.

Carleton lowered his head to his hands. The boy was his. He had no doubts on that score any longer. Harry had seen it too, earlier, when they had been eavesdropping on Peregrine's plans to dispose of him. Had looked at him with disgust and run off.

He had a son who hated him.

'My God, Helena, what have you done?' he groaned.

She might not have had the opportunity to poison his soup just yet, but she had spent the last six years poisoning his son's mind against him.

Not that he could entirely blame her, he supposed. Not now he accepted that his recurrent dream was no dream at all, but a hazy memory that had kept on trying to break through. He felt outraged even now to think of the ease with which she'd seduced him into her bed, when he'd never had any intention of consummating the marriage. No wonder he'd fled the scene and attempted to blot it out in alcohol. He would have been furious at her attempt to curtail his liberty.

Liberty! A bitter laugh escaped his lips. Only a man who had spent years as a prisoner of war could know what loss of liberty was really like.

He rubbed at the deep furrows ridging his forehead. And yet far from living it up at Lambourne Hall, as he had been imagining, Helena had been languishing on the verge of destitution herself. A condition she had spent years blaming him for, since she seemed to believe he had deliberately blackened her name and then left her penniless.

Hearing her light tread in the passage, he sat up straighter, his eyes fixed upon the door. She avoided looking directly at him as she marched across the room. The tray went down on the table with a slap that sent soup slopping over the rim of the bowl and wetting the handle of the spoon.

'Broth again?' he asked. She seemed to have a never-ending supply of it.

She glared at him. 'That is the last of it, and it is

mostly vegetables now. I will have to kill another chicken tomorrow if you want meat.'

'You look,' he said thoughtfully, 'as though it would give you a great deal of pleasure to kill something.'

Nell flinched as though he had struck her. 'I never enjoy killing anything. Even though I have to sometimes, to survive.' Her eyes slid away from him. 'Perhaps I could prevail upon Reverend Byatt to give me a ham tomorrow. He is a most charitable man…' She shook her head, the angry frown returning as she became aware of his gaze resting speculatively upon her.

'Not that you are interested in my problems, so long as your belly is filled,' she added waspishly.

'You have no idea what interests me.'

'What do you mean by that?'

'Just what I say.' Carleton had been steadily applying himself to the bowl, and now his meal was nearly all gone. 'Would you like to know?'

'Know what?'

'What interests me?'

'Not particularly. I just want you to leave.'

'So different from the first time we met. Then, you did all in your power to make sure I would never leave.'

'I have told you before—I did not!'

'You deny staying in a room with me all night, and

arranging for your aunt and various other house guests to discover us together the next morning?'

'Absolutely!' She lifted her chin, staring him down.

To her surprise, this time he did not begin to berate her for lying. Instead, he laid the spoon down in the empty bowl and said, 'Then how do you account for the fact that you and I *were* in that room all night, and that we *were* discovered?'

'Will you listen to me this time?' she asked, her knees suddenly growing weak. 'Will you really let me tell you how it came about?'

'This time?' He frowned. 'To my recollection we have never discussed that event.'

'Because you would not listen! You would not come anywhere near me until the day we met in church to get married. And then that night, when I tried to tell you how sorry I was, you just…grabbed me. I thought it was going to be all right after all.' But after he had slaked his passion he had reared back, a look of horror on his face. She felt her eyes sting with stupid tears. Angrily she blinked them back. She was done crying over this man.

'So tell me now.'

She blinked at him again, trying to judge his mood. He had been really angry with her earlier, but now he just looked…well, troubled was the only way to describe the expression on his face.

She sighed.

'It was all a dreadful mistake. My aunt wanted you

to marry Lucinda. She had been out for three years, and nobody had come up to scratch, and you were so…' She sucked her bottom lip into her mouth as she sought for the words to describe what Carleton had been like in those days.

'Green?' he supplied for her.

She looked at him apologetically. 'Well, yes, I suppose you were. You certainly fell into her trap like a ripe plum. She plied you with drink all night, and then watched to see where you passed out.'

'Passed out?' The woman had expected him to pass out? Since he had never, before that particular week, drunk to the point where that had happened, he could only draw one conclusion. 'She drugged me!'

Nell looked at him reproachfully. 'Carleton, you did drink an awful lot.'

'No more than many other young men of my acquaintance. And I was never so incapacitated as I was that night. Not before nor since.'

She tilted her head to one side, examining him. 'You were never quite sober. Not during any of our encounters.'

'During our few encounters I probably was not,' he acknowledged. 'But inebriation was *not* my normal condition.'

She considered his claim for a moment or two. It was not easy to let go of her opinion of him…but then it struck her that it would be equally hard for him to revise his opinion of her. Perhaps if she expected him to believe what she had to tell him she must be prepared to accept his version of events too.

Clearing her throat, she said, 'Well, in that case I apologise for calling you a drunkard.'

He did seem to relax a little. Encouraged, she went on, 'Anyway, after establishing that you were out cold, she came up to Lucinda's room and told her to take some books back to the library.'

'Knowing I was already in place?'

'Yes. Only it was rather a cold night, and Lucinda did not want to leave her room to traipse all the way downstairs to perform a task she thought better suited to one of the servants. So she sent me.'

'Why you? Why not a servant, if that was who she thought should have done the traipsing?'

'Because she loved ordering me about as though I *was* a servant.' Her shoulders hunched a little as she recalled her days of being at everyone's beck and call, made fully aware of her position of dependence every minute of each day of her dreary life.

'And then?'

'Then I took the books and went to the library, and put them all back on the shelves. When I tried to leave, I found the door was locked.'

He frowned. 'Your aunt was careless enough, after setting the trap, to lock the wrong girl in the library with her victim?'

'I was wearing Lucinda's shawl,' she sighed. It had been a gaudy thing, made up in Spitalfields. 'She had singed it on her candle that very evening, so she said I might as well wear it.'

He nodded again. In the unlit corridors of that Jacobean house, one dark-haired girl in a nightgown with a distinctive shawl about her shoulders might very well pass for another.

'And then, of course, I noticed you on the sofa. At first I thought you might be able to help me get out, but I could not wake you.'

'Drugged, then,' he nodded. And then said reflectively, 'The fuss your aunt made the next morning did seem extremely odd, considering she had obviously made sure several of the other house guests were there to witness our discovery. At the time I thought it was because you had abused her trust by entrapping me. That opinion,' he said, his eyes boring into her, 'was reinforced by the way your uncle later spoke of your behaviour. He seemed not to care whether I married you or not. He *did* ask me to leave, citing concern for the reputation of his own daughters should it be known what a rakehell he had invited into his home. But he said of you only that you were past praying for, and that he washed his hands of you entirely.'

Nell sucked in a sharp breath as her perception of her past shifted into a completely different pattern. She had heard raised voices coming from her uncle's study the morning after she'd been discovered in the library with Carleton. But she had always assumed her uncle had been insisting he marry her. Not that Carleton had… She frowned. Carleton had done the honourable thing! Much as he had despised her, he had given her the protection of his name. And even though he'd stayed well away from her for the next two years, until it was supposed he had died, he had housed her in considerable comfort. He had been perplexed to find her in this cottage too, mentioning a jointure…

'I understood,' he was saying now, 'his comments to mean that you had tried his patience to the limit already, with similarly wanton behaviour.'

'No!' For years she had been telling herself she did not care what he thought of her. But in the light of what she had just discovered it felt imperative she now seized the chance to clear her name.

'It was not my behaviour he objected to but my very existence! You see, he had not approved of the man my mother married. And was downright angry that when both my parents died he had no choice but to take me in. My aunt reconciled him to my presence by pointing out that I was old enough to do the work of a servant, and thus save him one set of wages. But he always made it very clear I was only there on sufferance.'

Carleton frowned as he imagined what her childhood must have been like. For the first time he could understand that she might have been overwhelmed by the desire to escape such miserable drudgery. Then he shook his head as he checked that line of thought. She was not offering him excuses for why she had trapped him into marriage. She was maintaining she had done no such thing.

'Don't you believe me?' she wailed. 'I am telling you I did not plan any of it. I was as much a victim of my aunt's scheming as you were.'

And if that were true—he shuddered—she had more cause to hate him than he had ever supposed. His subsequent actions must have seemed like the most appalling cruelty.

Seeing his shudder, Nell felt as though he had struck her. Sweeping the tray off the table, she darted out of the room before Carleton had a chance to say another word.

'Oh, my God,' he groaned. No wonder he had not heard her argue with Peregrine for long. If all she had said was true, and somehow it all fell so neatly into place he just knew it was, then he fully deserved her hatred.

He had comprehensively ruined her life.

A sheen of sweat broke out on his brow.

Peregrine would be back in a few days with the means to poison him. And all of a sudden he could understand why she might feel completely justified in giving it to him.

Chapter Four

Nell dunked the scrubbing brush into the bucket and slapped it down on the kitchen table.

Ever since the discussion they'd had the night before, when she had learned that Carleton had not deliberately ruined her reputation, she had been more determined than ever that somehow she must find a way to thwart Peregrine.

Just as she was now working the brush round and round, to scour the table clean, so she had gone over all the elements of the argument they'd had. She had quickly perceived how a confidence shared with just one person could have been taken up to become fodder for the gossip which had subsequently destroyed her. And, knowing her aunt's sly, scheming ways, she found it easier, somehow, to accept she had drugged Carleton than to keep on believing he had been a habitual drunkard.

And now that she'd learned Peregrine would stop at nothing to keep hold of Carleton's title, not even murder, she wouldn't be a bit surprised if much of what he had told her had not happened in the way he portrayed it.

Carleton certainly refused to believe his family would have treated her as Peregrine has assured her they would.

Would they really have welcomed her into their midst, though, and raised Harry as Carleton's heir believing him to be illegitimate?

She had not made up her mind about that, but one thing had struck her quite forcefully.

Peregrine's plot relied for its success on the fact that only she and he knew Carleton was alive.

So all she had to do to ensure her husband's safety was to broadcast the fact that he had returned.

To that end she had sent Harry to fetch Squire Jeffers. As the local magistrate, he would know how to go about reinstating Carleton to his rightful place.

Running the back of her hand over her brow, she lugged the bucket to the scullery so she could tip the soapy water down the sink. She had just upended it to dry when she heard Harry come banging though the kitchen door.

'He's coming up the path now, Ma,' he panted, only a split second before Nell heard a fist pounding on her front door.

Hastily tugging off her apron, she went down the

passage, tucking stray wisps of hair into the bun that was fastened neatly at the back of her neck as she did so.

'Well, Mrs Tillotson?' Squire Jeffers barked as soon as she opened the door. 'What is so urgent that I must drop everything and come to your cottage without delay? Or is this just another of your brat's ill-judged pranks?'

'N-no…it is not! I mean of course it is,' Nell stammered as the Squire barged in, forcing her to shrink back. He had taken off his hat and gloves, and was vainly looking round for a side-table on which to deposit them before she managed to quash her indignation at his attitude towards Harry sufficiently to say, 'That is, it *is* an urgent matter, sir.'

He glared at her as she squeezed past him in the narrow hallway to push the door closed, shutting out the cold air that had come gusting in behind him.

'I have to report a crime,' she explained. 'At least, there will be a crime…' She faltered. 'That is, there might be a crime if…'

'Ha!' he said, dropping his gloves into his hat. 'Knew it would turn out to be a wild goose chase. Do you think I have not better things to do on a cold winter's afternoon than—'

'Indeed, sir, it is not a wild goose chase,' she replied. 'Won't you please go into the parlour, where it is warm, so that I might explain?'

'May as well, now I'm here,' he conceded, thrusting his hat into her hands as she made to open the parlour door.

Carleton appeared to have been dozing, but his eyes snapped open at the sight of the portly, pompous man strutting in as if he owned the place. As the Squire examined him from head to toe with a critical eye, he pushed himself upright and lowered his stock-inged feet to the floor.

The Squire's eyes rested for a moment on the darns at his toes, before flicking up to the coarsely woven shirt that was hanging from his slender frame.

'Caught yourself a criminal, have you, Mrs Tillot-son?' he said. 'Damn fool thing to take a vagrant into your home, though, even if he does look as though a puff of wind would blow him over.'

'No, no—you mistake the matter. This man is no criminal. He is my husband…'

Both Carleton and the Squire looked at her sharply.

'Thought you claimed to be a widow?' said Squire Jeffers.

'Y-yes, I thought I *was* a widow. But apparently the news of my husband's death was a false report…'

'Hanged, was he not, your husband? For spying? 'Bout the only admirable thing I ever heard of that rakehell, if we really are talking about the late Viscount Lambourne.'

'I regret to have to inform you,' said Carleton, with such hauteur it was clear he found the Squire's manners as offensive as Nell always did, 'that I was never a spy. Nor was I hanged, as the French authorities intended.'

'But you do claim to be this woman's husband?' said the Squire, taking a snuffbox from a waistcoat pocket and helping himself to a generous pinch.

'I *am* Helena's husband. Carleton William Tillotson, Viscount Lambourne,' he declared icily.

'I suppose you have some explanation for how you come not to be dead, then?' returned the Squire with sarcasm, snapping shut the snuffbox and returning it to his pocket. 'And why you have decided to stage your resurrection here, in the home of a woman everybody knows you were about to divorce for her infidelities?'

He sat down, crossed one leg over the other, and eyed Carleton with scorn.

Nell held her breath. Carleton was not used to having his word questioned. Nor, in her experience, did he have much of a hold over his temper. She should have warned him that she was bringing the magistrate here. But then that would have meant discussing Peregrine's plot against him. She had not wanted to worry him with the knowledge that his life was in danger. Had he not been through enough?

Yet now she saw her attempt to protect him from further anxiety had been a grave mistake. He *should* know how important it was to get this man's sympathy and support.

She dropped onto the only remaining chair in the room, clutching the Squire's hat between tense fingers as she braced herself to witness Carleton's explosive temper blow her rescue plan out of the water.

But, in a voice that was as icily calm as Squire Jeffers's had just been, Carleton said, 'I did not part with my wife on the best of terms, no. There had been a series of misunderstandings, which were no doubt exacerbated by my youthful arrogance.'

Nell's breath went out in a great whoosh. It was not just hearing him speak in such measured tones that brought her such relief. It was the fact that those particular words indicated he believed her. He had finally accepted she had not deliberately trapped him into marriage. And, judging from the somewhat contrite look he shot her, he might actually be feeling some remorse for his own behaviour back then.

She settled back in her chair, feeling remarkably inclined to smile.

'I had been running with rather a wild crowd,' Carleton continued, as she ducked her head to hide the rising tide of pleasure she was sure must be written all over her face. 'And, deciding I needed to break with them before they dragged me down too far, I went over to Portugal with an old schoolfriend of mine. He had some interest in one of the regiments over there... But that is beside the point. You want details of my arrest, and how I managed to escape execution.'

Nell's head flew up. She longed to hear what had happened to Carleton during his long years of absence, but had never quite dared to ask him. The scars she had seen on his body were evidence he had been on the receiving end of some brutal treatment, but she could not imagine what sort of person would think they could get away with flogging a British peer.

'We were staying in Bilbao, which we believed was completely safe, when suddenly the French army appeared outside the city walls. The citizens panicked, and began to flee towards Portugalete. When I woke—for I was not in the habit of rising early, you understand—the streets were already choked with every kind of conveyance. And it was raining heavily.'

Nell could guess what was coming next.

Carleton had been far too concerned about his image in those days to have wished to give the impression he was panicking. The weather would have given him the perfect excuse. She could just imagine him saying, in that languid voice she had heard him use when addressing the other members of her aunt's house party, *Go out there? In this weather? And risk getting mud on these boots? Absolutely not!*

'I had no intention of joining that desperate throng in such inclement weather,' he continued, confirming her image of the always gorgeously apparelled young man she remembered. 'Besides, as a civilian I fully believed that whatever the soldiers were up to was nothing to do with me. I assumed that whoever was in charge of the French army would leave civilians out of things. And for a while, at least, that was true. There was some little inconvenience, but nothing to remark—until the Spanish mistress of one of the French generals was suspected of giving away information to a British spy she had taken as her lover. Rather than give him up, the woman named me as her partner in crime. Nothing I could say would persuade the General I was not the guilty party. And so, since I was not an officer of His Majesty's army, he decided to hang me.'

'Without a trial?' Nell asked, outraged. It was monstrous that a man could be sentenced to death without being given a chance to defend himself.

'Justice tends to be somewhat arbitrary when the military is in charge of a town,' he replied with a wry smile. 'Although in this case…' his eyes hardened, as though he were seeing something quite other than the shocked features of an English woman '…the General was in no hurry to bring a swift conclusion to his punishment of the man he believed was the cause of Juanita's double betrayal.'

Nell felt her stomach lurch. He did not need to spell out what form his punishment had taken. She had seen the scars on his wrists and ankles and torso.

He had been manacled and flogged, as though he were a common criminal.

He blinked, as though dragging himself back with an effort from a very dark place. 'Eventually I got tangled up with a batch of Portuguese prisoners of war from the garrison of Saragossa. One of them, a private by the name of José Tortuga, changed places with me on the eve of my long-delayed execution. Thus saving my life.'

The Squire harrumphed. 'Why should any man do a damn fool thing like that?'

'Have you ever seen a man with a case of gangrene?' Carleton enquired politely. 'Believe me, hanging is a preferable option to suffering a lingering death from putrefaction of the limbs. It is swift, and in this case gave a man who had been insignificant all his life an opportunity to achieve a magnificent end. José swaggered to the gallows wearing the clothes of an English aristocrat, knowing that everyone who watched his execution would believe him capable of not only stealing military secrets but of having done so by seducing a beautiful woman who belonged to a wealthy and powerful man. And, perhaps more importantly, he died knowing he had outwitted the French, whom he hated.'

'And I suppose you are going to say he bore a remarkable resemblance to you?' sneered the Squire.

'Not particularly.' Carleton shrugged. 'But you

have to understand that the French paid little attention to their prisoners. And that by the time José went to the gallows in my stead I was no longer under the jurisdiction of the General who bore me such personal malice.'

Carleton fell silent, his eyes taking on that faraway look that told Nell he was not really in the room with her but in the past, reliving a profoundly moving experience.

'After that,' he continued, though he still seemed not to be altogether fixed in the present, 'his comrades all seemed to regard keeping me alive as a symbolic way of continuing to fight the French. Whenever they obtained food they made sure I had more than my share. I never lacked clothes on my back or boots on my feet during our long forced march into France, no matter what they had to endure. We were put to work in the Western marshes. I hesitate to say the other prisoners dropped like flies. Flies were the only creatures that seemed to thrive in that abominable wasteland.'

It must have been a salutary lesson to him, thought Nell. The kind of men he would have scorned to notice in his privileged youth had sacrificed their own well-being to ensure his survival.

'When the other prisoners were freed and sent back to Portugal I went with them,' he said. 'I did try to tell the British officer in charge who I was, but he either could not or would not believe me. I could see his point, I suppose. I must have sounded like a raving lunatic. There was I, dressed in rags, amidst a batch of Portuguese prisoners, claiming to be an English viscount!' He smiled ruefully. 'My claim to be a civilian clinched it for him, though. If I had ever been an enlisted man I would have been the responsibility of some regiment. There would have been proper channels for him to process me through. So, instead of coming straight home when France was occupied, I was obliged to take a detour through Portugal, thus delaying my return until less than a week ago. And then, only because my Portuguese brothers banded together to pay for my passage.'

'Very affecting, I'm sure,' said the Squire, wrenching Nell from the wonder she had been feeling as she listened to Carleton's remarkably humbling experiences.

'Now I dare say you are going to put the seal on this farrago of nonsense by relating how you have a distinctive birthmark that only your wife knows about, the revealing of which will be irrefutable proof you are who you claim to be?'

'Birthmark?' Carleton looked puzzled. 'No, I have no such thing.'

The Squire clucked his tongue. 'You disappoint me. It is the usual climax to a tale of this nature, you know.'

'What are you implying?' Carleton frowned.

'Do you really think I am green enough to be taken in by tales of Spanish mistresses and spies, and people going to the gallows in the place of a complete stranger?' the Squire scoffed. 'Your tale is leakier than a sieve!'

He surged to his feet.

'Mrs Tillotson,' he said sternly, 'Viscount Lambourne warned me that you were another such as Mrs Green before you came to live here. So I have been half expecting you to get up to some such trick as this. But I am still shocked,' he said, snatching his hat from her lax grasp, 'that you should attempt to embroil me in what I can only assume is a scheme to oust a decent man from a position he fills with admirable probity.'

'Helena is doing nothing of the sort!' Carleton objected. 'All you need to do, if you don't believe us, is to contact my mother or my sister and bring them here. They will only have to take one look at me to confirm my identity.'

The Squire laughed harshly. 'If you really were who you claim to be, you would know that the lady you claim is your mother died last winter. And since her daughter is married to a diplomat, and conveniently out of the country, there is no danger of her exposing you as an impostor.'

He clapped his hat on his head and made for the door.

'If it were not for the season I would be very tempted to have the pair of you thrown in jail. As it is…' he paused on the threshold, eyeing them with contempt '…I give you fair warning that if you persist in trying to stir up trouble with your malicious lies I shall make your lives extremely uncomfortable.' He rounded on Nell. 'You have lulled us all into a false sense of security with your show of modesty and industry. But I have always known what you really are. We do not want your sort living in Barstow. When your accomplice is well enough to travel, I strongly suggest you remove to the city, where you will find more scope for your…' his lips curled into a sneer, '…talents.'

He whirled out of the cottage in a flurry of snow-flakes. Nell slammed the door behind him. She had never liked the horrid man! He had always looked down his nose at her and found fault with her at every available opportunity. She had been a fool to seek his help. She would have done better to apply to the vicar. Reverend Byatt would at least have given her a fair hearing.

It was just that she always thought of him as being so heavenly minded he was of no earthly use!

'I am so sorry,' she said, returning to the parlour where Carleton was sitting staring dejectedly into the fire. 'I thought the local magistrate would have the right connections and the legal experience to know just how to sort out your predicament. It never occurred to me that he would think we were making the whole thing up!' She slumped in the chair opposite Carleton, staring moodily into the flames.

She did not want to admit how badly it hurt to learn that no matter what she did everyone put the worst possible interpretation on it. She could imagine how the gossip must have flown round the village when Carleton had shown up. Nell Tillotson had a man living in her cottage, so he must be her lover. She could not possibly have taken him in out of compassion, because he was sick. Oh, no. Her years of living blamelessly were now seen as a deliberate attempt to lull everyone into a false sense of security so that she would find it all the easier to swindle them at the first available opportunity.

'You have no need to apologise, Helena,' Carleton said softly. 'It is entirely my fault that your reputation has been tarnished.'

Nell turned to stare at him.

'I often wondered,' he continued reflectively, 'during the years I spent as a prisoner of war, what I had done to deserve such suffering. Now that I have heard what you have endured in my absence...' He sucked in a ragged breath, his eyes skittering away from her. 'Whatever happens to me now, I can only feel as though I am reaping what I have sown. Although...' he flicked her a wary glance '...I should like to know why...' He took another rasping breath, his eyes looking unnaturally dark against the pallor of his cheeks. 'Why did you summon the Squire at all? Would it not have been easier for you to fall in with my cousin's plans to dispose of me? Permanently?'

Nell gasped. 'You know of his plans?'

Carleton nodded gravely. 'I heard him urging you to poison me. Why do you not seek to get your revenge upon me, Helena? It is only what I deserve. And there is nothing I can do to prevent you.' He spread his hands wide in an attitude of surrender. 'Why don't you strike while you have me at your mercy? While I am too weak to try and escape?'

'Stop it! *Stop it!*' she cried, getting to her feet. 'You cannot really believe that I would stoop to so foul a crime as murder! It is bad enough that you thought all the rest—though I am beginning to see why you might have acted as you did. But murder…' She covered her face, shuddering at the very thought.

'Were you not even tempted?' he persisted. 'I must confess if I had been able to get my hands on the Spanish woman whose lies condemned me to such hellish suffering I would have cheerfully wrung her neck.'

'No! Oh, no—you would not!' Nell fell to her knees at his feet. 'When you had a chance to reflect, you must have seen that she feared for her own life! You must have worked out that she would rather sacrifice someone she did not know to that horrid French soldier's brutality than the man she loved! You would not murder a woman in cold blood, Carleton. I know you would not!'

'You…' He frowned. 'You seem quite ridiculously determined to see some good in me.'

'But there *is* good in you!' she protested.

'You can say that?' he said wonderingly. 'After suffering such cruelty at my hands?'

'Well, but you never meant to be cruel, did you? You were just young and proud and hot-tempered. Like Harry.'

'Helena,' he breathed, reaching down to take her hands and pull her up so that she was sitting on the sofa next to him.

Emboldened by the fact that this was the first time he had ever reached out to her of his own volition, she blurted out, 'I expect you even had a really good reason for believing I had taken some other man to my bed?'

Carleton's hands clenched over hers so hard she winced.

'Yes, I did. Thank you for crediting me with that much integrity. It was Nicholas Malgrove whom I always believed was the father of your child.'

Nell wrinkled her brow in perplexity.

Carleton let out a stunned laugh. 'You have no idea who he is, have you?'

Nell shook her head.

'He was one of the crowd I brought down to the

hunting box with me. That weekend, when I was so determined to prove that even though I was married I could still behave exactly as I pleased, I rounded up the very worst of my acquaintance, conveyed them to your home, and let them loose to wreak what havoc they would. Though I want to make it quite clear, my dear, that I was not in the habit of throwing *that* kind of party.'

Nell's own fingers tightened on his. Had he just called her his dear? Had he meant it? Or had the endearment just slipped out? Perhaps he always peppered his conversation with females with such meaningless blandishments. She forced herself to concentrate on the conversation he was having with her, though she could not prevent her heart from beating very fast as she admitted, 'They terrified me.'

'I failed to take into account how very young you were,' he confessed ruefully. 'Scarce seventeen, was it not?'

She nodded.

'Dear God,' he breathed. 'How on earth did you survive?'

'Mostly by hiding in the staff quarters. After that first evening, when I thought—' She broke off, blushing.

When she had seen the coaches drawing up, and the sumptuously dressed people come tumbling out of them, she had assumed she ought to act as her husband's hostess. Though she had had not a clue how to fulfil this role, she had tried to do her very best. She had organised what she'd hoped was an adequate dinner, given that she'd had no notice Carleton was bringing guests down. But when she had entered the dining room later, dressed in her finest gown, it had been to discover one scantily clad female draped across Carleton's lap, while two other gentlemen were vying for another's favours. When they had seen her they had let out a hunting cry and come bounding towards her.

Thankfully, the dining room had been large, the floor highly polished, and her pursuers far from sober.

'I kept to the kitchens by day,' she said, thrusting that frighteningly unpleasant episode from her mind. 'And at night I took refuge in your housekeeper's rooms. You remember Mrs Took?'

Carleton inhaled sharply. If any of the staff from those days remained in service, they would be able to confirm or deny her story. Helena had continued to live in that hunting box, alone except for the staff, when he had returned to London. She had stayed there after Harry had been born. Until the day the false account of his execution had reached England and Peregrine had sent her here. His staff would know her character inside out. Yet she looked completely unperturbed by the prospect that he might check up on her. Like a woman with nothing to fear.

An innocent woman.

'My reason for thinking you had entered into the spirit of debauchery that ran rife that weekend,' he said, hanging his head as he ran his thumbs over and over the backs of her hands, 'was that I saw Malgrove coming out of your bedroom one morning, in a state of…undress.'

Carleton had gone to her room to tell her he'd had as much of his guests as he could stomach. That he was sorry he'd brought people into her home who had frightened her. To apologise for not behaving as a gentleman should and to assure her he was sending them all packing that very day.

He'd had some thought of maybe introducing her to his mother, who would train his young bride to behave in a manner befitting her new station in life. Or at the very least teach her to dress so that she might *look* the part.

'I heard a woman's laughter coming from within…'

'So of course you assumed it was me,' she nodded.

Oh, yes, he had. He had imagined Malgrove's limbs tangled with hers. That lecher breaching the innocence that rightfully belonged to him.

There was no punishment too great for such betrayal. He had vowed he would never forgive her!

And he'd been the one to leave, lest in his jealous rage he stormed into her chamber and throttled her where she lay!

'Are you not angry?' He looked up, searching her face for signs that she bore him some malice.

She shook her head. 'No, of course not. What you have just told me explains everything.'

'But it does not excuse it. I behaved abominably. I have given you nothing but grief…'

She tugged one hand free, raising it to his mouth to silence him. 'You gave me Harry,' she protested. 'From the moment I held him in my arms my life was transformed. I love being a mother.' She smiled. 'To know that I finally belong to someone, in such a special way…'

She turned eyes that were suddenly shadowed on him. 'From the day my parents died nobody wanted me. My aunt and uncle made sure I knew they had only taken me in on sufferance. I knew a man as handsome and rich as you would never even have noticed a girl like me, and that had it not been for my aunt's wicked plot to trap you into marrying Lucinda I would probably not have married anyone. But then Harry was born. And, however bad our marriage was, I was always grateful it produced him. He has been such a blessing to me…'

The shadows faded and she seemed to light from within. She looked so radiant that Carleton could not help himself.

He took her lovely face between his workworn hands and kissed her full on the lips.

Chapter Five

For a moment Nell was so surprised she could not react. Carleton was kissing her.

Her husband was kissing her as though he meant it.

'Wh…why did you do that?' she could not help blurting, the moment he stopped.

He looked down at her ruefully.

'Did you not like it?' He stroked her face gently, then ran his hands down her arms, squeezing her hands gently as his shoulders sagged in defeat.

But when he would have let go of her hands altogether, Nell gripped them tightly.

'It was not that I did not like it,' she explained. 'Just that you took me by surprise.'

'Surprise?' he repeated, studying the way her fingers were clutching his spasmodically. 'If I were to give you fair warning of my intent,' he asked with great seriousness, 'would you object if I were to kiss you again?'

'No,' Nell breathed.

'Quite sure?'

She nodded, blushing.

'Thank God,' he sighed. 'Because I find you irresistible. Even on our wedding night,' he mused, 'when I thought I hated you, it was the same.'

He took her in his arms and, far from making any move to escape him, she let her darkened eyes fasten on his lips. His last doubts as to whether she found his attentions unwelcome dissipated when she looped her arms about his neck and very inexpertly attempted to kiss him back.

In less than a heartbeat Nell was melting into the sofa cushions, Carleton sprawled half on top of her. She was trembling, and when he laid one hand upon her breast he could feel her heart pounding beneath his palm.

His own heart was racing too. In fact he was feeling quite light-headed.

'We are going to have to stop,' he panted, drawing back from her reluctantly. 'Else Peregrine will get his wish.' He lay back, letting his head loll against the sofa-back, his eyes closing.

Nell scrambled upright. 'Oh, dear,' she exclaimed, noting his pallor. 'I did not mean to harm you.'

'It is not your fault I got a little carried away,' he assured her. 'I know you would never do anything to hurt me. Nor anyone else, I suspect.' He opened his eyes and regarded her curiously. 'I do not think you have a malicious bone in your body, do you?'

Nell was so flustered by the unexpectedness of the kiss, the havoc it had wrought on her senses, and the flattering words coming from the lips of a man who had previously done nothing but sneer at her, that she found herself opening and closing her mouth like a fish.

'Helena,' he sighed, reaching for her hand. 'You are a rare treasure in this benighted world. You took me in and cared for me when anyone else would have left me outside in the snow. You have tried to restore me to what is lawfully mine, at risk to yourself and our son.' He found her hand and grasped it, his eyes suspiciously bright. 'You know it is no use, though, do you not?'

'No use?' Nell's heart plunged.

'No. From what you have told me I have come to believe Peregrine swindled and cheated and lied to get his hands on my title. We both know he is prepared to kill me to keep it. I am sorry… No, though, I am not!' A little colour was returning to his face, and his eyes burned brightly as he declared, 'I was going to say I am sorry I came here and brought all this trouble to your doorstep. And I *am* sorry that I have brought the trouble, but not that I have discovered you. We may only have a few days left to us, but I am so glad that we will be spending them together. We should always have been together, Helena. I wish to God I had not been such a colossal fool!'

'Nell,' she whispered, raising his hand to her lips and kissing it fervently. 'Oh, won't you please call me Nell? Whenever anyone calls me Helena I feel as though I am being told off.'

He laughed, and hugged her. 'Nell it shall be, then. Darling Nell, how I wish I had made the effort to get to know you better when we first married,' he said ruefully. 'Now it is too late.'

'Do not say that,' she replied, her fingers caressing his lean cheek. 'We will find a way…'

Carleton shook his head grimly. 'I have had more than my fair share of narrow escapes. And I don't think I really knew how little I deserved any of them until I saw myself through your eyes. Even on the voyage back to England I was still conceited enough to think I was about to embark on a life worthy of José's tremendous sacrifice. But it would have just been by being a fairer landlord to my tenants, maybe espousing a few charitable causes. I would soon have reverted to being the insufferably arrogant prig I was in my youth, considering myself better than everyone else because I was born to a position of wealth and privilege. But I'm not, am I, Nell?' He gazed at her solemnly. 'Even Squire Jeffers knows Peregrine has done a better job of being Viscount Lambourne than I ever did.'

'No, no—you must not say that!' Nell wished she had a tithe of the eloquence her well-educated husband possessed. But all she could come up with was, 'Peregrine is the most hateful person I have ever met!'

Carleton's face broke into a smile. 'You are a miracle. Do you know that, Nell? More of a miracle than a wretch like me deserves…'

He fell silent, crushing her to his chest so tightly she could hardly breathe. She felt as though her heart would burst with pleasure. She no longer cared what anyone else might say about her. Not now Carleton believed in her.

She would gladly have stayed like that, held tightly in her husband's arms all day. But after only a few minutes of being her cradled against his heart Harry burst in through the door. The expression of shock on his face, swiftly followed by disgust, had her pulling out of Carleton's embrace. Reluctantly he let her sit up, but he restrained her when she would have left the sofa altogether.

'I know I have not been exactly the kind of father you might have wished for, Harry,' he said. 'But I am your father, nonetheless. Can you find it in your heart to forgive me, as your mother has forgiven me?' He held out his hand. 'Will you shake on it?'

Harry's face worked furiously for a minute or two, before he simply turned on his heel and dashed out of the room.

Carleton let his hand fall to his side. Nell took it and cradled it between her own.

'He has a hot temper, but he will come round eventually. He just needs time to cool down…'

Carleton sucked in a sharp breath. Nell sounded so very much like his own mother—who had, he now realised, thoroughly spoiled him. She had never believed he could do any wrong, making excuses for all his youthful wildness. She had even sympathised with him when he told her how he had been tricked into marriage, never questioning his subsequent treatment of his wife.

When it had been so grossly unfair.

He sighed. Harry had every right to despise him. 'He is *my* son, Nell,' he said gloomily. 'He is quite capable of stoking his anger indefinitely.' Just as he had nursed his resentment towards Nell.

For years.

Early the next morning Nell received word that Peregrine was going to call the following day. Although she had no intention of falling in with his plans, his visit was still going to cause a momentous upheaval.

Carleton had settled into an attitude of defeat. He had been through so much, was still so weak from his last bout of illness, and there seemed to be no fight left in him.

'I do not suppose,' he had said the night before, when she had gone to spend a few minutes with him after Harry had gone to bed, 'that I will be celebrating Christmas at Lambourne Hall after all.'

Peregrine did not want him to see the inside of Lambourne Hall again under any circumstances, she thought, angrily crumpling the note into a ball and tossing it into the fire.

But the horrid man would not be coming till tomorrow. They still had today. And since it looked as though her tenure here was about to come to an end one way or another, with both Peregrine and Squire Jeffers ranged against her, she saw no point in being economical with the stores she had laid up to see her through the winter.

If this was the last day she could guarantee spending in her cottage with her husband and son, she decided, marching down to the chicken coop, then she was going to make it a day to remember.

Her last laying hen was soon plucked and stuffed and thrust into the oven, and her larder raided for suet and spices and dried fruits, which she blended and tied into a muslin cloth.

The wonderful aroma of roasting chicken and steaming pudding was soon wafting through the immediate vicinity.

She guessed it was the smell of dinner cooking that tempted Harry back to the house from wherever he had been skulking all morning. He checked on the threshold when he saw Carleton sitting at the kitchen table, scowling mutinously when he saw that three places had been set.

But his mood did not prevent him from making hearty inroads into the meal Nell set before them.

'That was wonderful, Nell,' said Carleton as she gathered up the plates both father and son had scraped clean of their first course. 'I cannot recall when I last enjoyed a meal so much.'

'There is still pudding to come.' She smiled, then experienced a strange pang when they reached for their spoons in unison, identically avid expressions on their faces.

'The taste of Christmas,' sighed Carleton rapturously, after taking his first mouthful. 'All we need now to make the occasion really festive is a pound of flour to make a bullet pudding.'

'Bullet pudding?' Harry echoed, his spoon halfway to his mouth.

Nell held her breath, marvelling that Carleton had managed to coax any response from the boy who was so stubbornly hanging on to his hostility towards his father.

'You can't eat bullets,' Harry finished scornfully, obviously deciding his father was talking nonsense.

'No,' replied Carleton. 'Of course not. It is a game. Haven't you ever played it?' He looked an enquiry at Nell.

When she shook her head, he said, 'Well, what you do is put a heap of flour on a plate, with a bullet on the top, and everyone takes turns to carve a slice away with a dinner knife. Eventually, of course, the bullet gets dislodged, and whoever cut the slice that caused it to fall has to nudge it from the plate with their nose. Which makes everyone else laugh, naturally.'

Harry was watching him with his head cocked to one side as he chewed on his own pudding.

'We used to play snapdragon too. You soak raisins in brandy and set them on fire. Then each player has to take turns snatching one out of the flames. You have to be quick for that one!'

Both Nell and Harry sat spellbound while Carleton regaled them with tales of Christmases spent at Lambourne Hall in his childhood—until suddenly he sagged back in his chair.

'I apologise,' he said, as Nell gathered up the dishes for washing, 'but I do not think I am up to helping you with those.'

'Think nothing of it,' she smiled. 'At least you managed to join us at table today. You are getting stronger all the time. By tomorrow…' She faltered, her face falling. By tomorrow Peregrine would have arrived with his poison, and no doubt a whole new batch of threats to hold over her head.

Harry stayed at table for a few minutes after Carleton had left the room, kicking his feet against the leg of his stool. But when Nell called to him from the scullery—'Time to help me with these dishes, Harry!'—he was nowhere to be seen.

Exasperated with him, Nell darted into the passage, hoping to catch him before he escaped the house. She was just in time to see him march into the parlour, a purposeful expression on his face.

She clapped her hand over her mouth to hold back a peal of laughter. He looked for all the world as though he meant to insist his father gave a strict account of himself.

Perhaps he did.

She returned to the kitchen, finishing the dishes and then preparing the chicken carcass for the broth they would be eating the next day. She dared not plan any further ahead than that. She sighed, wiping her brow with the back of her hand. What Peregrine would do when he found out she had no intention of falling in with his monstrous plans did not bear thinking about.

But at least Carleton appeared to be winning Harry over. They spent the afternoon in the parlour together, and when Nell eventually joined them she saw a new light glowing in Carleton's eyes. Harry still seemed a little subdued, but he was no longer being openly hostile. When darkness fell, and she sent Harry up to bed, she was gratified that for once he obeyed her without demur.

'He's a good boy,' said Carleton, his eyes still on the door through which Harry had just gone.

'He can be a very naughty boy,' retorted Nell, suddenly gripped by foreboding that his display of docility meant he was hatching some mischief.

'All boys can be naughty.' Carleton smiled. 'I would not want any son of mine to lack spirit.'

'He has that,' she said with some asperity, 'in spades.'

He laughed and drew her into his arms. For a few minutes they forgot everything but the delight of being with each other. Nell felt as though she had been waiting all day for this very moment. And she suspected from the way Carleton's eyes had been following her every movement that he had been counting the minutes till they could be alone too.

But at length she prised herself out of his embrace.

'I must go and tuck Harry in, and hear him say his prayers.'

Carleton kissed her lingeringly once more, then said with a twinkle in his eye, 'Do not take long. I need you…' he lay back on the sofa, artfully dislodging one of the blankets that were stacked on a side table with his elbow '…to tuck me in too,' he finished, as it landed in an untidy heap on the floor.

Nell floated up the stairs to Harry's little bedroom under the eaves. But her euphoria dimmed the minute she caught sight of her son. He was sitting up in bed, his face clenched as tightly as the fingers that kneaded the coverlet which he held up to his chin.

'What will happen now, Ma?'

She smoothed back an unruly lock of hair that had flopped into his eyes.

'I do not know, Harry,' she sighed. 'What do you mean, exactly?'

'The Viscount will be coming back tomorrow, won't he? With the poison?'

'Harry!' she gasped. 'However did you find out about that?'

A tear escaped the corner of one eye. He angrily knuckled it away. 'We heard you talking. We were outside in the garden. We heard everything. What are you going to do?'

Nell felt sick to her stomach. It was bad enough that Peregrine had tried to involve her in such a repulsive crime, but to think a boy of Harry's age should have overheard and been distressed by it was monstrous!

'You are not to worry,' she breathed, furious that her son must have been fretting about this for days. 'I will think of something!'

Harry's face cleared instantly. 'I knew you would, Ma.' He grinned, flinging his arms round her neck and hugging her fiercely.

When he lay back, she felt like weeping at the innocent trust he placed in her. She fumbled her way guiltily down the stairs, conscious that for the first time in his young life she had not been honest with her son. Far from having any idea what they should do, her mind was in complete turmoil.

She really must sit down and discuss the threat with Carleton seriously. There must be some simple solution that would stop Peregrine in his tracks. Or some person unknown to her to whom they could apply for aid. Even though Peregrine meant to leave his poison with her the next day, he would not expect to hear news of Carleton's demise for a while. In that time perhaps they could reach someone who could vouch for her husband's identity.

But when she opened the parlour door it was to see Carleton was fast asleep. She supposed she ought not to be surprised. It had been his first full day out of bed, she reflected, picking a blanket up off the floor and shaking it out. She sighed, bending to kiss his forehead as she gently tucked it round his slender form. And if Peregrine had his way it would be his last.

She sat down in the armchair after she had banked up the fire, just to watch him sleep. He was so handsome, even pared down by hardship and illness, that she could hardly believe he appeared to have grown so fond of her so quickly. It was just typical of her life, though, that when something as good as this happened to her it was only with the knowledge that it would soon be snatched away.

She could not bring herself to climb the stairs to her solitary bed and tear herself away from the husband who would only be hers for a few more hours. So she took another blanket and curled up on the armchair, with her head on the armrest. She did not care how uncomfortable it was. She did not want to waste a moment of the short time they had left together in sleep.

If only she could persuade Peregrine to just leave them alone! He could keep Lambourne Hall and the stupid title, for all she cared. So long as they were all safe. She was sure she and Carleton and Harry could carry on living quite happily here, in this little cottage. After the things Carleton had been through, it would seem like luxury! And Peregrine could not *really* want to have a murder on his conscience, could he?

She tugged the blanket up round her ears as a gust of wind rattled the windows, the sudden chill reminding her that such thoughts were foolish in the extreme. *She* might be content to live here, but Carleton had spent all day going on about how wonderful everything was at Lambourne Hall. He might seem as though he had accepted defeat, but that was only because the fever had brought him so low. Once he began to recover, the glowing fervour he held for his former home and position would flare up until it consumed all that stood in its path.

She shifted uncomfortably. In a way she knew she did not want to hold him back. Because Carleton *was* the Viscount, and whatever Squire Jeffers said Peregrine did *not* deserve to hold that position.

Carleton stirred in his sleep, flinging one arm up above his head. Nell sighed. Peregrine would never let them be. She had no chance of persuading him to be merciful. Carleton threatened all he held dear just by being alive.

It was just as dawn was breaking that inspiration struck her. She had been drowsily replaying the events of the past few days, holding each one up individually in her mind like precious jewels, when it came to her. She sat bolt upright, the blanket slipping unheeded to the floor. She would *beg* Peregrine to let them carry on living in this cottage. And then…

Her heart racing, Nell pelted up the stairs to shake Harry awake. For once she was glad he loved getting into mischief. He would take to the part she wanted him to play today like a duck to water.

To her immense pride, he grasped her plan quickly. They went over it several times while he was scrambling into his clothes, just to be on the safe side, but she was pretty sure that if it did not work it would not be Harry's fault.

The morning dragged endlessly. Carleton was reluctant to leave his sofa, explaining to Harry in a listless manner that he had exhausted himself the previous day. But when his eyes met Nell's she could read the despair in their depths.

Finally, she heard the church clock striking midday.

'Why don't you go out and play?' she said to Harry with a significant nod. 'It snowed so heavily during the night I am sure there must be lots of ways you can amuse yourself.'

'Thank you, Mama,' he said, stiffly polite. 'I shall go down past the church and see if the duck pond is frozen.'

She bent to kiss him as he exited the back door, whispering, 'You have not forgotten? The Rectory first…'

'And then the Manor,' he said solemnly. 'I'll fetch the vicar *and* the Squire for you, Ma, I promise!'

Tugging his cap down over his ears, Harry shot out of the door like a bullet from a gun.

Now all she had to do was prime Carleton. She entered the parlour hesitantly, wondering how he would react to the way she was employing their son. He was lying flat out, his eyes fast shut.

She backed away, closing the door softly so as not to disturb him. It was for the best that he should sleep through all that was to follow. Apart from the fact there was not really time to explain her scheme, she had grave misgivings as to whether he would go along with it. Just because he had kissed her once or twice, and called her dear, it did not mean he would suddenly become the sort of man who would believe a mere woman could outsmart a would-be murderer.

While Harry was out assembling all the principal players, Nell still had to set the stage. To that end, she went into the kitchen and began to pull random items from her sadly depleted store cupboard. Once her pastry board was liberally dusted with flour, there was nothing to do but wait. She sank down onto a stool, nervously chewing at the ragged edge of her thumbnail. As the minutes ticked past she went over her plan again and again, wondering if it really could work.

She had staked everything on the predictability of all the players concerned. But if Peregrine for some reason did not leave his carriage at the Blue Lion and sample their ordinary before walking over here, as he usually did…

Almost beside herself with nerves, she got to her feet and went down the passage towards the front door. She paused outside the parlour, her fingers lightly brushing the door panels. *I will not let him destroy you, Carleton,* she silently vowed.

And even as she made this promise she heard the sound she had been anticipating and dreading in equal measure. Booted feet marching up to her front door. Swiftly, before her visitor had a chance to raise the knocker and wake Carleton, Nell darted to the door and opened it.

Peregrine stood there, scowling.

'You have come to your senses, madam, I trust?' he said, not waiting for permission to enter but just barging his way in.

'Would you mind very much if we were to conduct our business in the kitchen?' she replied in a subdued tone. 'Carleton is asleep in the parlour, and I am sure you do not wish him to overhear us.'

Confident her words were a sign of capitulation, Peregrine smirked knowingly as he preceded her along the passage, leaving her to shut the front door.

'I have come up with a much better solution to your problem than the one you put to me when you were last here,' Nell announced, the moment she reached the kitchen.

He turned from tossing his hat onto one of the chairs, his face creasing with annoyance.

'What do you mean?' he barked. 'There is only one solution to my problem. Carleton must die!'

'Oh, no, sir! Please could you not spare him? Carleton has changed so very much during the years he spent abroad. He is not interested in reclaiming the title of Viscount Lambourne. He would be quite content to live here with me and Harry. Please,' she cried, 'do not compel me to kill him!'

'I know what this is,' he retorted. 'You are afraid

of being found out. I don't believe for one second that Carleton has changed one iota. You just don't want to hang if anyone were to find out you had done away with him. Well, let me tell you something,' he snarled, taking a small bottle from an inner pocket and slapping it down on the table. 'If I do not get word within two days that your husband is dead, I shall be making other arrangements. Do you understand me?'

He placed both hands flat on the floury table, leaning forward, his voice full of menace. 'Arrangements that will include you and your boy. Which is it to be, madam? Carry out this simple little commission for me, or be added to my list of irritating problems that need to disappear?'

'You would pay someone to kill me?' she gasped. 'And Harry? But he is a child!'

'A worthless bastard is what he is! Nobody will miss him.'

A commotion erupted outside the window. The back door flew open to reveal three people struggling on her doorstep. Harry, the Vicar, and the Squire.

Harry was tucked under one of the Reverend Byatt's arms, his limbs flailing like windmills. With his free hand the Vicar was vainly trying to hold Squire Jeffers back, though the spindly cleric had scant chance against a sportsman of the Squire's calibre.

'By God, sir!' thundered the Squire as he surged into the kitchen, dragging the other two in his wake.

'Mrs Tillotson warned me what you were about, but I did not believe her. Not till I heard you condemn yourself out of your own mouth!'

Chapter Six

Peregrine paled, but made a swift recovery. 'I do not know what you think you heard,' he said, drawing himself up to his full height, 'but I can assure you—'

'No, *I* can assure *you*,' drawled a coldly forbidding voice from the door to the passage, 'that if I or Nell or Harry should die in an untimely manner, these two gentlemen will know exactly where to point the finger.' Carleton stood in the doorway, his fists clenched. 'You are the one that will hang, not Nell.'

Peregrine rounded furiously on Nell.

'This is your doing! You want it all, don't you? The title, the wealth and the position you think you will have as his wife!' He laughed maniacally. 'Have you forgotten already what it was like the last time round? He will fill his house with whores and reprobates who will suck him dry. He will make your life a living hell, just as it was before I came to your rescue! My God, I should have let you walk the streets to keep bread in your bastard brat's mouth—'

He would no doubt have carried on in the same vein indefinitely, had not Carleton flown across the kitchen, punching him so hard in the mouth that he reeled back against the pantry door.

He raised a floury hand to the blood that welled from his split lip, his eyes darting from one hostile face to the other.

'Harry is my son,' Carleton panted. 'My heir. Even if you did away with me, he would still stand before you in line of succession.'

'Are you quite sure about that?' Squire Jeffers asked dubiously, as Reverend Byatt lowered Harry to the floor. 'That boy? Your heir?'

'Yes, quite sure,' replied Carleton, going to place an arm round Nell's shoulder and drawing her to his side.

Harry shot across the kitchen and flung his arms about Carleton's waist. With a smile, his father reached down to ruffle his hair.

'Lost your cap again, Harry?' he chided gently.

'Never mind the boy's headgear!' the Squire snapped. 'There are far more important issues at stake here.'

'I quite agree,' said Nell. 'Won't you come in, Reverend, and close the door?'

'Yes—yes, of course. Cannot think how I come to be standing on your step like this.' He shook his head in a bewildered manner as he shut the door against the wintry air.

'And we still have to decide what is to be done with him!' put in the Squire, with an angry gesture towards Peregrine, who was groping in his pocket for a handkerchief.

'It is a matter for myself and my cousin to determine between ourselves,' said Carleton firmly. 'I have no wish to bring scandal to our family name by having him arrested and charged with attempting to incite my wife to murder.'

'But you cannot mean to let him walk away scot-free!' blustered the Squire.

'Relinquishing his position when he welcomes me home to Lambourne Hall will be punishment enough, I should think,' said Carleton.

'Welcome you to Lambourne Hall?' Peregrine protested, his voice slightly muffled by the bloodstained handkerchief he was pressing to his lip. 'I shall do no such thing!'

'Oh, I think you will,' said Carleton coldly. 'The alternative would be too ghastly to contemplate. I still have friends who will recognise me. Either the Squire or the Vicar will be only too happy to convey me to them. If you force me to seek them out, I shall then have no compunction in relating how you deliberately blackened my wife's name so that you could wrest the title from my son, my rightful heir. And how spreading such scandal caused my mother to suffer such shame that it probably hastened her demise. By the time I have finished you will not be received anywhere.'

Peregrine's face was turning an alarmingly unhealthy shade of purple. 'You would not…pack of damned lies…not the behaviour of a gentleman…' he spluttered.

Carleton shrugged insouciantly. 'But then, if you deny me what is rightfully mine, I shall not *be* a gentleman any more, shall I? I shall be forced to live on my wits.' His eyes hardened. 'And I should warn you I have learned a thing or two about survival over the years.'

'Come, come, gentlemen,' put in the Vicar nervously. 'This is supposed to be the season of goodwill.'

'My goodwill,' replied Carleton, 'can only extend as far as not pressing charges against this man for the attempt he would have made on my life.'

'Yes, that's it! Let bygones be bygones,' Reverend Byatt babbled.

'I suggest,' put in Squire Jeffers sternly, 'that you take yourself off to Lambourne Hall right now, and make arrangements for the Viscount's return. And if I hear a whisper of anything untoward I shall be swearing out a deposition for your arrest!'

'You leave me no choice,' growled Peregrine.

'None, sir!'

With one last venomous glance at Nell, Peregrine scuttled out of the door.

Nell felt Carleton sway. For the past few minutes the weight of his arm across her shoulder had been growing steadily heavier, until she felt as though she was all but holding him upright. Now, at last, he made for one of the kitchen chairs, and with her help sank onto it, his face white as chalk.

'Do you think he really will give up his claim now?' said Nell, moving to the window and anxiously peering out at Peregrine's retreating figure.

'He had better,' growled the Squire. 'He won't want it getting around that he plotted murder.'

'Gracious heavens,' said the Vicar, sinking onto another chair. 'And Harry really is your son? Heir to the Lambourne estate?'

'He is that.' Carleton smiled with pride.

'My goodness,' said the Vicar, shaking his head in astonishment.

The Squire stood looking around the humble kitchen with open contempt. 'This is no place for you, my lord. Not while you are obviously still so ill. You should come back with me to the Manor.'

Carleton looked straight at Nell.

'Thank you for your kind offer, sir. It includes my wife, naturally?'

She whirled round, looking so appalled at the prospect of going to stay in Squire Jeffers's home that he said, 'Grateful though I am for your concern, I must decline your offer of hospitality. My place is here, with my wife.'

The Squire harrumphed, and shifted uneasily at the warmth of the look the couple then exchanged. But the Vicar clasped his hands, as though in prayer, his eyes misting over as he said, 'Indeed it is. Oh, indeed. Perhaps what we should do, Squire, is to help them be more comfortable? I am sure our dear Helena could use some provisions?'

'My most pressing need is for fuel,' she replied, instantly purposeful. 'And foodstuffs suitable for an invalid, of course.'

'I'll see to that,' said the Squire brusquely. 'Until your cousin makes the arrangements to have you removed to your proper sphere, I will make sure you lack for nothing, my lord.'

Nell smiled at him sweetly, but could not resist saying, 'That will make a pleasant change, sir. Thank you.'

They saw their guests through to the front door, lingering on the threshold until they reached the front gate.

The Squire had just turned from fastening the latch when a large, wet snowball struck him square between the shoulderblades.

The Vicar gasped at the language that spewed from the Squire's mouth as he turned and shook his fist at Harry, who promptly darted back into the safety of the house.

'Oh, Harry!' Nell's hand flew to her mouth. 'That was so naughty!'

But Carleton burst out laughing. To Nell's dismay, he then dealt with the scene by calmly flipping the door shut, turning to his son, and declaring proudly, 'Good shot, my boy!'

Harry stopped dead, whirled round, and offered up a tentative smile.

'No, Carleton,' Nell protested. 'It was quite wrong of him to act in such a defiant and impudent manner. The Squire is a man of standing in the community, who deserves respect...'

'He deserves horsewhipping,' argued Carleton. 'You have endured a great deal of hardship in my absence, and that man, from what I can gather, only managed to make it worse.'

Harry sidled back down the hall and plopped himself on the bottom stair, watching his parents avidly.

'Well, naturally he was not at all happy about having a woman of my reputation coming to live under his jurisdiction. He feared I would be a bad influence...'

'But he must have seen after you had been here five

minutes that you are a woman of remarkable integrity. If you had been *that* sort of woman you would not have been living here, so fiercely proud of your independence. You would have traded on your beauty…' he traced the outline of her cheek with his forefinger '…to assure your comfort. How he could have continued to believe those false rumours…' His face puckered in remorse. 'The rumours which I set about…'

Drawing in a deep breath, he turned to his son. 'Harry, it can be a very bad thing to act impulsively. Although I admire your aim, and can sympathise with your desire to avenge your mother, we Tillotsons adhere to certain standards of behaviour. From now on you must demonstrate more respect for your elders.'

Harry's little face crumpled with dismay.

'Do not worry, Harry. Nobody is angry with you. But we should like to be alone for a while, your mother and I, to have a little talk.'

'About going to live in Viscount Lambourne's house, now you are going to throw him out in the snow?' said Harry, cheering up again.

'I am not going to throw anyone out in the snow.' Carleton knelt down on the flagstone floor, bringing his face down to Harry's level. 'Can you not remember how unpleasant it was when you were threatened with that fate? Would you want me to make anyone else feel so scared, and angry, and resentful?'

'Even if he deserves it?' said Harry dubiously.

'It will be hard for him to give up a position he has come to regard as his own. That is punishment enough. To do more would only be cruel. I hope you do not believe your father could be capable of deliberate cruelty? That would make me no better than him.'

Harry sighed, looking a little disappointed. Scuffing his toe along the edge of the skirting board, he admitted, 'I suppose so.' Then, with a sullen expression on his face, he said, 'I don't have to go and live in Lambourne Hall with him, though, do I?'

Carleton reached out and grasped the newel post, his face losing what little colour it had, prompting Nell and Harry to support him to the parlour sofa, fluttering around him until their determined ministrations drew a brittle laugh from his throat.

'Enough, enough!' he said, waving his hand to indicate they should take to their own chairs. Nell chose the armchair opposite him, Harry a stool at his feet.

'Let me make some things clear,' he began. 'Harry, you must understand your life will change now. When you grow up you will have substantial estates to govern, and you need to begin learning how to do that. That is why you must spend time at Lambourne Hall.'

When Harry's face took on a mutinous cast, he added, 'It is a wonderful place for a boy to live. There is a farm, and some woods, and a lake. You can learn to ride and shoot and fish.'

Harry considered for a few minutes, then asked, 'Will I have to respect the Viscount…I mean that man who *said* he was Viscount Lambourne?'

'When you have cause to meet him I shall expect you to be polite. But I should not think you will see him all that often.' Carleton leaned forward, clasping his hands loosely between his knees. 'My cousin has a property in Northumberland. I hope to persuade him to remove there.'

Harry looked relieved.

'You can go outside and make the most of the snow now,' said Carleton gently.

'Wrap up warm!' called Nell after him as he dashed from the room.

As soon as she heard the back door slam, she turned to Carleton anxiously. 'What if you cannot make Peregrine leave Lambourne Hall? What then?'

'So long as we all spend Christmas there, it really does not matter. It is too late for him now to cancel the traditional celebrations that are held there. We shall meet all the neighbours, and from them the news of my return will spread like wildfire. His options then will be limited.' He made a dismissive gesture with his hand. 'And in any event, my estates and investments yield enough to keep us all in considerable comfort.'

'But if that was your plan all along, why did you threaten him with ruin?'

Carleton's face hardened. 'I had to convince Peregrine I was prepared to fight dirty. I had to put the fear of God into him, Nell, don't you see? To keep you and Harry safe! Nothing else matters.'

Nell twisted her hands together in anguish. She knew what Lambourne Hall meant to her husband. He could not possibly want to give it up.

'How can you say it does not matter? If you cannot get him out of your home—'

'Was he right?' he cut in. 'Did you only defend me because you want the title, the wealth and the status I denied you the last time round?' He stared at her, aghast.

'How can you even think that?' she cried. 'I do not care about any of those things! I never have! If you must know,' she said crossly, getting to her feet and pacing to the fire, where she took up a poker and began to thrust it into the logs, sending showers of sparks up the chimney, 'I would as soon stay here and keep chickens, and grow my own vegetables, and—'

'Never have to clap eyes on me again, I dare swear?' His eyes were pools of bleak despair. 'Oh, do not attempt to deny it,' he said when she whirled round, the poker still clutched in her hand. 'You never wanted to marry me in the first place, did you? How could I ever have been arrogant enough to think that you would go to such lengths to trap me?'

Nell made a great show of placing the poker back

on its stand. 'I…I did not play any part in trapping you,' she said, keeping her back to him. 'But I cannot deny I was not at all reluctant to become your wife. I had watched you, from the shadows where I was supposed to stay, and I had admired you. You know how handsome you were!' she admitted crossly. 'All the girls wanted you to notice them. I was not surprised when you believed I was the same. You were so used to that sort of pursuit. That girl who pretended to faint at your feet! What was her name?' She glanced at him over her shoulder.

'I cannot recollect,' he said diplomatically.

Nell turned fully round, clasping her rather sooty hands together at her waist. '*That* was why I came to your chamber on our wedding night. I did not want you to think I was like them. I wanted you to know the truth. And I hoped that we could become friends, and find a way to deal with what my aunt had done to us both.'

He groaned. 'And I made yet another error in selfishly taking what I assumed you had come to offer. Then compounded my sins by attempting to blot out the whole episode with brandy.'

With a stricken look, Nell crossed the space between them and silenced him by laying the tip of her finger against his lips.

'You were not selfish. You were wonderful. You were so tender with me. Took such care of me and brought me such delight…' She blushed, then busied herself removing the sooty fingerprints from her husband's mouth with a corner of her apron. 'I foolishly thought you had decided to make our marriage real. Only the next morning you left in such a terrible rage…'

'Only to return with that degenerate rabble…' He shook his head in remorse.

'I was so pleased to see you that first night,' she admitted shyly. 'I thought you were introducing me to your friends, that I was going to act as hostess…'

'And instead—' he groaned '—you were faced with the sight of me with that trollop on my knee…'

'I do not want you to feel guilty any more,' she said, looking him straight in the eye. 'I understand you were trying to demonstrate that you intended to go on living exactly as you would have done were you not married. Although…' She frowned. 'How you expected me to believe you were *that* dissolute, when I could see how uncomfortable the behaviour of the other gentlemen made you…'

'Could you? Then you were the only person who has ever guessed what a half-hearted rake I was.'

'That is because I was used to observing, rather than joining in. I always knew…at least I *hoped* that you were a better man than the way you behaved led others to believe. After all, they believed totally wrong things about me.'

'As did I.'

'Yes, but I had the advantage of knowing that you were a victim of my aunt's plot, so it was easier to understand how trapped and angry that had made you.'

'Nell,' he said irritably, 'all you have said has re-assured me that you have forgiven my past treatment of you. But it is not enough. It means…' he ran his hand over the crown of his head '…almost nothing!'

Nell flinched back from his angry gesture, her insides clenching in a cold hard knot.

'You took me in and nursed me back to health simply because it was the right thing to do! And fighting to get me recognised has had the effect of securing Harry's future.' He looked haggard. 'It does not mean you care about *me* at all!'

He turned towards her, grabbing her hands and looking into her face with a kind of desperation. 'Nell, don't leave me without hope. Tell me that one day you might come to feel some affection for me.'

'Have you not heard a single word I have said?' she replied softly. 'I already love you. With every fibre of my being.'

'Nell…' he gasped. 'Nell!' He seized her and crushed her to his chest. 'I love you too. So very much!'

'Don't be ridiculous!' She pulled away from him, her eyes wide with shock. 'You barely know me! You have scarce been here six days…'

'Six days is quite long enough to fall in love with a woman as brave and loyal and clever as you.' Especially, he reflected, now that he knew the woman he'd been dreaming of, who'd kept him warm through all the long, lonely nights of his imprisonment, his perfect bride, was this angel. Oh, in the cold light of the morning he had pushed her away, replaced her in his mind with an image of the scheming woman he thought he'd married—Helena. But each night Nell had loved him all over again. How could he fail to love her back now that his eyes had been opened to see her as she really was? The embodiment of all he had ever wanted in a wife.

'The trap you set for Peregrine this morning…' He shook his head, his eyes lit with such admiration it warmed Nell to the core. 'It was quite a brilliant piece of strategy to get both the Squire and the Vicar to overhear Peregrine ordering you to murder me.'

'No,' she demurred, 'it just came to me after Harry confessed he had been lurking in the garden with you, eavesdropping. What was brilliant was the way you convinced Peregrine you would stop at nothing to wrest the title back.'

It was Carleton's turn to shake his head. 'Mere posturing,' he disclaimed. 'The truth, if you will hear it, is that we make a good team. Nell,' he whispered, lowering his head to drop a kiss into her sooty palm 'give me the chance to make amends. Let me spoil you.

I want to replace this threadbare homespun—' he fingered the folds of her skirt '—for satins and silks. I want these work-worn hands—' he ran his thumbs gently over her callused palms '—to never have to lift anything as heavy as a garden fork again. You will have your own maid, Nell, to care for your clothes and dress your hair. And you shall have jewels too— whatever your heart desires. Only tell me what you want, and I will make it my life's mission to give it to you!'

Nell turned her head away, blushing rosily. 'A baby,' she said. And then, when there was no immediate response from her husband, she plunged on. 'I do not think it is right for Harry to be an only child. I have been inclined to spoil him, and have begun to fear he will grow up a hellion. Now, if he had a little brother or sister…'

Her homily ended in a muffled squeak as Carleton seized her and kissed her passionately. Only when she had wound her arms about his neck did he pause.

'A little girl,' he mumbled against her mouth, as though he could not bear to be more than a whisper away from her skin. 'I hope we have a little girl next, who looks just like her beautiful mother.'

'I shall not care what she looks like. I shall love her for herself!'

'As you have loved Harry,' he agreed. 'Even though he was *my* son.'

'No,' she murmured back. 'It was never that way. When I thought you were dead, I mourned you. It felt as though all I had left of you was Harry.'

'Oh, Nell,' he said, crushing her in his arms. 'I do not deserve such happiness. I cannot believe I have been so fortunate as to find my way back to you.'

'Well, Christmas,' she said, 'is the season of miracles.'

Outside in the passage, Harry punched the air, doing a silent dance of victory. He had a father, a proper father, who could see how wonderful his ma was at last. They would all go to live in a big house, where he would have as much to eat as he could ever want, and play in woods where nobody could tell him he was trespassing.

Then suddenly he realised how significant it was that his ma had said Christmas was a time for miracles. His pa had come back right after he had challenged God to send him a father for Christmas. Dashing to the kitchen, he stuffed his feet into his boots, then ran, slithering and slipping over the icy ruts, all the way down the lane to the churchyard.

This time he paused long enough to snatch off his cap *before* he barrelled in through the door.

He was greeted by the smell of freshly cut greenery. A group of village women were tying bunches of holly onto the choir stalls in readiness for the Christmas services. When they saw who had come in, they turned back to their work, contemptuously ignoring the outcast son of, as they believed, the village's scarlet woman.

Wouldn't they be sorry when they found out he was going to be a viscount when he grew up!

His heart swelling with emotion, Harry made his way down the central aisle until he stood beneath the stained glass window of the Madonna. He grinned up at her as she smiled serenely down at the Christ child in her arms.

Very quietly, so the gossiping women could not hear him, he said, 'Last time I came in here I told you I didn't believe in Christmas. But I do now. You sent me my pa back—my real pa—which is even better than what I asked for. And he's going to give Ma a baby, so we will be a proper family. Thank you.'

Having paid his dues, Harry turned, stuffed his hands in his jacket pockets, and sauntered back down the aisle. He had just got to the door when his face lit with a mischievous grin.

'Phew!' He chuckled, glancing one last time over his shoulder. 'When you decide to answer somebody's prayer, you don't do it by halves, do you?'

* * * * *

Dear Reader,

Although I've always loved the holiday time of year and all the parties, presents, decorations and festivities, I think the real reason that Christmas is my favourite holiday is the feeling of hope that surrounds us then. Hope that we'll see family members and friends we haven't lately seen. Hope that we'll find just the perfect gift for that special person in our lives. Hope that the coming year will be filled with health, happiness and everything important to us.

So, it is with that hope in mind that I invite you to read my novella, "Blame It On the Mistletoe". It has all the elements I think are so important during this time – family, friends, presents, hope and, most importantly, love.

I wish you all the happiness and health and good things that this season can bring to you and hope that you find yourself among friends and family to celebrate.

Merry Christmas and Happy Holidays to you!

Terri

BLAME IT ON
THE MISTLETOE

TERRI BRISBIN

I'd like to dedicate this story to another pair of young lovers, my son Matt and his wife Carrie. They fill my life with reasons and opportunities to be a better person and a better mom, and they fill my holidays with fun and love and hope for a fabulous future. To Matt and Carrie – may your love fill your life together with the same happiness you've brought me.

Chapter One

The flames soared over the wide bowl, sending blue transparent sheets of searing heat above and distorting the faces of those bending closest to plan their attack. As Julia Fairchild watched the antics of the young men gathered around the table in her brother-by-marriage's drawing room, she wondered if they'd lost their wits as a result of too much imbibing of spirits, or if they'd simply been born without them.

Well, they were Englishmen, she thought with a sigh, so it could be either.

The next one designated—a Mr Jeremy Stockton, if she remembered his name correctly, pulled up his sleeve and wiggled his fingers, readying them for his attempt. Waving his arm over the flaming brandy, he then plunged his hand in and successfully plucked one of the floating raisins from its surface. Those watching and those awaiting their turn cheered him on for his achievement as he popped the heated sweet in his mouth.

Julia was about to turn away from the frivolous behaviour when she glimpsed a familiar face above the flames. She dreaded giving the appearance of interest in the antics being played out in part because of her, but she wanted a closer look at the man across the drawing room, and stepped closer to the group surrounding the table and bowl. He stood stiffly next to one of the windows, peering out at she knew not what, and leaning slightly against the ornate carved trim around the ceiling-to-floor window.

Julia studied his face from the side and tried to decide if he truly was Iain MacLerie. Before she could, those playing Snapdragon cheered, and she glanced over to see what had caused this new uproar. Apparently Mr Stockton was not satisfied with one successful grab; he'd gone again and burned the hair on his forearm.

Stupid fop, she thought. She might even have mouthed the words to herself, never dreaming someone would notice her impolite behaviour. But in that moment the man across the room chose to turn and meet her gaze. Even from here she could tell he fought the smile that tried to alight on his face as he recognised her words.

It *was* Iain! He was here!

Now Julia could see his whole face, though he was older and more changed now than the last time she'd seen him, she knew him immediately. Without much thought to proprieties, she left the small group of women with whom she stood and walked across the room to speak to him. Only when she moved closer to him did she spy the thick walking stick in his left hand.

There was so much more than a few years between them now, for that piece of wood spoke of his months and months of pain and recovery after a carriage accident had nearly taken his life four years past. It had taken his parents' lives. Four years during which he'd withdrawn from his family and from life to work diligently on his recuperation—one that physicians had thought impossible. Now he stood before her so much more a man than the boy she'd been half in love with for as long as she could remember.

A man who'd seen her discourteous insult a few minutes before. A man she wanted to throw her arms around and welcome back to their annual Christmas gathering. A man who, as though he could read her thoughts, gave her a warning glance from his steely grey eyes that said he would not or could not accept sympathy or pity easily or well.

Julia dipped in a polite curtsy before him, and watched as he bowed in reply. The years of struggle and pain were etched on his face and in those eyes, and the changes were obvious to anyone who had known him as a younger man.

'Miss Fairchild,' he said softly. So formal, then?

'Mr MacLerie,' she answered. Damn the man!

'You have just thought something wicked, have you not? I saw that familiar flash that usually speaks of a regrettable lapse in your behaviour.' His words teased and spoke of a shared past, even if his tone wasn't as welcoming as she'd hoped when she'd spied him.

'A lady never tells, sir.' Julia peered round at the others in the room, before leaning in to offer a conspiring whisper. 'And neither would a gentleman if he were to witness a lady's indiscretion.'

'I could write a book about your—' he began, before she placed her hand over his lips.

'Iain, please!' she whispered.

He lifted her hand away, but did not release it immediately. Instead he held it out and tilted his head, inspecting her from the tips of her pale blue slippers to the matching ribbons entwined in her hair.

Such things had never mattered to her; she wore them more as a favor to her sister than because of any real interest on her own part. But now, after seeing the strange glint in Iain's eyes as he took in her appearance, Julia was gladdened that she had taken time at her toilet for this evening's festivities.

'You look lovely, Julia.'

She felt the unwelcome heat of a blush creeping into her cheeks and lifted her hand from his. 'And you look well.'

Was it the wrong thing to say to him? His expression seemed to harden before her eyes, and he appeared ready to bolt from her side at this reminder of his condition.

'Iain, wait—please,' she said. 'It was not my intention to make you uncomfortable. I simply wished to greet you and tell you that I am… I am…' The words swirled in her brain, and each one sounded more personal and pitying than the last. At last she settled on the plainest. 'I am glad you are here, Iain.'

He nodded at her words, and shifted his position as though uncomfortable. 'And I am glad to see you too, Julia.'

Just as she was about to enquire of his plans—plans she'd already learned of from his aunt, Lady MacLerie—and express her unbecoming curiosity, the very same person approached.

'The Countess has announced there will be dancing in the red parlour, Julia, and she wishes you to join her there. This game is nearly done—and none too soon for my tastes,' she continued. She scorned stupidity as much as Julia did, and this game seemed the very height of it. 'Will you escort us there, Iain?'

She'd said it so matter-of-factly that Iain seemed to take no notice, and certainly no offence at it. He smiled, revealing the face Julia had known before, and shook his head.

'No, Aunt Clarinda. I fear my journey here today has done me in. I am sure,' he said, as he motioned to someone standing nearby, 'that my uncle will no doubt like that honour.'

'And will claim several dances for myself before relinquishing you to any other man,' Lord MacLerie said, smoothly taking hold of his wife's hand and offering his other arm to Julia. 'Anna has promised waltzes in addition to the customary country dances, and I know how much you like to waltz.' Somehow he'd managed to say the words so that he referred to both women, but Julia knew it was Clarinda of whom he spoke.

'Until the morning, then, Iain?' Clarinda asked as they began to walk away. 'The staff here know what a real breakfast meal is, and it is something not to be missed.'

'Until then, Aunt Clarinda, Uncle Robert.'

Julia slowed her steps, hoping to hear one more name. If Lord or Lady MacLerie noticed they did not indicate so. And then it came at last.

'Miss Fairchild.'

She nodded without looking back, and then picked up her pace once more, unable to comprehend why hearing Iain say her name should be so important to her. It was not as though she had been waiting for him or watching for his arrival at the Christmas festivities. It was not as though she'd asked anyone about the possibility of his attendance here.

She had not. But once the chance of it had been mentioned, in a casual comment made by her sister Anna to Lady MacLerie, it had been all she could think upon. At last she would have a chance to see how he had fared since his accident.

Her letters to him had been returned unopened, and reports on his condition had come only through her sister or Lady MacLerie. They had been vague and sometimes disconcerting. Julia had always been certain they were keeping the worst from her, and his appearance now only confirmed her suspicions.

As they walked down the long corridor and up the stairs leading to the large parlour that would host the dancing this evening, she realised that Clarinda and her husband whispered only between themselves, and did not press her for any comments. Which, considering she had none to offer, was a good thing.

And that worried her even more—for she was never without words on a subject. Be they comforting or sharp or witty words, as the situation needed she had them. Until now. Try as she might to convince herself that she had no other reason for feeling a tightly wound sense of anticipation within her, Julia could feel that Iain's attendance here meant something more than just renewing an old acquaintance. She would put her mind to it and discover the reason for these strange feelings in the pit of her stomach.

They entered the parlour just as the musicians tuned their instruments, and the younger son of Lord and Lady Sutcliffe greeted Julia. He'd reserved a dance as soon as dinner had finished, and he held out his hand to guide her to the dance area in the centre of the room.

Soon the room whirled in time to the music, and Julia lost herself in the dance and the company and the evening's festivities—without ever realising that Iain watched her from the edge of the door.

It was not my intention to make you uncomfortable.
She'd spoken the words out of simple considera-tion but the pain of seeing Julia now tore a hole through his heart. *Uncomfortable* would never describe the humiliation he suffered knowing that he was less a man now than when last they'd met.

Iain had been hoping that the silly game would cover his arrival, but then she'd looked over and made that mischievous comment meant for no one to see, and caught his gaze. He'd prayed through every moment of their encounter that his leg would not fail beneath him, and that he would be able to smooth the grimace his face usually wore into something more appropriate for polite company.

More than anything he did not wish to embarrass

his uncle and aunt, who had been his stalwarts of support over these last four years of hell. If not for them, Iain would be locked still in his world of darkness and unyielding torment, unable to function or even remain on his feet as he did now, or worse— dead. Their relentless pursuit of new medical treatments for him and their refusal to allow him to curl into a ball and die when it would have been the easier path for him had earned them more than his love, it had earned them his gratitude and respect.

And his absolute word of honour that he would never fail to try his best for them.

So this evening, when he'd arrived and wanted nothing more than several large glasses of brandy, each with a dash of laudanum to ease his way into sleep after such an arduous journey, it had been their invitation to the gathering that had given him no choice. And when Julia had approached him with that look of wonder and concern on her lovely face it had been their presence, watching the exchange, that had given him the strength to remain on his feet.

But then, as he'd looked up the stairway to where all the guests had gone to reach the parlour for dancing, it had been that expression of wonder in Julia's luminous blue eyes that had made him begin the gruelling climb up. Lady Treybourne had arranged for a room for him on the main floor, so that using the stairs to reach most of the meals and gatherings would not be necessary.

Iain had followed at his own pace, and each spasm that shot through his left leg and into his hip had taunted him with the possibility of failure and falling. Watching her float up the stairs on his uncle's arm, carefully lifting the edge of her gown so that she did not trip, had made him want to take the chance to see her swirling like an angel around the dance floor. She had no idea of what her simple words had meant to him.

By the time he'd reached the second floor and made his way to the red parlour he was out of breath and sweating. Now Iain paused by the door, and took a glass of something from a passing servant's tray without caring that it was anything but wet. After downing it, he tugged his handkerchief from his pocket and dabbed at the moisture on his face. He rested most of his weight on his good leg and then looked around the room.

Couples in lines of four made their way through a country dance to the music of several violins, a cello and a pianoforte. He could see Julia in the second row of dancers, and watched as she made her way through the figures of the dance. She moved now with a gracefulness that in no way exposed her dreadful lack of it as a child. It was a difficult challenge to see any of that rumbustious child now, as she laughed and nodded in agreement at some comment made by her partner.

Iain caught his breath, watching as long as he dared

to—for someone would surely catch him gawping like a schoolboy soon—and then took a deep breath and prepared for the struggle ahead to return to the main floor of the house. As his leg screamed in protest with each pace away, and as he cursed himself for being such a fool, his heart answered the question he asked himself silently with every step.

Yes, it was worth even this much pain to see her dance.

It took some time to make his way safely down the staircase, and it took all his concentration to keep his leg from buckling under him. So much concentration that he didn't see her standing above at the railing, watching his every move...

'Well, that did not go as I expected it would,' Anna, Countess of Treybourne, offered.

'You never listen to me, Anna,' replied her best friend Clarinda. 'I told you that Julia's reticence regarding attachments of the heart was not as steadfast as you thought. You chose to ignore my words of wisdom.'

Anna and Clarinda stood in the hall along from the parlour, far enough into an alcove so that her sister could not see them but they could watch her. And they did.

No sooner had Clarinda's nephew left the parlour and begun his journey down the stairs than Julia had followed him out of the parlour, watching him through the railing of the staircase. Anna thought it did not take a scholar to recognise the look on her younger sister's face.

'I never said never, Clarinda. I always suspected that the right man would break through her resistance—much as Trey did mine.'

They stood silently and watched the longing on Julia's face increase with each step away that Iain took. Neither wanted to say what they were both thinking. Then Anna did. Julia was, after all, her sister and her responsibility.

'Regardless of any tender feelings, he is not the right man for her.'

'Regardless,' Clarinda replied, nodding in agreement.

'For so many reasons,' Anna added.

'For ever so many reasons,' Clarinda said, with a sad tone in her voice.

Anna felt the sting of tears burning in her eyes and blinked them away. 'But it is Christmas time. There will be time for the realities of life after the holiday is over.'

Clarinda stepped out of the alcove with her and nodded, her own eyes glassy with tears too.

'And there could always be a miracle. A Christmas miracle of a sort.'

Anna glanced at her dearest friend and agreed. 'A Christmas miracle, indeed.'

And as they passed Julia at the railing they looked away, offering up a prayer for just such a thing.

Chapter Two

She woke at dawn, as was her custom, but the sun sitting low in the winter sky did not offer much light to the morning. Its pale rays barely had the strength to pass through the curtains into her rooms, and it was more habit than signal that bade her seek out the new day.

Stretching within the thick cocoon of her bedcovers, Julia thought about the possibility of seeing Iain this morning—and that spurred her to climb from the warmth of her bed.

Dressing in a sensible day gown, short boots and a woollen shawl, Julia refused the maid's attempts to arrange her hair in some elaborate style and chose a simple chignon instead, leaving a few strands loose around her face. Draping the shawl around her shoulders, she let the ends of the plaid fall loosely over her arm, and made her way to the smaller dining room on the first floor of the house, where breakfast would be served in a more casual way than in the formal dining room above stairs.

As she reached the room, she took a deep, calming breath and stood in the corridor, savouring the last moment of peace she would enjoy for the entire day. Gathering her shawl tighter, and wrapping her formidable sense of humour around her, she glanced at the footman attending the door. It had taken her more than a year to break the habit of opening doors for herself. More than a year before she stopped trying to make the footmen laugh or move. And more than a year before she could force herself to speak openly in front of the too-numerous-for-her-taste servants as though they were not present.

She did not belong here.

The passage of the more than five years during which she'd lived with her sister and her brother-by-marriage the Earl of Treybourne had not lessened those feelings within her heart and soul. She could not survive in this world of nobility and wealth and pretence. Her sister had become accustomed to it, for the love Anna bore her husband had eased her transition from a comfortable but tenuous life in Edinburgh to this secure and more worldly one on the Earl's Northumbrian estate. Or any of his others.

She did this only for the love she bore Anna and Trey.

As she nodded to the footman to open the door, she reminded herself again of the debt she owed her sister and brother-by-marriage. If not for Anna, simply put, she would have perished. If not for Trey she'd not have enjoyed the education and the many luxuries and opportunities his wealth and his name had been able to provide her and her sister—and their causes.

Julia entered the dining room and paused. Every young man she'd sought to avoid sat at the large oval table, and the one she sought did not. They stood at her entrance and bowed courteously. Returning their polite gesture, she looked for a place to sit and noticed only two or three women at table. It was not Anna's custom to miss breakfast, and her absence surprised Julia.

In the next instant every man save one had scurried around the table, pulling out any empty chair for her. Then she spied Trey, sitting at the opposite end of a table made for thirty and clearly fighting the urge to laugh. Without hesitation she walked to the open chair nearest him, and allowed Mr Sutton to assist her.

'Good morning, my lord,' she said as she eased into her chair. 'I hope this morning finds you well?'

'Good morning, Julia,' Trey replied. He folded his newspaper and laid it down, and gifted her with a mischievous smile. 'So what, pray tell, are your plans for the day?' He paused, but she could tell he had not finished. She was not out of danger yet. 'Have you found a partner yet for charades this evening?'

Spoons clattered on fine porcelain. Conversations halted. Heads turned, eyes stared, and ears perked up all round her. Julia smiled at Trey—a smile she hoped gifted him with all the promises of retribution she felt at that moment, but one which appeared pleasant enough to those looking on. He knew how distasteful this entire Marriage Mart excuse for Christmas festivities was to her. But he also loved his wife, and would do anything for her—for Julia too, for that matter, especially if he believed it to her gain.

'I thank you for your interest, my lord. I have chosen a partner, but would prefer not to reveal a name for fear of the displeasure of the rest of your esteemed guests.'

Julia turned and smiled demurely at the men who watched their exchange. If she held it for much longer she swore her mouth would freeze in such a position and never move again. One of the butlers placed a plate in front of her, so she unfolded a crisp linen napkin and dropped it in her lap.

'Thank you, John,' she said quietly, and she waited for him to step away before continuing. Turning back to Trey, she noticed his sheepish expression and seized on his apparent guilt. 'And you, my lord? Who will you be partnering for the games this evening?'

Trey sipped from his cup before answering. 'I will be but a watcher, Miss Fairchild. It would hardly seem fair to oppose my own guests.'

'Just so, my lord.'

She let the conversation wane as she ate the perfectly seasoned coddled eggs and slices of bacon and fried bread. When the butler had removed her plate and filled her cup with her favourite brew of tea, she leaned back.

'What are your plans for the day, my lord? Had I heard correctly about a visit to your new stables?'

'Yes, Miss Fairchild. Lord MacLerie and I have invested in a new racer. I have invited the men to view its arrival today.'

'How exciting!' She looked across and down the table at the young men there, and gifted them with her most feminine smile. 'I do envy you all, but I must see to Lady Treybourne and aid her in her plans for this evening's festivities.'

Julia gave them no chance to intervene with her escape as she stood and waited for the butler to assist her with her chair. Trey rose and offered a courteous bow, as did every other man in the room. Trey could stop her in her place if he wished, but apparently he'd teased her enough this morn. With a nod of acceptance, she walked out as quickly as she could without appearing unseemly, and made her way to her sister's chambers.

Inhaling the scent of the many pine branches and wreaths that decorated the doorways and windows, Julia smiled. In spite of Wesley Hall's size, her sister managed to make it seem small and homey. Different from their simple Edinburgh townhouse, where she'd spent the Christmases of her childhood, or the Highland estate of the MacLeries, Trey's manor was far larger and grander. Only Anna's small touches— using some of the smaller rooms for family gatherings, bringing their most favourite furnishings from Edinburgh and gathering their dearest friends and family around them—made it less overwhelming.

Reaching the first floor above, Julia walked down the corridor that led to the family's rooms and passed the door to Trey's chambers. She knew, as did everyone at Wesley Hall, that her sister and her brother-by-marriage shared a bedchamber, but Julia would never presume to call on Anna there. Reaching the last door, she knocked softly and waited. When no one answered, she opened it a crack and spoke her sister's name.

'Anna?' Then, when no reply was heard, she called a bit louder. 'Anna?'

The sounds emanating from the dressing room between the lord and lady's chambers enlightened her to several things at once. First, Anna was ill. Second, Anna was ill in the morning. And third, and most happily, Anna was carrying another child. Julia recognised the sounds and symptoms from Anna's last two pregnancies, and knew her absence from breakfast this morn would be the first of many.

Mary, the maid who served her sister most closely entered from the dressing room and took note of Julia as she walked to the bed and began straightening it.

'The Countess is a little ill right now, miss. If you would call on her later? Perhaps when she meets with Mrs Herman to discuss this evening's plans?' Mary smiled softly then, reassuring her of the situation. 'I will tell her you were here.'

Ah. Everything was well in hand if the capable Mrs Herman had control. Wesley Hall's housekeeper had magical powers, or at least it seemed that way to Julia, for nothing was impossible for the woman. Any request from family or guest was fulfilled. Any special arrangement handled. Any help needed—especially by a young Scottish girl new to this English nobleman's life and home—was provided, and sometimes before it was even asked for.

For now, Julia had some time to herself, and decided that the Earl's spacious and well-filled private library was the place to hide away from the maddening attentions of the young men in residence for most of the Christmas holiday. Once back on the main floor, she turned and went in the opposite direction to the dining room, hoping to arrive in her hiding place before the men left for the stables. The voices in the hall as she pushed the door closed warned her of their approach.

Once they'd passed her refuge, she sought out her

favourite place in Wesley Hall: a small alcove, separated from the rest of the library by two free-standing bookshelves that reached from floor to ceiling. Tugging the large cushioned chair there closer to the windows, Julia claimed her current book and curled up in it. With her book resting on her lap, her woollen shawl wrapped around her shoulders and the sight of the snow-covered fields in the windows before her, she relaxed for the first time in many days.

Keeping up the façade of enjoying these traditions of courtship was tiring. The constant and requisite smile, the need always to be present and the requirement to be pleasant to any and all buffoons and idiots who happened to be male, of any age, with a certain level of fortune or title, were not things that came easily to her.

But she would do almost anything for her sister, and if allowing this pursuit of men with thoughts of marriage was something that pleased Anna, she would tolerate it. Julia knew more than either Anna or Trey would ever admit about the price of Anna's support of her little family during the years when Julia had been too young to worry about such things. Julia knew what Anna had suffered to keep her and her aunt in a decent house, with food on the table and clothes on their backs. And, though she could never openly acknowledge it, Julia would honour her for that cost nonetheless.

Even if it meant acting the proper English young lady and accepting a husband of her sister and brother-by-marriage's choosing.

Julia shifted in the chair and drew her legs up, tucking them under her and arranging her gown so that there was no hint of this small impropriety visible. Leaning her head back against the cushions, she sighed.

The thought of ringing for chocolate drifted out of her mind as the urgings of lost hours of sleep crept in. Soon Julia found herself dreaming of dancing with Iain in the ballroom above, not worrying about doing the correct thing or about being the unwanted Scottish marriage prize.

Chapter Three

Iain watched as the group of young men, led by his uncle and the Earl, left the house and strode off in the direction of the stables. The coating of snow made it a slippery going, but no one seemed to have difficulty with it. Iain now had some time to finish his review of the contracts he carried for his uncle's signature before he returned from the outing.

The pang of loss struck once more as he envied the men who could walk without pain and ride a horse as he'd used to. Now he was condemned to constant pain and to never pursuing his favourite pastime of riding. Taking a full breath in, and letting it out, he tried to release the anger that sat deep within him at moments like this.

He was alive, he told himself.

He could walk.

After allowing himself a brief time to accept once more these changes and challenges in his life, he shook off the tendency to wallow in self-pity. With his satchel in one hand and his walking stick in the other, Iain followed his uncle's directions to the Earl's private library. From the expression in his eyes earlier, Iain suspected his uncle would use a need to meet Iain as his excuse for escape during the tour of the stables. Lord Robert MacLerie did not suffer idle young men well.

With the assistance of a footman after a turn down the wrong corridor took him to the kitchen, Iain reached the library and opened the door. Stepping inside, he caught sight of two matching desks on the far side of the room. So the gossip had not simply been worthless speculation, then? The Earl and the Countess did work together on their many financial concerns, including his orphanages and her schools. And on their magazine, the *Scottish Monthly Gazette*.

Making his way across the library, he laid his satchel on the larger desk and took a moment to examine the room more closely. As he ran his hand over the mahogany desk he turned and leaned against it, using it to support his weight. The smaller desk, with its vase of hothouse roses, was not the only feminine touch in what he would have assumed to be a bastion of masculinity.

Portraits of children and family groups filled one

wall, and Iain recognised them as being of the Earl and Countess's two sons and the Earl's natural daughter. Large cushions, colourful and embroidered, padded any piece of wooden furniture throughout the library. In the spirit of the Christmas festivities, holly and ivy encircled the candles on the mantel, and several smaller tables spread around the room.

Inhaling deeply, he savoured the scents that filled the room and created such a pleasurable ambience before sitting down to his work. It was as he walked to the other side of the desk that he noticed it—a scent that did not match the others. Instead of Christmas puddings and trimmings of pine, it reminded him of the fields of summer lavender near his home in the Highlands.

Looking around for some sachet left behind by the Countess, he found none. It was then that he spotted it—masked by the tall bookcases, a secluded sitting area near the windows at the corner of the room. Indeed, the corner of the house. Iain noticed that the scent of lavender grew stronger as he approached the nook. When the sound of soft snoring could be heard, he knew he was not alone. Reaching the first bookcase, he leaned round and peeped within.

The soft rays of morning sun dappled her hair, making it appear to be a multitude of colours—wheatgold, blonde, and even a touch of the palest of browns.

Most of it was caught up in some kind of bun, but soft wisps curled around her cheeks and framed her face.

Last evening she had had every appearance of a proper English young lady, but this morn—this morn she looked like a country lass fresh from the Highlands, wrapped in a tartan shawl, with a plain dress. He could imagine her walking the halls of his uncle's home or sitting in their library—though it was not as impressive as this one—or running wild in the tall summer grasses of their lands.

Julia's head lay back on the chair, and her mouth was open slightly, relaxed in sleep. None of the boyish lass of childhood could be seen now as he watched her silently from his place. She spoke and shifted in her chair, and Iain waited for her to wake. Instead she settled deeper into the large chair's cushions, and slept on, unaware of his perusal.

Knowing that his uncle's arrival was fast approaching, Iain took a step closer to wake her. Before he could, her eyelids fluttered and opened. Her surprise could not have been more than his own as she spoke his name in a sleep-deepened voice that sent tremors of awareness through him.

'Iain.'

Desire pierced him in a way he'd not expected possible at the sound of his name on her lips. He'd taken several steps forward before the sleep cleared from her eyes and she realised he was standing before her. He watched as the realisation struck her and she sat up, straightening her gown and shawl and placing her once-hidden feet back on the floor.

'Oh, Iain, it is you,' she said softly, becoming the English young lady once more. 'I did not hear you come in.'

With a spurt of true devilment aimed at trying to replace the hunger and desire that filled him, he leaned closer and whispered to her. 'Miss Fairchild, I fear you snore in your sleep.'

She did not attempt to rise from the chair, and he did not move back to give her room to do so. He'd left his walking stick on the desk, so he used the arms of the chair for support, bringing him into closer proximity to Julia.

'I could hear it from the other side of his lord-ship's library.'

'Surely not,' she whispered, looking around as though checking to discover if only he had heard it. 'A gentleman would not mention something so personal, sir.'

Not certain if that reminder was for him or for herself, he laughed softly. 'I mention it only to aid you in your attempts to present yourself as a proper lady, Miss Fairchild.'

His teasing went awry, for a flash of hurt filled her eyes and she gasped, 'I *am* a proper lady, Iain,' she said. Her voice did not carry the conviction of her words, though. It trembled even, and he felt the meanest cad for teasing her in a way that obviously caused her pain. But her words revealed more to him than most men here would understand.

'Do not ever let them convince you that you are not as proper and as much a lady as any raised in one of their households, Julia!'

He could not hold back the anger in his voice. He'd faced the jibes and slanders of the ignorant, aimed at his so-called 'barbarian' background, but had never thought it would affect Julia. Her manners, her appearance, even her voice spoke of being gently born and raised—and were not those that polite society seemed to expect from Highlanders. Or Scots, for that matter. He'd have hoped that the Earl's protection would have prevented such hurtful behaviours, but Iain knew the truth—it had simply driven it out of sight, it had not put a stop to it.

Iain stepped back then, allowing her to stand, but his balance was not good and he shifted, trying to regain his equilibrium. Never a shy flower, Julia reached out and grabbed his waist to keep him from falling to the floor. Clutching the fabric of his jacket, she held onto him until he could right himself.

She stood nearly tall enough for the top of her head to fit comfortably under his chin. If he allowed her to stand so. But, as the humiliation of his disability sank in, he wanted to distance himself from her, and not allow such weakness as afflicted him to show so clearly. Stepping back once more, he found her still gripping his jacket, and his step back was followed by her step forward, doing nothing to increase the space between them.

'Do not worry, Iain,' she said, looking up into his eyes. 'I have you now.'

He rested his hands on her shoulders then, not certain who was holding up whom in that moment. His heart pounded in his chest, and though he'd have liked to convince himself it was because of his exertions, he knew better.

It was her.

In this near-embrace of a stance he could inhale her scent, even feel the rise and fall of her own breathing. When she gazed at him so, he forgot their years spent as children together, and his attempts to free himself from the entanglement offered by a coltish young girl with doe eyes. He forgot their years spent apart and the differences between them. He forgot the pain and the suffering in his life.

All he could think of was her.

But when she lifted her face to his, tilting her head back and positioning her mouth exactly where it needed to be for him to kiss her, Iain forgot all of it. And he nearly forgot his place. For the temptation to touch his lips to hers, to taste her and to feel her mouth against his, grew strong so quickly.

He was a disabled man from the wilds of Scotland who would never walk without pain.

She was the young ward of a powerful nobleman, destined to travel the world.

He had no prospects other than those his uncle gave him.

She would marry well and live in the highest levels of society.

He had loved her for years.

She would belong to another.

Even as those thoughts flashed through his mind, even knowing everything that kept them apart, at this moment he wanted to believe she was his and his alone. And that meant kissing her, as he'd wanted to since he'd seen her across the drawing room last evening, with mischief in her eyes and the face of an angel.

Fighting the growing urge within him with the same self-control that had seen him live when given no chance, he closed his eyes and inhaled her scent again. A grave mistake, that. Waves of lavender teased and tormented him, then released him to follow his desire. Tilting his head, he captured her lips with his own, feeling their softness beneath his.

If it had ended then and there it would have been enough to last him his whole life, but it did not.

When Julia slid her hands under his jacket and around his back he could not step away. Oh, he could have broken free of her grasp—but, damn his fool heart, he did not want to leave her embrace. It was the sigh that she made, the softest of sounds, that destroyed any hope he had of holding on to his control and allowing her to leave unscathed.

Iain turned his face, allowing him to touch her mouth more fully and to tease those bow lips into opening for his tongue. Once more she missed an opportunity to slow him down or to stop him with her welcoming gestures. He felt her fingers rubbing small circles on his back, felt that male part of him harden and lengthen in anticipation of more, and felt her breathing become faster and lighter as he kissed her deeply.

Sweeping his tongue into her mouth, he tasted her essence and knew he would never be satisfied with another. She imitated his movements, touched and tasted his mouth, sucking gently on his tongue and opening wider as she did. His body was ready to proceed. He could not get harder than he was. But his mind knew they could go no further along this path.

Julia felt her body melting against his—her legs seemed to buckle beneath her, and only by holding on tighter did she keep her balance. The heat of his mouth as he tasted her fired something deep within her body and soul, and she wanted more. She felt his hands leave her shoulders and slide down over her arms to rest on her waist, drawing her closer to him. Meeting him thigh to thigh and chest to chest, she recognised the changes in his body and wondered at those inside hers.

An aching had begun deep within her, and it connected somehow to the throbbing between her legs. Her breasts grew sensitive. Even his encompassing embrace seemed to make them swell and the tips grow tighter and tighter. Julia's body wanted…wanted *something*… She leaned against Iain, seeking it.

His mouth left hers and she tried to follow, but his lips kissed the edge of her jaw and then moved back towards her ear. She trembled as shivers pulsed up and down her spine. Just when he reached the ticklish spot below her ear, she noticed the door to the library open behind them.

'Julia,' he whispered, and as he kissed her there, sending even more tremors through her.

'Iain?' Lord Robert called from across the room.

She felt his surprise, and then his awkwardness as he released her and stepped back. Julia forced her hands to let him go, and watched as the soft expression on his face as he'd kissed her changed into something she could not decipher.

Humiliation?

Regret?

Pain?

Whatever it was, he drew it back, and soon a polite smile sat there in its stead. Sheltered from his uncle's immediate gaze by his position, Julia smoothed the loose strands of hair from her face and took a deep breath. In spite of the abrupt ending to their embrace and to his kiss, her body ached for more.

She was about to break the uncomfortable silence by saying something when Lord Robert stepped into the breach.

'Ah, Julia. You are here. Clarinda was looking for you just now.' Without pause he turned back and opened the door, calling out to his wife. 'Clarinda— Julia is here.'

The short interruption gave them a chance to regain their senses, and Julia gathered her shawl around her, taking a deep breath and letting it out. She watched as Iain tried to stabilise himself, and realised he needed his walking stick. She spied it on the desk and brought it to him. A curt nod was his only response.

By the time Clarinda entered the library, they stood a respectable distance from one another. The emotional chasm that had opened between them as their kiss was interrupted was much wider, for Julia could almost feel him drawing away from her.

'Iain…' she said. She paused, knowing that some line had been crossed, yet not knowing what to say to him.

A proper young lady should be scandalised to have been kissed in such a manner. A proper young lady should have pushed him away and fought any inappropriate advances. A proper young lady would never have enjoyed such unseemly and inappropriate liberties as he had taken with her. But she had enjoyed every scandalous second of his touch, of his embrace, of his kisses.

'Julia, I should not have—' he whispered, stopping as his aunt walked to his side.

'Your sister has quite recovered from her bout of…' Clarinda paused, clearly unsure of how much to reveal about Anna's delicate condition. 'Illness…' was the word she settled on. 'She asked me to find you.'

'And Iain and I have business to discuss, so we will detain you no longer,' Robert added gallantly. Opening the door wider, he stepped back and allowed Julia and Clarinda to pass.

Julia had no choice but to follow her sister's friend from the room. Although no words had passed between them, she could tell that Iain had been as affected by their encounter as she had. His eyes carried a confused expression, he stood stiffly and ill-at-ease, and she would swear it was not related to his injury. His body had responded to hers.

Although her sister would most likely be shocked, Julia understood what Iain's body had done when he kissed her. She had not gained this many years without hearing the comments of the young women at Anna's School for Unfortunates in Edinburgh. Or without noticing the realities of life in the country while visiting the MacLeries' Highland estates. Without overhearing Anna telling her closest and dearest friend about losing her virtue while in service as a governess.

He desired her.

In spite of the years that had separated them. In spite of the trials that he had faced in those years and the growth she'd experienced. In spite of his plans for his future and her sister's for hers.

He desired her. As a man desired a woman.

A certain awareness of the change between them flooded her senses. No more child and pest—a lass chasing at his feet, a nuisance to be borne. She was a woman, and he recognised it. But more importantly for the first time she *felt* it.

Clarinda stopped and faced her, and Julia nearly lost all the self-confidence his kiss had given her. Could Clarinda tell from just looking at her that something was different? She did not feel guilty about what they'd shared, but did it show?

Clarinda's exclamation and expression said it all. 'I told Anna not to put mistletoe in that secluded corner!'

Julia could not resist the urge to touch her lips— for surely they had given her away? Or the blush that heated her cheeks—had that been the sign that exposed her actions to Clarinda? Turning back towards the library, Julia noticed for the first time the mistletoe branches tied in bright ribbons hanging from the ceiling over Iain's head.

Robert closed the library door with a nod at her, and Julia faced Clarinda once more.

'Come now, Julia. Anna is waiting for you,' she said, dragging her up the stairs towards her sister's chambers. As they reached the landing at the top, Clarinda paused to readjust Julia's hair and then winked at her. 'Remember, if she asks any questions blame it on the mistletoe.'

Chapter Four

Iain had to respect his uncle's ability to bide his time and ignore the obvious breach of proper behaviour.

They'd been at their meeting since this morning, reviewing supplies and orders, planning for additions to the Laird's estates in the Highlands and his house in Edinburgh, as well as expanding their market in England and Wales. Robert MacLerie had taken over the MacLerie clan and its businesses on his father's unexpected death just over a year ago, and he had not looked back.

And the new Marquess of Douran had dragged Iain into the thick of it, kicking and screaming.

No excuse worked to make the Laird lose interest in his orphaned and poor relation—neither Iain's near-death carriage accident, nor his lack of business training and even the formal education usually needed for such a post, and not even his advisors' arguments against giving his nephew such responsibilities had worked.

Now, hours after Robert had observed the kiss, Iain waited uncomfortably for the inevitable reprimand to come. Why had his uncle been the one to witness his lapse? A juvenile sense of guilt filled him—not unlike the time his uncle had caught him kissing the kitchen maid at Broch Dubh.

However, Miss Julia Fairchild was no kitchen maid.

Realising his leg was beginning to tighten, Iain pushed back from the desk and stood. Using the edge of the desk for support, he tried to stretch the muscles before they became completely enveloped in pain. Too much sitting, too much standing—too much of any activity or lack of it—caused the terrible spasms to begin.

Taking a few careful steps around the desk, dragging his right leg and putting most of his weight on his left, Iain paused to gain his balance before standing up straight.

'The journey yesterday took its toll, then?' his uncle asked.

When Iain looked up, he saw that Robert had been watching his every move. 'It did—more so than I ever expected.' His leg began to buckle then, as if to answer the question itself. 'I did not mean to interrupt your reading, sir.' He nodded at the pile of papers in front of his uncle.

'And you did not. But the words seem to be dancing on the papers, out of focus. I think it is time for us to finish for the day.'

Robert gathered up the papers before him and started to organise them. Iain took a step towards the desk. It was his job to handle the Laird's business files, after all. But his uncle stopped him with a shake of his head.

'Walk a bit—stretch your legs. I can see to these.'

Iain accepted the offer and walked slowly to the far wall pausing to examine the paintings as he passed. Iain had not realised how different this household was until just this morn and the children depicted here spoke of its unconventionality.

The Earl was of noble English blood, while his Countess was Scottish gentry. The Earl's family could trace their heritage back to the Conqueror, while the Countess made no such claims. The Earl had been raised among the wealthiest in the land, while the Countess had earned a living as a governess before beginning her own business among the working class.

Yet here they merged family backgrounds, business and charity interests, cultures and even children. Though it was a practice not accepted by most polite society, the Earl of Treybourne had dispensed with the usual hypocrisy of such a situation and recognised his natural daughter. Even more surprising, the Countess allowed her to be raised alongside their legitimate children. And if a few society hostesses did not include them on their guest lists, the Earl and the Countess took no mind, seeking only the company of those who would raise no issue of it. Of course only the foolish did not include the wealthy and influential Earl of Treybourne, who also happened to be the heir to the Marquess of Dursby.

Reaching the far wall and turning back, Iain discovered his uncle once more watching his every step. Taking in a deep breath and letting it out, he decided to broach the subject that they had so studiously avoided for hours.

'I intend to apologise to Miss Fairchild and leave as soon as we conclude our business, sir. I understand how…' His words drifted off, because the wrong ones kept coming to mind.

Lovely.

Desirable.

Delicious.

All ways he would describe the kiss *and* the young woman, but none appropriate when trying to mitigate one's behaviour.

'I know you two spent much time together when she visited Broch Dubh as a child, but I thought it was nothing more than a childhood fancy.'

Iain could not lie to this man. 'As did I. Aunt

Clarinda and the Countess passed on a few letters from Julia during my convalescence, but I did not read them and have not spoken to her for five years.' He walked closer and smiled. 'Until I saw the bewitching young woman across the room last evening I had no idea of the beauty she'd grown to be these last years.'

'Iain,' Robert said as he stood and approached his side. 'The Earl and Countess have expectations…' Robert stuttered then, as though his words were jumbled in his brain. 'Several of the young men included in this Christmas gathering…'

Taking pity on his uncle, who was clearly as uncomfortable discussing the situation as he, Iain shook his head. 'Sir, I understand the situation fully. I only wish I could explain why I did it,' he glanced over at the secluded corner and back to his uncle.

'Heh?' His uncle laughed then. 'Any fool with eyes could tell you why you did it, Iain. Even an old married man like me cannot miss the appeal of such a one as Miss Julia.' Putting a hand on his shoulder, his uncle continued, 'But appreciating such a young woman and acting on it are two different things.'

Instead of bringing comfort, the hand felt heavy, weighing down Iain's heart in a way he could not explain. 'I understand, sir. Truly.' He turned now and faced the Laird. 'I do not aim for something I cannot attain.'

Walking back to the desk, he stumbled on the last step. His mind was already rebelling against the possibility of never seeing her again.

His uncle's strong hand on his arm steadied his stance. 'I would expect nothing less from you, Iain. But I know that your aunt knows what happened between you and Julia, even if she saw nothing. I will have to answer her questions when next we meet. I simply wish to remind you of your duties and of the lady's honour.'

Iain nodded his head and picked up the remaining folders on the desk, stuffing them somewhat haphazardly into his satchel. 'Would you like to continue after dinner, then?'

'From the look on your face, I think we have done enough for this day. Give yourself a rest tonight and we can finish in the morning. Another day or so and you can continue on to London.'

Not certain if that was a dismissal or a reprieve, Iain picked up his satchel, grasped his walking stick in his hand, and offered a slight bow to his uncle on leaving.

In that moment he wished more than he ever had in the years since the accident that he could run. His chest burned with unreleased pain and he wanted nothing more than to drop his satchel and his stick and run: down the hall, out of the Earl's country house and away. Far enough away to avoid the truth he now knew—he had much stronger feelings for Julia than he could have dreamed possible.

* * *

Robert MacLerie, Marquess of Douran, watched his nephew's confusion as he gathered up his belongings and left. The pain he spied on Iain's face was not all physical, and not all caused by the terrible damage the overturning carriage had caused. Running his hands through his hair, he worried on what else he had witnessed in the Earl's library this morning.

Not just the kiss exchanged by Iain and Julia.

Oh, aye, that kiss was enough to worry over, but Robert had seen something in Iain that he'd thought the pain and suffering had obliterated—a young man's longing for a lovely young woman. Something he had never dared hoped to see after the physicians' dire predictions.

That, along with Iain's obvious interest in Julia, told Robert that trouble was on the way.

Of course after watching his nephew struggle away from death's door and his intense and anguishing recuperation, he was thrilled at this very normal reaction in Iain. And part of him—the part of his heart that loved Iain as a son—cheered on this milestone in his recovery.

Instead of the grimace of pain that never quite left his nephew's face, always shadowing his gaze, a healthy flush of colour filled it even now. Instead of the living ghost of the young man he was meant to be, an Iain he had only prayed to see had shown himself.

But now, instead of hope and expectation between two young persons for their future together, he saw defeat take hold once more, just before Iain turned from him.

Robert looked around the library for something to drink. He needed something to fortify him—nay, more to wash away the bitter taste his words of warning had left behind. He'd like nothing more than to encourage Iain on his path back to normality, but a future with Julia was not to be part of that. Still, the signs that Iain could be interested, could pursue something in this personal nature of things, gave him a renewed sense of hope for the boy.

Knowing that Trey kept a potent bottle of his own personal favourite whisky stored in a cabinet here somewhere, Robert searched until he found it and helped himself to a generous portion of the *uisgh beathe*—he would need it before facing his wife and the Countess to discuss this morning's incident.

Sitting behind the Earl's desk, and savouring both the taste of the brew and the strength of purpose it seemed to give, Robert spotted the bundle of green and red hanging from the ceiling over the secluded corner and groaned.

Damn the Countess's mistletoe!

Chapter Five

Julia did not see Iain for the next two days. She looked for him in the mornings, but he did not join the rest of the group for their early meal, nor the noon one either. Nor the evening one.

He did not join in the entertainments, nor in outings to the neighbouring estate to make the Earl's annual visit. And he certainly did not attend the evening balls and dances arranged for the guests' pleasure…and for her sister's purposes.

Now, peering out through the red salon's windows and watching the fat snowflakes drift down from the sky on their journey to the ground, she wondered if she would ever see him again. The only good thing about this downturn in the weather was that it assured his travelling on to Town did not occur.

Julia shook her head at that reference. She was, she

feared, becoming more English every day. Thinking of London as 'Town' was only one more proof of it. Not that she didn't enjoy the pleasures it had to offer, both in culture and society, and in the more intellectual pursuits as well, but the fact that she thought of it in that way just pointed out how much of her Scottish upbringing was eroding.

Lady Sutcliffe's complaints over the snow invaded her private thoughts. The older woman was decidedly against the thought of venturing out into the cold day, which only convinced Julia more of the rightness of the plan. Though she'd renewed her efforts to be the perfect lady after her 'lapse in judgment', as Clarinda referred to it, she already grew bored of it.

She wanted nothing more than to throw off the raiments of society and frolic in the newly fallen coating of snow. Glancing back at the boring company in the salon, Julia longed for nothing else.

Well, that was not totally true. She longed for another kiss from Iain. She longed to test the attraction she felt for him now that he'd demonstrated he was not immune to her. Folly, surely? But how else could she know the truth and depth of her feelings? Feelings that threatened everything her sister was so carefully guiding her towards even now.

She did not think ill of Anna's efforts to find her an amiable husband—one who would provide for her and who would hopefully develop soft feelings for her. If she was being a sensible, pragmatic young woman, as was her customary behaviour, Julia would admit that she stood to make a brilliant match because of her position as the ward of the Earl of Treybourne.

But ever since that kiss…

She could think of no one else but Iain. And though the thought of sharing another intimate moment with him made her heart race and her skin tingle in some new and strangely enjoyable way, the thought of doing that and more with someone else was equally distasteful to her.

That kiss… She sighed, leaning her face closer to the window and hoping that the chilled pane of glass would help cool her heated cheeks.

Clarinda had warned her not to say anything to Anna that day when they'd reached her rooms, and though she had doubted it was the right course of action initially, the sight of her sister's pale and ill face had convinced Julia to accept Clarinda's advice. She did not need to add to Anna's distress. And she did not need a lecture. Julia quite clearly understood that she should not have kissed Iain.

But she had, and, oh, that kiss!

Touching her fingers to her lips now, she wondered what would have happened if they'd not been interrupted at that moment. The kisses he'd placed along the skin of her cheek and jaw had sent shivers through her as much as the touch of his lips on hers. Perhaps even more? And he'd touched—nay, *licked* the soft, sensitive spot below her ear. The one that tingled now. What would he have done next? she wondered, even while trying to divert herself from such invigorating thoughts.

As if her thoughts had conjured him, Julia watched as Iain walked up the path outside the house towards the door. He took each step with care, placing the tip of his walking stick judiciously along the snow-covered lane. He never once looked up from his task, and she sensed that a lack of concentration would result in danger for him as he made his way back. Tempted though she was to knock on the window and gain his attention, she contented herself to watch him as he passed below her. Her heated breath began to fog the frosty panes, making it difficult to see him without wiping the condensation away.

Knowing he would pass by this room in order to reach his, she adjusted her shawl around her shoulders and left her place near the window, walking slowly and as though without a particular destination. Circling the room, she listened for the sound of his walking stick on the hard wooden floors in the hall. She'd just reached the doors when she heard his approach. Nodding to one of the footmen, Julia waited for the right moment before leaving the room and encountering him—by accident.

'Mr MacLerie,' she said brightly. 'Have you just

returned from the out-of-doors?' Of course he had—
but she needed to find some way to converse with him.
The entire group of women in the salon behind her
could hear her words, and they must seem polite and
not planned.

'I have, Miss Fairchild,' he replied, after a short
delay that included a bow to her.

'And how did you find the weather? Is it terribly
cold now that the snow has begun?' Stupid, witless
questions, she knew. But at least it gave her an opportunity to speak to him, to watch his face as he
answered. To watch his lips move and to remember
how they felt against hers.

'No, not too cold. Not the biting cold you might
remember from your visits to Broch Dubh. Comfortable enough if you are warmly dressed.'

'I should not keep you from your plans, Mr
MacLerie, especially since you've just returned from
the cold. Will we see you at dinner this evening?'

A look of distress flitted over his face for a brief
moment, and then was gone before he answered, 'I
fear not. But thank you for asking.'

'The evening's entertainment, then? Lord Treybourne is arranging a card tournament of sorts for the
gentlemen,' she offered. Somehow making certain he
was included was important to her. 'If I remember correctly you have some amount of skill at whist, or was
it commerce?'

'You are too kind, Miss Fairchild. I fear I am out of practice with either game, and would only be a detriment to any partner assigned to me. But, again, I thank you for asking.'

If she had to be polite to him for another moment, she would lose control, and with that breach also lose every bit of pretence that she—they—managed to create after their scene together. But in spite of her efforts to draw him back into the company of the day, he made certain that he stayed out.

'If you will excuse me now, Miss Fairchild? My uncle awaits my return, and I would not keep him waiting.'

He bowed politely and did not wait for her dismissal before walking away from her. Unwilling to let it end without some meaningful words between them, she followed him. He must have realised it, for he stopped several yards down the corridor and turned back to her.

'You know this cannot be,' he pleaded in a low voice, with no attempt to prevaricate. 'Please, Julia, allow this to fade away between us.'

Inwardly thrilled by his acknowledgement that there was indeed something more between them than had been there before the kiss, she felt her heart hurt at the thought of it never being anything else…

'Iain, I…' She wanted to protest, but the look in his eyes told her of the futility of it. Worse, he seemed to accept it. Already an inescapable burden to her sister, she would not be one to this man who had borne too much in these last few years. 'Very well, Iain. Forgive me,' she said softly.

Julia was about to leave him when the women who'd been having tea and cakes in the salon now followed her path down the hall. She tried to think of some polite dispatch, some clever or pithy way in which to end their encounter, but the unhappy Lady Sutcliffe came to life.

'Ah, my dear Miss Fairchild! See where you and Mr MacLerie have stopped!' she called out, in a voice loud enough to draw more observers.

Julia looked to where she pointed and gasped. Another of her sister's boughs of mistletoe hung above their heads. How many had Anna ordered to be placed? Iain did not move, but she could see the slight shake of his head.

What better way to say farewell than with a kiss? It could not be the one she wished they could have, but a kiss was a kiss. And she would take it and savour it in her memories as their last one.

'Mr MacLerie, you do observe this custom in your lands, do you not?' Lady Sutcliffe asked, referring to the Highlands as though they were a foreign country.

Although Julia wanted to question why Lady Sutcliffe would goad them into such behaviour, she also wanted to thank the intrusive woman for almost demanding it.

'Of course, Lady Sutcliffe,' Iain replied. 'Ne'er let it be said that a Scotsman doesna ken the way of doing things.'

Julia smiled. He'd thrown in an extra measure of Scots' accent to make her believe she was correct, but it was the smile that began to lift the corners of his mouth that intrigued her. She waited as he took the step towards her necessary to position them within kissing distance. Although she wanted to throw her arms around him and hold him as close as she had the first time, she understood that this would need to be different.

He held out his hand to her and she placed hers there. With only that polite touch between them, he leaned in and touched his lips to hers—a gentle touch only, without the passion she knew he held in check, as did she. Then he stepped back, dropped her hand, and bowed.

Their small audience clapped and smiled, but inside Julia wanted to cry. It had been nothing like their first kiss, and not the kiss she always wanted to remember. Before she could say anything, Iain bowed to the group and left. Julia leaned back and cursed the mistletoe above her.

It was the most difficult thing he'd done in his life. And the most painful as well. Far more difficult than fighting the constant pain in his leg and hip. His heart was more tender than the rest of his body, it would seem.

First inflicting that sham of a kiss on her, and then turning and walking away. But he knew that he must do what he could to protect Julia's reputation and her honour and if he must do it in spite of her own folly, then so be it. How it felt to carry out such noble intentions was the unpredictable thing, he discovered.

His uncle was indeed waiting for his return, so, after leaving his greatcoat with a footman, he made his way back to the Earl's private library. The snow had made the roads worse, nearly impassable now, and would delay his journey onward. Instead of three days, his stay here at Wesley Hall would now extend to at least four more.

Putting him into Julia's path frequently enough to be dangerous. Dangerous to his heart and dangerous to the plans her family had for her. But he must do his best to keep her from losing the opportunities that life held for her, even if he did not want to.

His chance to do that came much more quickly than he had expected, for a glance at a window as he walked down the hallway found the very woman, walking in a manner best described as skulking away from the house towards the stables. It brought a smile to his face, and memories of her attempts to follow him and his cousins on the adventures of their youth.

Memories of the way things had usually ended on those adventures—badly.

Catching the footman before his coat had been stored away, Iain shrugged back into it and followed her path out into the snow. The fluffy, slippery coating—now a few more inches, by the look of it—made his progress slow, and he was winded when he arrived at the stables, but he made it. Stepping inside the huge building filled with heat and smell of the Earl's horses, he rested for a moment to catch his breath. Peering down the length of the single corridor, Iain could neither see nor hear Julia.

Admiring the stock for no more than a brief moment, he made his way to the back of the stables. He was nearly there when he heard a side door slam shut. It took him a few more minutes to find it, and when he looked out he could see only a stableboy running towards the lake with skates in his hand.

Oh, dear God above, he prayed as he recognised the figure in those boy's clothes—it was Julia!

She'd always loved the snow when she visited Broch Dubh in the Highlands at Christmas as a child. And she had been one of the best skaters when the temperatures had dipped cold enough to freeze the nearby loch to ice. Now, watching her receding figure, he knew he must follow her. If he gauged the distance correctly, the lake was at least several leagues away.

He'd not walked that far since his accident.

He did not know if he was capable of doing it now; he only knew he must try. A deep sense of foreboding hit him in the gut and, watching her walk further away with each passing second, Iain knew he had to move.

A half-hour later he reached the snow-covered bank of the lake and observed her gliding along the far side. He stayed in the shadow of the trees, far enough back that she would not see him. With his lower body screaming at both the distance covered and the relentless pace he'd kept to, he paced slowly there, so that his legs would not seize up completely. Her voice, calling out to someone, grabbed his attention.

A child, a boy, had joined her on the ice, and he watched as they chased each other across the frozen surface, mindless of the cold and the new snow falling around them. Years ago he would have strapped on his own skates and raced with them on the ice. He sighed, realising again that his limitations and disability would forever keep him from the things he'd so enjoyed in his youth…and from her.

Some minutes passed, and though he was near exhaustion, he did not tire of watching her—her sense of enjoyment in this simple activity, the way she treated the child from the village, the grace with which she moved, even the scandalous way that the boy's clothing outlined the womanly curves of her body. It was more joy than he'd had in many months, and even if it was tinged was a sense of seeing what he could never have, he would treasure every moment of it.

Julia and the child had skated to a different section of the lake when he heard it. The ice cracked and sent its ominous warning of danger over the surface. He looked across at the skaters, their sudden pause and obvious searching for the origin of the sound, telling him they'd recognised the danger.

He was about to shout out a warning when Julia screamed and disappeared from his view.

Chapter Six

The child fell to the ice, and Iain knew he must act or lose them. Realising that his legs simply would not support him on the ice, he quickly staggered to the edge of the lake and slid along as much as he could without losing his balance.

'Julia! Hold on, Julia!' he called as he moved awkwardly out onto the ice in their direction. He did not see Julia, but the child heard him and called her name again.

He could not delay, and trying to remain on his feet was doing just that. Possibly the only good thing to come from his injuries was the strength he'd built in the muscles of his back and chest and arms, so he tossed his walking stick aside and threw himself forward on the ice. After the initial shock of his hard landing, he pulled himself along the slippery surface, using any roughness he could grab onto.

Although it seemed as if time had slowed, and his progress was even slower, he could see he was closer with each second, and soon he could see the frightened child sitting on the ice, calling out to Julia, who must be in the water. Once he neared the edge of the break in the ice, he pulled himself up on his knees—knees now numb from the cold and wet—so he could see over it. Sheer terror filled him at the sight of Julia in the icy waters.

'Are you hurt?' he asked the boy. 'Did you fall in as well?' Moving carefully closer, he inspected the boy for any sign of injury.

'No, sir. But the lady...' The child shook—probably from both icy wetness and fear.

Iain grabbed the boy and slid him over to the edge of the lake. 'Go. Run and get the Earl, and bring him quickly! Tell him to bring rope.' He prayed that the Earl had kept to his usual schedule of visiting the stables each day at about this time.

'Aye, sir!' the child called, and he scampered off the ice towards the stables.

'Hurry!' Iain yelled, though it was not necessary, for the child covered the distance quickly.

Turning back to the water, he saw that Julia's eyes were closed. Not certain if he was too late, he pulled himself as close to the edge as he dared and called her name.

'Julia! Open your eyes, lass!'

Her eyes opened slowly, and he saw the shivers that shook her. 'Iain,' she sighed.

'Julia, open your eyes and look at me, lass!' He reached out and waved his hand in front of her. 'Give me your hand now!'

He thought he'd lost her in that moment, for she sank a little lower in the water. Then, as he shouted her name once more, Julia opened her eyes and lifted her hand. It was blue, as were her lips and most of her face. She was freezing to death in front of him. He could not wait for help to arrive.

'Give me your hand,' he said again, and as he reached out to grab it. He barely had a moment, for her strength seemed to fail at that moment. But he did manage to grasp it and pull her closer to the edge of the ice.

'Julia, we have done this before, you and I.' He spoke slowly to her as he manoeuvred his body into a wider position, spreading his weight before trying to pull her out. 'Do you remember when Collin slipped in Loch Dubh?' He hoped she would focus on his words and stay conscious. He could not do this alone.

'Iain,' she sighed again. 'It is so cold.' He felt her hand loosen its hold on his, and could feel the fear growing in his heart.

'Aye, love, it is cold. But you must help me get you out of the water. *Now*, love,' he said sharply. Her eyes fluttered and shut once more, in spite of his words. 'Julia, please help me!'

He saw her gaze clear then, and took advantage of the moment.

'Can you lift your legs? Try to kick them up to the surface.' He could slide her from the water more easily than lifting her in his present position and condition, and he had no assurance that the ice beneath him would not give way and topple him into the water.

He saw the water near her move, and watched as she did manage to kick her legs closer to the top. Holding onto her hand, he began inching his way back from the edge, guiding her body along the thinner ice and onto the thicker part. It was a near thing more than once as he heard the ice groan beneath their weight. He paused for a moment, before continuing to slide back and away from the gaping hole.

His chest was tight, and he found it hard to breathe, but he could not give up yet. His body, not used to this kind of exertion, screamed in protest, but he would not give in to the need to rest.

Once he'd moved them back from the edge, he sat up as best he could and pulled her into his lap. At least the numbing coldness presented him with a pain he could handle. He would worry about the rest later, once she was safe.

For minutes that seemed hours, he wrapped his arms around her and held her close. Her features resembled those of a porcelain doll now, ghostly white and fragile. He tugged the hat she still wore from her head and held her against his chest.

Her tremors shook them both. Until she was out of those wet clothes and dry, she could not begin to recover. He felt the cold seeping into his own bones, but focused on keeping her awake.

'Julia, open your eyes, lass,' he said softly. Tugging his glove off with his teeth, he stroked her cheek gently. Lifting her hand in his, he blew on her fingers, willing them to warm. 'Do not worry, Julia. I have you now,' he whispered, while gathering her closer.

She'd spoken the same words to him, just before he'd kissed her days before. The whimsical thought clarified in her cold-muddled brain, and Julia struggled to reply to his assurance.

It was just too cold. She wanted nothing more than to let the threatening sleep overtake her, to settle into its grasp, but he kept interrupting, forcing her to hear his words and to open her eyes.

She did look at him, even while her body shuddered from the piercing cold. 'Iain.'

'You must stay with me, Julia. Help is coming, but you must not give up to the cold,' he urged.

The frown that furrowed his brow told her of his worry. And the way he touched her cheek and held her hand, though truly she could barely feel it, spoke of his concern.

The strangest thought entered her mind then. He held her so close she could see only part of his face, his mouth, and she wanted him to kiss her. To warm her, to make her feel something before she slipped into the darkness that waited for her.

So that she had something to remember if it was the last memory she would have.

'Kiss me, Iain,' she whispered, hoping he would.

At first she couldn't tell if he had kissed her or not, her face was numb, but then the warmth of his mouth on hers seemed to wake her skin. The heat of his mouth warmed hers, and she felt the tip of his tongue moving deep inside her mouth, seeking hers. *This* was the kiss she remembered.

No, this was the kiss she would *always* remember.

He lifted his mouth from hers and held her close as the shivering shook her over and over. She needed to tell him how she felt, about the feelings that had grown in his absence from her life, about the life she pretended to enjoy so as not to disappoint her sister.

Instead she simply lay in his arms, allowing his strength to seep into her, hoping that he'd found her soon enough. Soon though, it was too much for her, and she could fight the cold and exhaustion no longer.

'Iain…'

She whispered his name, and then lost consciousness.

* * *

It could not be! He shook her and called her name, even slapped her cheek to get her to wake up, but none of it seemed to work. She'd spoken his name and then collapsed against him, no longer awake. He was not even certain she still breathed.

No! She could not die! Not because of his disability!

If he'd been whole he could have pulled her out of the water and carried her to safety. If he'd been whole, he could have caught up with her and kept her from harm in the first place. If he'd been whole…everything would have been different.

The pain welled inside until he could not keep it within him any longer. Leaning his head back, he roared out in frustration, in agony—both physical and emotional—and in fury. And still she did not move. He slumped over her, shielding her body from the growing winds, praying that help would arrive soon.

As the snow continued to fall in silence, he finally heard people approach, and he called out to them to hurry. He recognised the Earl and his uncle, and some of the servants.

'See to Julia,' he called out. 'She has fallen unconscious.'

The Earl reached them first, and with help managed to get them off the ice and onto solid ground. Then Lord Treybourne peeled Iain's arms from around his sister-by-marriage and lifted her into his own.

'She needs heat, my lord. And dry clothes too. Quickly.'

If anyone thought there was anything strange about a commoner ordering an earl to do his bidding, no one said it. All actions were focused on getting Julia to the house, where they could warm her and see to her condition. When they began to see to him, Iain brushed them aside.

'Uncle! Please help her. Get her to the house,' he ordered again.

Instead, his uncle and one of the stablemen pulled him to his feet, tugged his soggy greatcoat off his shoulders and replaced it with several thick woollen blankets. Taking one arm over each of their shoulders, they began to walk back towards the house, balancing him between them.

''Twas my fault, sir,' Iain confessed. 'I chased her from the house by my behaviour and it led to this.'

His thoughts were disjointed at that moment, but clearly his rebuff of her attentions had pushed her away and into this situation.

'Iain, the boy said you saved him from drowning,' his uncle argued. 'Hardly your fault.'

'Sir—' he began, but when his head began to spin and his legs gave out beneath him he could say no more.

'There will be time to sort this out, lad. Let's get you inside and cared for, and we can sort it all through.'

Iain did not have the strength to argue the point. He could feel himself slipping away with each attempted step. And, after only a handful of paces away from the lake, he could no longer fight the exhaustion and the fear and the pain.

Chapter Seven

The story was changed slightly before being put out for the rest of those at the Earl's Christmas festivities.

The Earl's young ward, along with their Scottish guest, had gone skating on the lake with a stableboy as attendant. When the ice had cracked and Miss Fairchild had fallen through, Mr MacLerie had been able to pull her from the water while the boy ran for help.

This version was more acceptable than the one that had Miss Fairchild dressed in a boy's clothing, skating with one of the villager's children when the ice broke. Iain's participation remained the same in both versions: pulling the unconscious Miss Fairchild to safety while awaiting help.

Neither version included his improper handling of her when they were alone, or the passionate kiss shared by them before she had fainted, or the part when he had roared against fate in a voice that had sent chills down the spines of those who'd heard it as they approached the scene of the accident.

Protecting the reputation that Julia had fought so hard to maintain seemed of the utmost importance now—especially as her life teetered so dangerously close to the edge. Two days passed before her survival was thought to be a certain conclusion to the unfortunate accident. And her sister did not leave her side during those dark hours, praying all the while, and caring for Julia the whole time.

Clarinda watched it all with a heavy heart, knowing that she had ignored the warning signs of trouble coming. Julia could be headstrong, but she was usually pragmatic about the important things. But Clarinda had seen this very situation before—she'd watched Anna go through the same thing when she had not recognised her own feelings towards the Earl of Treybourne. It was easier for someone standing a distance away to see things that could not be seen by someone standing too close.

Julia was in love with Iain.

Iain, she suspected, returned the feelings.

And neither one thought it was a good idea.

Neither did their relatives.

Now Iain was recovering from injuries sustained in his rescue of Julia from the lake, and she'd never seen him so blue-devilled. He had taken more laudanum than she'd seen him take in months over the past two days, and did not speak except to answer simple questions. Never once had he asked about Julia.

Pacing outside Julia's bedchamber now, Clarinda knew she needed to speak to Anna about him. But she did not know how to broach such a sensitive subject. Expecting a servant when the door opened, she was surprised to find Anna leaving her sister's bedchamber.

'Anna.' Clarinda embraced her friend and then held her at arm's length to examine her more closely. 'How do you fare through this?'

'I do what I must,' she replied, looking back at the closed door. 'She sleeps now, and Trey has ordered me to my own bed.'

'You need to have a care for your own condition, Anna. Do you wish me to sit with Julia for a while?'

Anna frowned at her. 'And Iain? Who sees to him?'

'Young men do not take well to the eager attentions of their uncles or aunts. I have done what I could before he dismissed me as unneeded.' Clarinda let out an exasperated breath. 'So much pride in their abilities, and shaken to the core when they are not able to perform as they expect to.'

'What is wrong, Clarinda? Come. Accompany me to my bedchambers and tell me the whole of it.'

'You will not like it, Anna. I worry about your reaction.'

At her candour, Anna shrugged. 'I nearly lost my beloved sister two days ago. Is what you need to share worse than that?'

This was the practical, calm friend Clarinda knew. A woman able to face difficult situations and deal with them without hysterics or fear. All would be well.

'No. Actually, nothing so horrible as that.'

Anna linked arms with her and they walked in silence to the Countess's suite at the end of the corridor. Surely they could find a way out of this?

Iain closed the door and rested his head against the wooden frame. It had taken two days of laudanum and then three more days to gain control over his need to dull the pain since Julia's accident. His control had slipped away when he'd been faced with the terrible spasms and the fear that she'd died in his arms and he'd taken too much, numbing him to most sensations. The constant ache in his heart reminded him that drugs did not help every sort of pain.

He'd made his decision in the moment when the Earl had lifted her from his arms: if they survived, he would walk out of her life for ever. She deserved better than he could offer, better than he could ever be again, and he would neither ask nor expect her to make that choice.

Her sister offered her every comfort and every opportunity for a wonderful future, and he would never deny Julia the chance for that. Even if she did not realise her good fortune, he did. He'd travelled enough for his uncle, seen enough of the poverty of women's choices, to know that although he had nearly cost her her life he would not make her sacrifice her happiness.

Once Christmas had passed he would make his way to London and fall back into his usual schedule. Work on his uncle's business interests, work on his estate, work on his farms. A simple life.

One without Julia Fairchild in it.

He'd lived without her for years; he could do it again.

Sound permeated the wooden barrier of the door as though it was not there, and he could hear the music from above stairs. He remembered her as he'd seen her that first night—floating around the room on the arm of one or another gentleman. For a brief moment he allowed himself to imagine her on *his* arm, following him through the steps of a dance, conversing politely and gifting him with the smile that was hers alone.

Iain hummed along with the music for a minute before pushing off the despondency that threatened him. He tugged his cravat loose and pulled it free from his neck. Tossing it on the bed, he shrugged out of his jacket and unbuttoned his waistcoat. Although he'd forced himself to walk more today, his legs still pained him.

Just as he was about to sit down to remove his shoes, he heard a scratching at his door. Crossing the room, he pulled the door open.

She stood before him, looking not at all as she had the last time he'd seen her. Her face was full of colour, and not the ghastly blue-tinged hue of when he'd held her in his arms. Though dressed in a simple gown, she could not have looked more beautiful to him. His hands left his sides and reached for her before he could even think, but luckily he stopped them before he touched her.

'Julia,' he said. He clutched the side of the door and braced himself against it—partly to balance himself and partly to keep her in the hall. 'You look well.' Surprised that his voice did not shake, he peered down the hall to see if anyone waited for her. 'Why are you not at the ball?'

'I needed to speak to you, Iain,' she said softly.

'You should be at the ball,' he repeated, nodding his head towards the music that he could hear clearly now that his door was open.

She met his gaze then, and Iain lost his breath. He recognised a vulnerability there now that was new. The confident Julia had been chased away, leaving this new uncertain one in her place.

'You saved my life, Iain. I cannot find the right words to use to thank you for such an act.'

He stepped from his room completely then, not

trusting himself if she entered his chambers. Tugging the door behind him, he cursed himself for his current state of undress. Lowering his voice, he remembered his decision to leave her.

'I nearly cost you your life, Julia. Assign no heroic actions to my account.'

She twisted her hands in front of her, standing head bowed. 'Billy told me what you did. I did not know you had followed me that day, or why, but I do know that I would be dead now if you had not.' Julia lifted her eyes to his. 'I can never repay you for saving my life at the risk of your own.'

His anger surged then, for she was ascribing the wrong motives and reasons to his actions of that morning. Clenching his hands into fists, he shook his head at her.

'First I chased you from the house with my disregard. Then I could not follow you to stop you from your folly.' She began to speak, but he shushed her with a shake of his head. 'I could not follow you, Julia! Any man can walk fast enough. Any man has enough strength in his legs to walk a few furlongs. Yet I do not.' He forced the words out through clenched jaws. 'You fell through the ice and I could neither run to your side nor lift you from the water.'

He ran his hands through his hair and groaned at the memories of her disappearance into the frigid water. 'My legs gave out, Julia. My *legs*, damn them.

They gave out and I could not walk on the ground or on the ice to reach your side.'

'Iain,' she said, 'you saved me that day. Billy said you pulled yourself along the ice and then slid me out of the water to safety.'

He clenched and shook his fists. 'I could not walk to you, Julia. You fell into that water and I could do nothing.' Did she not realise his horror at his inability to help her when she'd needed him the most? 'What will happen the next time an accident befalls you? Must I stand by and watch you die?'

Iain dragged in a ragged breath and shook his head at her. He noticed the tears in her eyes, but he must make her understand the danger of continuing any alliance between them.

'I cannot be the cause of harm that might come to you because I cannot walk…like any other man can. Or because I don't have the strength to reach you… like any other man can. Please, Julia, do not ask me to stand by and watch…' His voice trailed off. He could not bear to see the disappointment in her gaze, his failure once more reflected in the eyes of someone he loved.

He *loved*.

'You expect too much, Iain,' she whispered. 'Most other men would have died from the injuries you received. Most other men would never have survived what you have faced, and you are stronger for it.'

'I am no hero.' He knew he must end it now. 'You will find your knight in shining armour, Julia. And he will be able to ride his horse and walk at your side and dance with you at your ball.'

The strains of music echoed down the hallway to them. It seemed a perfect and poignant reminder of what he could not do.

She reached up and touched his cheek with her fingers. He fought the urge to turn his face into her palm and feel her skin against his. 'I have faced death and thought I would never wake when I fainted in your arms, Iain. And it was the loss of you that grieved me most. I swore that I would not let you go without telling you…'

'Julia, please do not say something you will regret.' His heart wanted to warn her off, and yet wanted to hear the words she threatened to speak. 'Please.'

'I have always loved you, Iain. I know it began as a childish obsession, but it grew into something else. I hoped you'd wait for me, but you moved on with your life.' She paused and stepped close enough that he could see the rise and fall of her chest as she breathed. 'I have always loved you, and hoped you could love me too.'

Time did not move. The very air around them grew still as he heard the words that any man would be thrilled to hear from her. Any man who could offer her a life and his love in return. But he could not be the man she needed, the man she wanted, the man she deserved.

'I cannot return your love, Julia,' he whispered, lying with his words even as his heart screamed out the truth from within him. 'I do not.'

She flinched as though struck, and he was certain his words had hit her as surely as if he'd raised his hand in a blow. The colour seeped from her face then, and her hand slipped from the caress so recently given. In spite of his rejection, she shook her head at him.

'You are afraid, Iain. I understand that—I do. But together we can…'

Afraid? He was terrified inside at the thought that he could be the cause of harm to her because of his disabilities. But not so tied up by it that he could not see what he must do.

'This is not about fear, Julia. I have faced death myself—too many times to count in these last few years—and I have found a way back. This is about the impossibility of something more between us.'

She would not back down, it seemed. No matter that he had insulted her and rejected her love and her heart, she came back at him in ways unexpected.

'Not afraid?' she asked, stepping back a few steps and holding out her hand to him. 'Then be by my side and dance with me.'

The musicians had tuned their instruments for a

new dance and he recognised it immediately—a waltz. The strains of it floated down the hall and encircled them like some kind of mesmerising spell. A chance to hold her in his arms and to believe that she could be his… His heart raced in his chest and the blood pounded in his head as he stared at her hand and considered what she offered. He was not certain that he could take even a few steps of the dance she offered, but he wanted to try.

All he would need to do was take her hand and her love.

His palms itched to move; his feet ached to step forward to her side. His heart demanded again to take her love, and to give his in return. But it was his cold, rational mind that gave the answer.

Iain took a step back into his room and closed the door behind him, leaving Julia with an expression of disbelief and devastation in her eyes. Leaning against the door, he waited and listened. After a minute or an hour, he knew not which, he could hear the sound of her feet padding down the hall.

Better, he told himself a million times, to disappoint her now than to risk her life and her safety later. The words and the sentiment rang hollow to his ears and to his heart, and he knew they would sound no better when Christmas Day dawned over Wesley Hall the next morn.

Chapter Eight

She could not breathe.

It felt as if the icy water was swallowing her again, the cold pulling her down and chilling her to the bone. No matter that she told herself she was safe, and her ordeal was over, Julia shivered as she watched the door close in her face.

Certain that he only needed the reassurance of her love and support to consider their future, she'd held out her heart to him. Iain had thrown it on the ground and stamped on it.

Tremors shook her once more, but she waited. He would open that door and come to her side—she knew it. He loved her—she was certain of it. He would...

He did not.

The silence deafened her. She closed her eyes, wrapped her arms around herself and shook even more. The tears burned her throat and her eyes and she felt them trickling down her cheeks.

Music pierced the silence that held her and grew in intensity, and Julia knew that the waltz was nearing an end. Soon people would come looking for her. She'd promised a dance to two of the young men at her sister's request, and they would notice her missing.

This time she did not want to be found. The pain that flooded her heart and ripped her soul in two grew, and she could face no one in that moment. What good was there in realising that the feelings one had felt and thought only infatuation were something stronger, something more substantial, and then to have them disregarded in such a fashion as this?

Julia had thought Iain would at least hear her out. She knew enough about men to understand their sense of pride. Iain continued to argue that he was not able to be like other men, but Julia knew it for the lie it was. While lying in her bed, recovering from the incident that had nearly taken her life, she had learned many things.

She loved him. As simple as her declaration had been, it was a powerfully true statement.

She wanted him. Inexperienced though she was, her body had come alive beneath his touch, and kissing him simply made her want for more.

She wanted the kind of life he could offer her. In spite of the chance to experience the luxury offered by her brother-by-marriage's fortune and title, Julia did not need the same in order to be happy. Iain would have a respectful income from his work for his family's businesses and could support her comfortably. And though she'd travelled the length and breadth of England, visited London and Paris, and had savoured every moment of those experiences, if she never left Scotland again—whether the Highlands or its cities—she could live quite happily.

With Iain.

Julia shook her head, finally accepting that he would not return and accept her, and walked down the hall to the Earl's library. Nothing at the Christmas Eve Ball appealed to her any longer.

Closing the door behind her, she made her way to the corner collection of chairs and sat in one of them. The same one where she'd sat the day when Iain had kissed her. Looking up, she lifted up on her toes to reach the now offensive branches above her. Tugging once, she pulled the bundle of mistletoe free and tossed it on the floor in the corner. Then, curling up in the cushions, she leaned her head back and watched the Christmas snow fall silently outside the window and form a new layer on the old one there. The lake's shiny surface in the distance seemed to mock her sadness and remind her of how fragile life could be.

Trey left Anna in their chambers and went off, as she had requested, in search of Julia. It was not difficult to guess where he would find her. Although Julia had seemed to regain her strength after her accident, something had changed in the girl—and he suspected he knew what it was. It did not take a scholar to recognise a young woman in the throes of first love.

Nor the look of a young man in the same condition.

Trey felt very much the man in the middle now, watching his wife and her sister struggle to make others proud and happy while ignoring their own wishes. Julia, he knew, went along with Anna's matchmaking because she felt beholden to her for the years when Anna had given up her own happiness and dreams to protect and care for her sister and aunt. Anna, after dealing with years of deprivation and need, wanted to make certain that Julia never faced the same desperate situation, and so she looked to arrange a marriage that would take care of her in that regard.

Noble sentiments, acceptable behaviour, and yet she was too stubborn to see the wrongness in her actions or the ultimate unhappiness that could and would result from it. Unless someone who loved them both could make them see the truth.

Someone like him.

His attempts to draw Julia fully into their family had met with measured success—although he thought of her almost as a daughter, there were times when she seemed to hold herself apart from them. At first she'd seemed to enjoy the changes that his marriage to Anna had brought. Even the addition of his natural daughter to their household had pleased her, for it had given her a playmate and a sister to replace the one he'd stolen away as his wife. Then, as she's travelled and met more of those in his circle of friends and society, Julia had seemed to grow more and more discontented.

Anna had read this as a challenge to see her happily settled, and once she'd reached eight-and-ten years of age Anna had set off as on a mission from the Almighty to find her sister a husband. Now, if either or both did not stand down, the results would be catastrophe or broken hearts or worse.

Trey walked quietly to the corner of his library and peered down in the darkness at the sleeping girl. The tracks left on her cheeks by tears were obvious even in the low light from his candle. Her face was pale, paler than this last day, when she'd risen from her bed and returned to a more usual schedule. She needed rest, a good night's rest, and a chance to recover more from the shock of facing death.

Placing his candle on the table, he crouched down in front of her and said her name softly. Repeating it again, he watched as her eyes fluttered open and she recognised him.

'Come, Julia. Allow me to escort you to your chambers,' he offered as he stood. 'Anna is worried about your condition so soon after your accident. I told her you are as stout and steady as a workhorse, but she doubts my word on it.'

She did smile then, just for a moment, in a hint of how much younger her face looked when not so tense and burdened. 'A workhorse, my lord?' she asked. 'Surely you could have come up with something more stylish?' She tried to keep her tone light, but sadness crept in. 'I did not mean to worry her, Trey. Truly not.' She pushed out of the chair and stood before him and he could see some new pain there in her eyes.

'Julia, what has happened?' he asked.

Tears poured freely down her cheeks and she began to shake. Opening his arms to her, Trey held her close, soothing her much as he did his young sons. 'Julia, sweet, tell me what has happened.'

'He does not want me, Trey. He does not want me.'

She sobbed now, leaning against his chest with her tears soaking into his dressing robe. He let her finish, and when she raised her head and stepped away from him he knew she was ready to discuss it with him.

'Do you think that is his problem?' he asked. He'd learned long ago never to protest the innocence of the man involved when women decided a man was wrong.

'He is so proud, and yet so corkbrained at the same time.'

'Is that not your complaint about most men of late?' Trey shrugged. 'How is he different from the rest of us?'

'Oh, Trey!' she said. 'I do not think of you so. You have only treated me with the best of intentions and attentions. And although you do sometimes succumb to the weaknesses and peculiarities of your gender, I think you are one of the most sensible men I have ever met.'

'Thank you,' he said, with a nod of his head. 'But you have not told me young Iain's problem.'

She took in a ragged breath and released it, sitting down and motioning him to take a place on the other seat there in the corner.

'He saved my life, yet he refuses to see his own worth!'

'He still struggles back from his injuries, Julia. 'Twill take some time, I suspect, before he gains confidence in any physical abilities.'

'Trey, Billy told me that Iain dragged himself across the lake using only his hands. He is stronger than he realises, but will not listen to anyone who speaks of it.'

'You tried, then? Tonight?' he asked.

'Yes. He did not come to see me after the accident, so I went to see him, to thank him for saving me...' Her voice trailed off, leaving out the part she did not wish to speak of, but the part he could guess—she'd offered Iain her heart as well and been rejected.

'Sometimes a prideful young man needs time to accept that he is not the failure he believes himself to be.'

'Oh, Trey, how can he not see it? He is indispensable to his uncle. He is competent. He is talented and thorough. How can he not see that?' She wiped her eyes and leaned back in the chair.

'He was gravely injured. He did not know if he would survive and he suffers with serious pain every day of his life. Everything he did with ease before that terrible day he can no longer do. Every step he takes threatens to land him face-down in the dirt. That is enough to make him doubt everything he knows or thinks he knows about himself and his abilities.' Trey reached over and lifted her chin so that she met his gaze. 'Surely you can allow him that much? He has the best reasons for doubting himself.'

'Then why does he doubt *me*, Trey. How can he doubt me?'

Her words were almost whispered, but the depth of the pain there told him so much. She waited for words to give her the reassurance she so desperately needed. Could he give her that? What if Iain had other reasons not to accept the feelings between them?

'If he cannot trust himself he can trust no one else, Julia. Not his uncle, not even you.'

'But I love him, Trey,' she protested.

Surprised at the strength of her feelings, he said, 'And you told him of your feelings?'

'Tonight. When I went to see him,' she said, nodding.

His reaction should be to admonish her for seeking out the company of a young man, but he could see the love she felt and the pain it was causing and he did not have the heart, especially as Christmas morn approached, to admonish or reprimand her.

'I would say, then, that he needs time to accept his situation, his future and your feelings…his as well. For I suspect that he does have tender feelings for you, Julia.'

She took some comfort in his words, and a smile lit her face. 'Do you think so?'

He reached out, drawing her near, and kissed her on her forehead. 'Aye, Julia, I do. My question to you is this: is he a man you could settle with, or is this just a passing fancy for you? I would urge you not to trifle with him if the love you say you bear for him is less than genuine. This is not the first time you've spoken of love for him—yet you came to regret that, as I recall.'

She leaned back and met his gaze. 'Oh, Trey! You heard that story second-hand, and you know that I was only ten years old when I said it to him that summer.'

'True, it did not match the seemingly rational young woman I met when I was courting your sister. Still, are you confident in your feelings for him now?'

In that moment Trey knew the truth of the matter of her heart and where it was leading her. The love that shone in her eyes told him that she had grown up and fallen in love even while he had been watching her these last five years.

'Then we must wait and watch for some way to convince Iain of the folly of his ways,' he promised. She smiled then, and he stepped away and lifted his candle to lead her to her sister, who needed reassurance of her well-being. 'Come. Anna awaits word of your condition. Tell her what you have told me, so that she can rest more easily over the matter.'

'If only more men were as sensible as you, Trey,' Julia teased.

He did not rise to her baiting this time. Let her believe that men could not understand the tender feelings of a woman's heart. Let her think he did not see the proof of it in her eyes. And, Lord above, let not Iain make the same mistakes he had.

Christmas Morning brought her sister's young sons and stepdaughter to Julia's chamber door, where, along with several of the servants' children, they sang carols for her. As they moved along the hall, Julia stretched under her covers to wake from her troubled sleep. As each guest was awakened in the same manner, Julia realised that their Christmas celebrations combined the best of both English and Scottish traditions.

The part she loved—exchanging gifts—would come during their family breakfast in just a little

while, and then they would all attend church together
in the nearby village. Pushing back the covers, she ran
to the window and looked out on the new day to find
another newly fallen and very thick layer of snow. It
would make travelling to the village difficult, but since
Anna and Trey took their duties as lord and lady seriously at Christmas, it was something not to be missed.

Walking to her chest of drawers, she searched in the
top one to make certain her gifts were wrapped and
ready. She'd chosen a Belgian silk scarf for her sister,
a cravat pin for Trey, a hand-made box for his
daughter Maddy, to keep all her drawing pencils and
colours in, toy horses for her nephews and several
other gifts for her maid and the other servants here.
For Clarinda and Robert she'd sketched a picture of
Broch Dubh, Robert's ancestral home in the Highlands.

Glancing over at her wardrobe, she realised she'd
left Iain's gift there. Going to it, and pulling the box
from behind some of her gowns, Julia ran her hand
over the smooth leather satchel that she knew would
be of use to Iain in his work. She'd planned this for
months, hoping against hope that this would be their
first Christmas together since his accident and
knowing that he would appreciate something to make
his work easier.

Did she dare give it to him now? Was everything
so changed between them—with her recognition of

her feelings and his rejection of them—that she should ignore the tradition of exchanging gifts? Listening to the soft voices singing songs about the Lord's birth and the joy of the season convinced her to carry on with her plan.

Even if he could or would never accept her love, they were still friends, and they had spent many childhood years together and exchanged many gifts to mark this day. Shaking her head, she called for her maid.

Nay, this was Christmas morn, and she would proceed as they'd always done—a family breakfast, the exchanging of gifts, services at the village church and a wonderful dinner later in the day. And if Iain could not face her, then he would have to deal with that.

Chapter Nine

Although he'd been absent from it these last few years, Iain knew that Anna and Clarinda planned Christmas Day festivities a certain way, and he'd learned early on not to argue, plead or complain about it. Secretly, Iain enjoyed every moment of the special day and had longed to be included once more. Of course that had been before Miss Julia Fairchild had decided to pledge her love to him and he'd rejected it.

As he washed and dressed, he wondered if he would be barred from the family observances once his actions became known. When his aunt sent word that they were waiting breakfast for him, Iain worried that they knew and were planning some sort of retribution, or if Julia's midnight visit to his rooms had gone unnoticed. Making his way down the hall to the small dining chamber, he found everyone there but for him.

Instead of a dubious or lukewarm welcome, Lord Treybourne and his Countess greeted him as family and invited him to sit. Once the servants began placing bowls of thick, honey-sweetened oatmeal, loaves of steaming bread, crocks of butter, honey, jams and preserves, as well as cuts of cold beef and chicken and sliced cheeses all around them on the table, the mood became festive, and memories of their last Christmas all together—the Earl's first one as Anna's husband—filled his thoughts.

Time and time again his gaze met Julia's across the wide table. In spite of the dishes being passed round, the presence of the children and the number of separate and intertwined conversations occurring around them, he could only hear her voice and see her expressions. At first he told himself that it was just to ascertain if she was angry or still hurt over his rejection, but then, as the meal progressed and he actually engaged her in a discussion about the newest writer gaining Edinburgh's attention, he knew it was because he enjoyed her company.

She'd grown so much—changing from hoyden to young woman, gaining an intelligence he'd not noticed before from both her education and her travels. Clarinda had spoken to him of her when she visited, and brought news of Julia's accomplishments, but nothing could have prepared him for the woman she'd become in his absence.

And nothing could have prepared him for the depth of his desire for her. Or the love he knew dwelt in his heart.

She laughed at something his uncle said, and her eyes lit and sparkled. She wore a simple gown in a vibrant red colour, and it made her hair look even paler than usual. Drawn up and held away from her face, the style of it softened her face and brought out the shape of her eyes and chin. So caught up in his perusal of her was he that he did not even notice his uncle calling his name.

'Lord Treybourne has said that the roads closest to the estate are of the best condition in the area. Most roads leading south are completely impassable now.'

Unable to decide if he should be unhappy that his escape had been prevented, Iain nodded and accepted the news it truly meant—he would be here most likely until Twelfth Night now. It would prolong the pain of knowing he would not see her again when she did not belong to another man, but it promised him some measure of pleasure in watching her blossom during these festivities. Either way, he would have memories to keep him for a long time.

When they moved into one of the parlours, he knew it was time to exchange gifts. He stood by the window and watched as the Earl and Countess gave gifts to their children and then to Julia and his aunt and uncle. The one presented to him was a surprise—a pair of boots, a greatcoat and leather gloves.

'You ruined yours in saving my dearest sister, Iain. We are happy to replace them. But your real gift will come later,' the Countess said, and she exchanged some meaningful look with her husband.

He would have argued, but they moved on and gave the head servants—the butler, the cook, the housekeeper, the ladies' maids, the nurse and the governess and the Earl's valet—their additional stipends, along with small personal gifts for each. The women received scarves and the men received gloves.

Then it was Julia's turn, and each of her gifts was well received. When she walked over to him and stopped there, he was surprised.

'This is for you, Iain. I hope you find it useful,' she said softly.

He took the box—the rather large box—from her, and offered her the gift he'd bought her. 'And this is for you, Julia. I hope you enjoy it. Happy Christmas.'

She smiled as she accepted it, and he thought of their many happy Christmases, celebrated either in Edinburgh or at Broch Dubh. He waited for her to open the package, wanting to see her expression. It was the only one of the gifts he had to give out that morning that he had chosen himself. His aunt had helped with the rest of them, but he had known this was for Julia as soon as he'd seen it in a shop in London on his last trip there.

Julia was never gracious about waiting to tear open

a present, and this morn was no different. When the torn paper revealed a book, she nodded and smiled.

'This is wonderful, Iain. Where did you find it?'

He'd found a copy of a traveller's guide to Italy—a place that Julia had always longed to visit when she was younger. This one, with drawings of local historical sites of interest, as well as a commentary on the social aspects of the country and its capital city, was very popular.

'In London,' he replied. 'I know a shop there that specialises in travel books and the like. When I saw Italy in the title, I thought you might like to read it.'

'I visited there last summer—perhaps you did not know?' she asked, while motioning at the box he still held. 'Aunt Euphemia and I travelled to meet her cousin, who has a wonderful villa in a small town on the southern coast.' She made a gesture with her hand and spoke a foreign word to him. *'Bene.'*

The Earl and the Countess laughed then, and he realised they were laughing at Julia and her accent.

'It was the only word in Italian she could speak,' said Anna. 'Even after two months there. And the only word she would use for quite a while upon her return.'

'But, Anna, *bene* can be used in so many situations I never felt the need to learn more.' She turned back to him. 'The food? *Bene!* The weather? *Bene!* The scenery? *Bene!* So useful, with so little effort.'

Iain laughed too, and nodded. 'Languages were never my strongest suit,' he said. 'I can appreciate finding such a useful word.'

'Go on, Iain. Open your gift.'

He pulled the ribbon on the box loose and lifted the lid. Inside he found a well-tooled leather satchel, one meant to carry papers and such. His own was several years old, borrowed from his uncle and worn, with the stitching coming apart at one corner. This gift would be much appreciated…and more so because it came from her.

'This will come to good use, Julia. Thank you for it,' he said. *And it will always remind me of you.*

She met his glance then, her cheeks flushed and her eyes bright, and he did not or could not look away. Nor did he want to, for in that moment he wished he could be the man for her.

The Earl interrupted, giving instructions about leaving for the church services, and Iain put the lid on the box so he could carry it back to his room. A footman offered to do that, so he relinquished his hold on it. He already had his coat and gloves for the trip, and was about to find his hat when the group all became silent. Peering across the room at them, he shrugged, not quite knowing what the cause of their interest was.

They were all staring above him, and then at him and the woman next to him there in the doorway—

Julia. Another bundle of mistletoe was draped over the door, decorated with ribbons.

The youngest began chanting first, then the others until he could not ignore them. Whether a-purpose or accidental he knew not, but he was not fool enough to miss this chance. When Julia nodded, he took a step closer, leaned down and kissed her softly on the lips.

Although everyone in the room seemed satisfied, he was not. But it would have to be enough—for it was the only way he would get to kiss her again.

With much laughter and festivity, the whole group proceeded out to the portico and to the sleighs waiting to take them into the village church. If a sleigh would hasten his departure, he would have commandeered one to get him to London. But they were not made for that kind of journey, and worked best only on packed snow and ice, so long as the horses pulling it could keep their footing.

Soon they arrived at church, attended the services, and returned to Wesley Hall with the vicar in tow as a guest for their Christmas meal. The house was ablaze with candles in the windows, and huge fires blazed in the hearths of each room. Iain, who had thought he could not eat another bite after their morning meal, found his stomach grumbling when he entered the house and smelled the appealing aroma of well-cooked food from the kitchen. Turkeys roasted and stuffed with bread and raisins and sausage, beef swimming in a red wine and garlic sauce, many kinds of fowl, along with accompaniments of all sorts, filled the tables to groaning, and Iain joined the others in eating his fill once more.

Since the day was Christmas, card games were not offered. Instead, the children were allowed to play several games, including an easy version of Oranges and Lemons and even Hunt the Slipper—with the slipper being hidden in the more obvious places that a child could spot. At a pace Iain would not have thought possible the day came to a close, and after a busy and thoroughly enjoyable day everyone sought their beds.

But rest would not come for him.

The events of the day ran across his thoughts over and over, and when his leg began to tighten in cramp, Iain decided to walk a little to ease the seizing. Only the servants remained busy, cleaning up after the feast and the celebrations, but they did not pay him any mind as he walked the length and width of the lower floor of the large country house.

He was on his second turn down the hall when he came face to face with Julia.

'Iain, I see you are not abed yet either?' she asked.

'No,' he said, shaking his head. 'I needed to walk to loosen up my leg and back.' He should probably not be mentioning body parts to a young woman such as she, but he knew it would not offend her. 'And what is your excuse?'

'I cannot sleep after such a wonderful Christmas. I thought I would come down and get my book to read. I left it in the parlour when we went to church.'

'Come, then,' he said, nodding in the direction of the front hall. 'Let us walk there and find it.'

As they walked, in what seemed to be a companionable silence, the need to address his behaviour of last evening pressed heavily on him. Should he apologise for refusing her, or would that make it worse? Should he try to explain once more why it could never work between them?

He was not paying heed to the small step needed to reach the parlour, and he stumbled when his walking stick caught in the space between the wooden slats of the floor and the step.

Julia reached out to steady his stance as he tripped on the step. He recovered quickly, but she left her arm under his as they walked, and he did not remove his from hers. They followed along the hall until they reached the front parlour, where they'd opened their gifts this morning. The servants had already put this room to rights, leaving only the candles in the window left to put out on their final round of cleaning before bed.

She left him for a moment, and walked over to the table in the corner where the gifts had been piled. Her book was on top. She turned back to find him directly behind her.

'What was your favourite part of visiting Italy?' he asked, then added with a laugh, 'Other than *bene*, of course!'

She opened the book and glanced at several of the sketches inside it. 'The food was magnificent. The weather was warm, with soothing breezes along the shore.' She looked around, as though searching for anyone listening, and then said, 'I even got Aunt Euphemia to walk into the sea!'

'Scandalous!' he said, as though it was an enticing thing. 'And did *you* walk in the sea?'

'The waters were so warm, Iain. Aunt Euphemia swore that the warmth eased her pains and keep her knees from cracking. Perhaps it is something that might benefit you as well?'

'It may.' He nodded in agreement. 'The doctors have suggested it, but I am not ready to travel there.' He met her gaze and she noticed the dark intensity in his. 'I would not go in an invalid chair.'

Although she wanted to argue with him about his worry over the look of such a method of travel, she knew that was not what he needed to hear. Sympathy seemed to work in the other direction when it was given to men—especially young, proud men.

'Well, now that you have come so far in your abilities, it may be time to consider it again. I can tell you the names of some wonderful villages we visited there.'

She had some pride herself, and she marvelled at how calmly her words came out. Especially since he stood so close now. Close enough that no one could fit between them. She watched as he fought some inner battle before speaking again.

'Julia…' he began, but his words faded after he spoke her name. He took in a breath and let it out before speaking again. 'I need to offer you an apology for last night.'

'Iain, please do not speak of it. I should not have come to your room. I should not have imposed my wishes on you—especially when I owe you so much.'

'Julia, this is not your sin to confess. I am the damaged goods here—'

'I have thought on your words and my actions today, and have realised that it was presumptuous of me to expect you to simply accept my declaration of love,' she explained, not allowing him to continue.

She had thought of nothing else since last night. And she had realised that she was simply not the kind of woman Iain would want as a wife. Why else would a man refuse all that she had offered?

'I have a number of tendencies that offend men— my interest in education and learning, my outspokenness, even my appearance,' she said.

'Your appearance?' he asked, while examining her from head to toe. Warmth surged through her at his perusal. 'What is wrong with your appearance?'

She told him what she'd heard while sitting in the alcove outside the ballroom on the upper floor. 'I look too Scottish, and not as fair and pale as a good English lady should be.'

He muttered under his breath then, and part of it was not polite. 'Who said that to you?'

'It matters not. It is only one of my flaws. The other comments were that I speak with too much of an accent and that I intimidate men with my intellectual accomplishments. There is not a man among the guests who would consider me a suitable wife if it were not for the settlement that Trey offers and the connections such a marriage would bring.'

Although she'd planned this to be a discussion about him, she'd just revealed her biggest fear—she would end up marrying a man who cared not a wit for her, but would do so only for the money and connections she brought. And, though this was clearly acceptable in Society, she had never thought she would be subjected to such a marriage. Poor Julia Fairchild, raised in Edinburgh by her sister, would never have had to worry over such things. But the Julia whose sister was now a countess, the wife of one of the most powerful men in the kingdom, did.

'Julia, you cannot seriously think that?' Iain asked, shaking his head.

She'd revealed more than she'd planned, and now

the insecurity within her grew and made her uncomfortable. 'I find I am fatigued after all, Iain.' She held out the book and nodded. 'My thanks again for such a thoughtful gift.'

Julia stepped around him and walked to the door. This time he followed her and stood close beside her.

'You will find a man who cares about you, Julia. Fear not, and do not let your unease make you worry.'

He paused and looked above them. There was yet another sprig of mistletoe, hanging over their heads. Luckily no one was there to see it, so they were not forced to kiss again.

His lips on hers surprised her, as did his hands on her shoulders, holding her still. He did not stop at just a polite and expected kiss. No, he tilted his face and covered her mouth with his, claiming her and teasing her lips until she opened to him. When she did, he moved his tongue, and she could taste him even as he did her. It was just as her hands crept up to encircle his back that her name rang out from above stairs.

They jumped back away from each other in a fraction of a second, and then looked up at the mistletoe. 'Is it my imagination, or is the mistletoe increasing throughout the house?' he asked.

She did not wait to answer. Julia scooted around him and walked quickly to the stairs, climbing them without ever looking back. She'd never thought herself a coward until just then, but she was not willing to ask the rest of her question about marriage—*why* did he not want her as a wife?

Chapter Ten

The next days passed quickly as everyone planned their gowns for the Twelfth Night Ball. Anna had made certain to have enough help and materials on hand for any sewing needs. Some of the women had brought appropriate gowns with them; some would dress up their current gowns with fripperies and decorations provided by Anna's seamstresses. The men would be suitably handsome in their evening clothes as well.

As the Christmas season wound down, she knew that Julia and Iain were no closer to resolving their attraction than at their first meeting a few weeks before. Anna and Clarinda had spoken on the matter. Anna and Trey had spoken, even Robert and Clarinda had shared their thoughts and concerns. The only person who'd not spoken on the matter was Julia.

Trey had revealed the incident that had occurred just after Julia's recovery, but her sister had still not shared her own feelings in the situation with her. Until she was certain of her sister's heart and mind Anna could go no further, and would allow no other interference.

The mistletoe had gotten out of hand. It seemed that the entire household spent more time kissing under it than doing anything else! Her idea of making it possible for Iain to court Julia without Julia's realising it had taken a different turn as Anna watched the passion between them grow. But even when she'd ordered the servants not to place any more it still appeared, and appeared—more frequently in more rooms.

Since Iain would leave in a day or two, Anna knew she needed to find out the truth about what existed between these two. She could not force them together, but no two people—other than possibly herself and Trey—were more perfect for each other. Fear and pride seemed to keep them apart, but what could bring them together?

It was the morning of the ball when she received the answer and guidance she needed. Watching her sons playing hide-and-seek with their older sister in the alcove next to the ballroom, she knew exactly what she would do.

He was miserable again. Standing here, watching Julia as the Queen of Twelfth Night while another man stood as King, was killing him. But it was her future, and he would not be part of it. They had reached a comfortable peace between them this last week, never speaking of anything too personal and never being alone together. But that did not mean they did not spend time together, and he'd kissed her more than a dozen more times because of the strange appearance of mistletoe boughs all throughout Wesley Hall.

Now, though, Lady Sutcliffe's son had found the bean within his piece of cake and was serving as King, immediately choosing Julia as his Queen. She'd sat next to him at dinner, and then danced several times with him, making Iain want to drag her away and beat the man for ever presuming that she could be his.

Knowledge of the stupidity of that notion was not long in coming, and his common sense and control kept him from beating the man senseless. Not from the wanting to do it, though.

Just when he thought he could take no more, when the sight of her on another man's arm was eating him from the inside out, his uncle called him aside. Rather than try to talk over the music, Robert led him out into the hall and down to a small alcove where they could speak.

'Do you still plan to leave on the morrow, Iain?' he asked when he'd drawn the curtain to give them some privacy.

'Unless you have some other need for me to be here, sir,' Iain answered.

'Do you have anything you wish to say about Julia?' Robert asked him.

Iain let out a breath and shook his head. 'No, sir.'

'That is all you can say? "No, sir".'

Iain dragged his hand through his hair. 'I do not know what you expect, Uncle. I do not want someone in my care when I cannot even take care of myself. I cannot endanger someone I love because of my shortcomings.'

'Someone you *love*?' he asked. 'If you love her, then how can you leave her behind for some other man to snatch up?'

'Uncle, it is exactly because of the love I feel for her that I will do it. I cannot live every day with the dread of thinking I could in some way cause her harm, or at the least not be able to keep her from it.'

His uncle shook his head. 'Do you not think that I live in fear of something happening to your aunt or our children after seeing what happened to you and your parents? I lost a beloved brother in that accident, and his wife, and nearly his son that day. To this day, every time I put Clarinda or the children in a carriage my heart seizes and I can hardly breathe.'

'What?' Iain asked, shocked at such a disclosure. 'I did not know.'

'Your father would not want me to let fear ruin and run my life, and he certainly would not want it to rule yours, Iain. So, every day, when I want to drag Clarinda out of a carriage for fear of what might happen, I think of your parents and let her go.'

Before he could reply, he heard voices approaching outside the alcove. When he would have opened the curtain to reveal their presence, his uncle stopped him with a gesture.

'It is cooler out here, Anna,' Julia said. 'Would you like me to get you something to drink?'

'No, I just need a few moments away from the crowd and the heat. Come, sit with me.' Iain could tell that they had sat on a small couch positioned across the corridor from where he and his uncle stood.

'Will you be glad when everyone leaves in the next few days, Anna? I know that it has been a difficult pregnancy so far, and you must long for some peace and quiet,' Julia said.

'I will be glad when I know that you are settled, Julia. I had hoped you would speak your heart and mind to me, so that I would know how to proceed.'

'Anna, I will marry whoever you think I should marry,' Julia said, her voice sinking low. 'I will accept your guidance in this.'

'I did not and do not ask you to simply follow my wishes, Julia. I know you are not happy about this, and I know you do not share your heart's truest feelings with me. I only ask that you do now, so that I can know what to do.'

'My heart's wishes matter not, Anna. He does not love me enough to take me to wife.'

She spoke of *him*. Iain turned, wanting to say something to her, but his uncle stopped him once more.

'He does not trust me or his heart enough, and so he cannot accept what I offer him.'

The words sounded sad, but resigned. He needed to tell her that it was his failing and not hers, but she continued.

'I thought I could be the wife he needed, but I am not that woman.'

'Julia, I think he does not want to take you away from all you could have and all you could do. Could you be happy if you did not travel or did not go to balls and move in society as you have for the last few years under Trey's sponsorship?'

'Anna, I have done most of that for you. I would do anything you asked of me for I owe you so much! I know what you did to see Aunt Euphemia and I safe and protected. I know the price you paid for that.' Julia paused as Anna gasped at her words. 'I would honour such cost by accepting your wishes over mine.'

'But I want only your happiness and security, Julia. I do not expect you to give up your dreams and the man you love simply to suit my wishes.'

Iain held his breath, waiting for Julia to answer, but it did not happen. Instead his aunt called out, and the two women left the corridor. His uncle pushed the curtain aside, and they watched as Anna and Julia followed his aunt back into the ballroom.

His uncle placed his hand on Iain's shoulder. 'So, Iain, will you allow fear to rule your life? Will you forsake the woman you love and who loves you because you are afraid of what could happen?'

Robert walked around him and back into the ballroom before Iain could say a word.

He'd had no idea about how his uncle felt, and how much fear had changed their lives. Yet his uncle was strong enough to live and to face that fear every single day of his life. For the last four years Iain had lived in fear—in fear of dying, afraid to live, afraid of pain, afraid of not feeling anything. Worse, he was afraid to let love into his heart for fear he would lose it.

Julia had offered him her heart and her love—was she strong enough to help him face the fears he lived with? Would she remain at his side and help him to stand every time he fell? Was he man enough to let her close to him and then face the fear that he might lose her?

No matter what, he knew he could not face a life without her. But would she still accept him? There was only one thing he could do.

Walking slowly back into the ballroom, he found the Earl and begged a favour of him. Then he made his way to where Julia now sat with the 'King', and waited for the moment.

The musicians paused, and then another dance was called—this time a waltz. He watched her face, and saw the confusion there as he approached her. Iain bowed before her and then, in a simple gesture that would change his life, held out his hand to her.

He prayed that she understood—that she knew he was asking for so much more than just this dance, that he was offering himself, with all his limitations and his flaws. That he was asking for her heart and her love.

Her eyes filled with tears, but she blinked them away before smiling at him. She let her love pour forth as she rose from her chair and nodded. Instead of waiting for him to lead in the steps, she positioned herself to take the lead in most of the dance's movements. As he stepped closer, placed his hand on her waist and lifted her other in his, she laughed softly and changed them, so that she was holding his waist.

'Do not worry, Iain,' she whispered to him. 'I have you now.'

That first step was the most difficult one he'd taken in his life, for it meant trusting her with himself. Trusting her not to let him fall. Trusting her not to laugh at his efforts. Trusting her to love him as much as he loved her.

Once he got past that, the rest of the dance was easy. And if he did not move smoothly through the pace of the dance, if they did not keep in time with the vigorous music, if they said a word or not during the entire dance, neither seemed to notice—for they were too busy falling the rest of the way in love to fear such things again.

Anna leaned against Trey and felt tears begin to burn her eyes and her throat. He wrapped his arm around her, heedless of the heads that turned at such a blatant display of affection for his wife.

'I told you he would do it,' Trey offered.

'I told *you*,' Anna countered.

'I was the one who told you they would work this out,' Clarinda said as she and Robert approached.

'But I was the one who suggested using the alcove,' Robert said.

They laughed together, and stood watching Anna's beloved sister and Robert's nephew take their first real steps in the dance of love that would take them through life. Although Iain faltered once or twice, it was clear that Julia was indeed holding him up. Anna knew they would do well together, and now that she knew Julia's heart she had no second thoughts or misgivings about them.

'What I do not understand, though, is the mistletoe. I told the servants to take it down, yet it continued to be replaced. And even more added every day.' Anna looked at her husband and friends, trying to determine which of them had decided that more mistletoe kisses would help bring the two young people together. 'So which of you is responsible?'

They all appeared shocked at her allegations—until someone cleared her throat behind them. Turning, they discovered Aunt Euphemia, watching them watching the couple waltzing.

'Even I could tell they only needed a small push, Anna. It was not only old married couples who could see the love they had for each other.' Anna watched as her aunt adjusted her looking glass and nodded. 'I knew it when they were children. Anyone with eyes in their head could see it. It just took some time to work out.'

'And some mistletoe?' she asked, wondering if her aunt had done anything else to encourage Iain and Julia.

'Kisses under the mistletoe at Christmas are simply the best, don't you think?'

Anna looked from her aunt—her maiden aunt, who'd never spoken of kissing before—to her husband, who had been enjoying the effects of the mistletoe as well, and smiled.

'Yes, Aunt Euphemia. Mistletoe kisses are wonderful.'

* * * * *

Regency

High-Society Affairs

*Rakes and rogues in the ballrooms – and the
bedrooms – of Regency England!*

Volume 1 – 6th March 2009
A Hasty Betrothal by Dorothy Elbury
A Scandalous Marriage by Mary Brendan

Volume 2 – 3rd April 2009
The Count's Charade by Elizabeth Bailey
The Rake and the Rebel by Mary Brendan

Volume 3 – 1st May 2009
Sparhawk's Lady by Miranda Jarrett
The Earl's Intended Wife by Louise Allen

Volume 4 – 5th June 2009
Lord Calthorpe's Promise by Sylvia Andrew
The Society Catch by Louise Allen

Volume 5 – 3rd July 2009
Beloved Virago by Anne Ashley
Lord Trenchard's Choice by Sylvia Andrew

Volume 6 – 7th August 2009
The Unruly Chaperon by Elizabeth Rolls
Colonel Ancroft's Love by Sylvia Andrew

Volume 7 – 4th September 2009
The Sparhawk Bride by Miranda Jarrett
The Rogue's Seduction by Georgina Devon

NOW 14 VOLUMES IN ALL TO COLLECT!

M&B

Regency

HIGH-SOCIETY AFFAIRS

*Rakes and rogues in the ballrooms – and the
bedrooms – of Regency England!*

Volume 8 – 2nd October 2009
Sparhawk's Angel by Miranda Jarrett
The Proper Wife by Julia Justiss

Volume 9 – 6th November 2009
The Disgraced Marchioness by Anne O'Brien
The Reluctant Escort by Mary Nichols

Volume 10 – 4th December 2009
The Outrageous Debutante by Anne O'Brien
A Damnable Rogue by Anne Herries

Volume 11 – 8th January 2010
The Enigmatic Rake by Anne O'Brien
The Lord and the Mystery Lady by Georgina Devon

Volume 12 – 5th February 2010
The Wagering Widow by Diane Gaston
An Unconventional Widow by Georgina Devon

Volume 13 – 5th March 2010
A Reputable Rake by Diane Gaston
The Heart's Wager by Gayle Wilson

Volume 14 – 2nd April 2010
The Venetian's Mistress by Ann Elizabeth Cree
The Gambler's Heart by Gayle Wilson

NOW 14 VOLUMES IN ALL TO COLLECT!

www.millsandboon.co.uk

M&B

millsandboon.co.uk Community

Join Us!

The Community is the perfect place to meet and chat to kindred spirits who love books and reading as much as you do, but it's also the place to:

- ■ Get the inside scoop from authors about their latest books
- ■ Learn how to write a romance book with advice from our editors
- ■ Help us to continue publishing the best in women's fiction
- ■ Share your thoughts on the books we publish
- ■ Befriend other users

Forums: Interact with each other as well as authors, editors and a whole host of other users worldwide.

Blogs: Every registered community member has their own blog to tell the world what they're up to and what's on their mind.

Book Challenge: We're aiming to read 5,000 books and have joined forces with The Reading Agency in our inaugural Book Challenge.

Profile Page: Showcase yourself and keep a record of your recent community activity.

Social Networking: We've added buttons at the end of every post to share via digg, Facebook, Google, Yahoo, technorati and de.licio.us.

www.millsandboon.co.uk

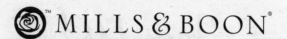